PLAYING FOR KEEPS

A Texas Scoundrels Novel

JAMIE DENTON

JAMIE DENTON

ISBN: 149235273
ISBN-13: 978-1492315278

*This book can only be dedicated
to two very special women*

*Kristine Mason - the sister of my heart
and
Kristi Avalon - my other oldest*

*You are my inspiration, my greatest encouragement
and my dearest friends. Thank you for always
always having my back.*

ONE

GRIFFEN SOMMERFIELD'S FINGERS trembled. She'd been dreading this moment. Although she'd known it would happen eventually, she just hadn't expected the foreclosure notice from the bank for at least another month.

She scanned the document, her stomach roiling. Reading the fine print wasn't necessary. All she needed to know was how long until the bank ripped Antiquities away from her.

Forty-five days? Seriously? That was it? The seventy-five hundred dollars the bank was demanding might as well have been seventy-five thousand. In another month, the price would be closer to ten thousand dollars. She silently cursed her soon-to-be ex-husband. Ross had cleared out every one of their accounts when he'd left, her business accounts included. As much as she hated the thought of giving up, she'd just run out of options. The wolves pounding on the door had changed tactics and were already sucking enough air into their lungs to huff and puff and blow her world apart.

The bell over the door to the shop jangled, signaling a customer. A *buying* customer, she hoped.

She slipped the foreclosure notice into a cubby on the roll top desk, then snapped her laptop closed. The ledger on the accounting program was filled with more red than black these days. Taking a deep breath, she adjusted her silk blouse, then left the small office. Maybe Charlotte Carter had returned to purchase the Louis XIV table she'd been coveting for the past six months. The sale wouldn't solve all of her problems, but the tidy sum might buy her some time until she could think of a way to save her shop.

She stepped into the showroom to find a short, portly gentleman she didn't recognize. He stood eyeing the rainbow of colored perfume bottles in the glass display case, arranged atop the emerald brocade fabric she'd used in conjunction with St. Patrick's Day. On the opposite end, resting against a cream velvet background lay a Victorian jewelry box filled with gold and emerald trinkets. A pot of gold, something she doubted any wily Leprechauns would be dropping at the end of her rainbow.

She walked around the counter and summoned a welcoming smile she was nowhere near feeling. "Can I help you?"

The gentleman looked up and studied her through smudged glasses. Pulling them from his beak-like nose, he wiped them on a tissue. "Mrs. Somerfield? Griffen Hart Somerfield?"

Apprehension balled in her stomach. *Now what?* Six months ago, she never would have reacted with such fear, or constantly be waiting for the other shoe to drop. First Ross wiping her out financially when he decided to indulge in a clichéd mid-life crisis with his twenty-two-year-old secretary. Then the past due notices and threatening letters followed. Spitefully, she'd let the bank repossess Ross's fancy sports coupe. Why would he need a sports car living on the white sandy beaches of Jamaica anyway?

She pulled in a deep breath. "I'm Griffen Somerfield. And you are?" she asked, aiming for a polite, business-like tone.

"Cyrus Morton." She took the hand he extended, and he pumped as if he were trying to get water from a well.

She retrieved her hand before he yanked her arm from its socket. "What I can do for you, Mr. Morton?" She resisted the urge to massage her shoulder.

He smiled, revealing a speck of pepper between his teeth. "I have something for you." He handed her a business card with the words Morton Investigations in bold, bright red letters emblazoned on the front. In the corner were the words investigation, surveillance, service of process.

Great. Now she was being sued.

He hefted a briefcase onto the counter and flipped open the latch. "You had a sister, a..." He lifted the lid and rifled through papers. "Just a second, it's right...oh yes. Danielle Hart?"

"That's right." Dani, her sweet, darling older sister, had been gone over nine years. Leukemia had cut her gentle life short, but Griffen would always have the single sacrifice her sister had made. Austin.

"My client is First Trust Bank of Mississippi. When your sister was a college student at Ole Miss, she'd opened a bank account there. She also had a safety deposit box."

Against the advice of her team of doctors, Dani had insisted on not only going to college, but she'd broken ranks and the family's long standing Baylor University tradition. Instead, she'd opted for the University of Mississippi and a business degree in advertising.

More unfulfilled dreams and wishes, Griffen thought sadly.

"My client has been attempting to contact Ms. Hart and only recently learned that she's been deceased for a number of years. You're listed as her primary beneficiary." Cyrus pulled a document from his briefcase and set it on the counter. "If you'll just sign here, I'll be on my way."

"Why did it take so long?" Griffen asked, taking the pen Cyrus offered.

"A routine advertising mailing. The last known address my client had for your sister was the college dorm. The correspondence was returned with 'deceased' written across the front," Cyrus explained. "The bank manager checked into it and discovered your sister had died."

"Doesn't anyone ever investigate inactive accounts?"

"Not as a rule. People open savings accounts all the time and leave them alone for long periods."

Griffen nodded and signed the document to release the contents of Dani's safety deposit box to her.

Cyrus asked for identification and verified the signature. Apparently satisfied, he opened his briefcase again to retrieve a thick manila envelope, which he placed on the glass counter. "There's a cashier's check inside, payable to you for nineteen hundred and sixty-three dollars. That's seventeen hundred and seventy dollars from her savings, plus nine years of accrued interest, less the rental on the safe deposit box, of course."

Nineteen hundred dollars? Granted, it wasn't much, but it would help keep her and Austin afloat for at least another month until she sold the business and found herself a nine-to-five job.

"Thank you, Mr. Morton." She took the envelope and held it to her chest. Nineteen hundred dollars would help, not much, but it would help.

"Are those authentic?" he asked, pointing to the atomizers in the display case.

"Yes, they are. Can I show you something in particular?" Maybe her luck was changing. She was curious as to what was in the envelope, but that could wait. If Cyrus wanted an atomizer, then she'd certainly sell him one.

"My wife likes those little perfume bottles. How bad would that blue one set me back?"

"Not as much as you might think," Griffen said with a smile. She reached into the case and retrieved the circa 1910 atomizer. When he didn't haggle over the cost, but asked her to wrap it, she nearly shouted with glee.

Ten minutes later, Mr. Morton left with an expensive gift for his wife wrapped in delicate floral tissue paper tucked inside his briefcase. Envelope in hand, she locked the door to the shop and flipped the sign to closed. She had about forty minutes to make it over to the gymnasium for Austin's basketball game.

Back in her office, she sat at her desk and carefully opened the envelope. She caught the faint aromas of vanilla and musk. Memories assailed her of the short time they'd had with Dani. Her eldest sister had been as sweet and delicate as a fragile hot house orchid. Her goal had been to work at one of the advertising firms in Dallas, but she hadn't lived long enough to fulfill her dreams. At the age of twenty-one, she'd given birth to a son, Austin. Having Austin had taken what little strength Dani had left and she'd never fully recovered. By the time Austin was two, Dani could hardly take care of herself let alone an active toddler, so Griffen had stepped in and cared for the adorable dark haired boy with huge brown eyes. When Dani had asked Griffen to promise to raise Austin as her own, no one in the family had been surprised.

Griffen had easily made that promise. Despite the fact that Ross had never wanted children, he'd insisted they legally adopt Austin. Dani hadn't objected. Austin Hart Somerfield was in reality Griffen's nephew, but in her heart, he was her son. A son she now raised as a single parent.

The anniversary clock on the top of the desk chimed the half hour. With plenty of time before the game, she reached inside the envelope. Resting on top, as promised, was the cashier's check. She tipped the envelope and two more envelopes, both sealed, tumbled onto the desk along with a glossy photograph.

She picked up the photograph, and her stomach rolled again. No. It couldn't be. But she couldn't think of any reason why Dani would have *his* picture, unless...

Griffen's heart thumped wildly. Dani had always refused to say, but Griffen had often wondered about the identity of Austin's father. Never in all of her wild imaginings would she have even believed it could be *him*. What would her younger sister, Mattie, and their father, say if they knew? It didn't matter. Griffen had no intention of telling them, or anyone. Especially Austin.

She stared at the black and white publicity photograph, at a familiar face. The handsome face of the man her son idolized, of the unnamed man Dani had claimed to love—Texas Wranglers' star quarterback, Jed Maitland.

She set the photograph aside. At least now she knew

where Austin had gotten his dark, good looks and a jaw already showing signs of becoming square and strong. Now she knew why at thirteen, he was nearly as tall as her own five-foot-eight inches and would no doubt top her by at least another two before the coming summer would draw to a close. But what she simply could not understand was what Dani had seen in Jed Maitland. They were so opposite, it just didn't make sense. Fourteen years ago when Austin had been conceived, Maitland had been a hot shot quarterback, the number one draft choice out of Ole Miss, snapped up by the Texas Wranglers in the first round. Young and cocky, he'd become a target for the press, the same press which now claimed Maitland was headed toward forced retirement. According to Austin, being cut from the team was a fate worse than death.

Had Dani tried to contact Maitland to tell him about his son? Had he refused to acknowledge his own child? Griffen wouldn't put it past someone like him. He'd already been sued once for paternity. As far as she was concerned, Maitland was a hard living, hard drinking, has-been womanizer.

With trembling fingers, she carefully slid the rose colored paper from the envelope addressed to her. A knot the size of a football churned in her stomach.

Dearest Griffen,

I know this probably seems rather morbid, reading a letter from the grave and all, but I can tell you now what I couldn't when I had the chance. As much as I love you, Griffen, I couldn't bear to see the disappointment in your eyes when you learned the truth about Austin's father.

Despite what the press and media say about him, the man I knew and loved really is a good man. I know in my heart that if he'd known about Austin he'd have done the right thing. I chose not to tell him for my own reasons, so please don't hold my choice against him. If you haven't already guessed, Jed Maitland is Austin's father. I know that I was wrong and probably should have given Austin the chance to know his real father, but I knew you would be the perfect mother and role model for him.

When Austin is old enough, he may want to know the truth. I planned to tell him, but that will now be up to you. Austin deserves the chance to know about his father, his real father.

I want you to do two things for me. Tell Austin how much I love him, and that the short time we had together were the happiest days of my life. The envelope for Austin contains my journal and I want him to have it in hopes that he may know how very much he meant to me.

My other request will be much more difficult for you, but I know you well. You always do the right thing. Please let Austin know about his father. Jed doesn't have to know, but Austin does deserve to at least know who his father is, and how much I loved them both.

All my love,
Danielle

Sweet heaven. What was she going to do now? The other shoe had totally dropped and managed a swift kick right to her gut before it hit the floor, bounced up and hit her square in ass. She leaned into the low backed chair and stared at the photograph of Jed Maitland. Her son's hero was also his father. The entire situation was too surreal to comprehend.

For one, how on earth had Dani gotten these things into a safe deposit box hundreds of miles away when she obviously knew she was dying? And why? Why not just give them to her? Or will them to her?

Her head ached and she had no answer as she folded the letter and placed it back inside the envelope, along with Dani's diary, the letter for Austin and the photograph of Maitland, then stuffed them in her oversized bag. She doubted if she'd ever figure out that particular puzzle.

The anniversary clock chimed the quarter hour. Austin's game started in fifteen minutes. She'd think about this later. Much later.

Like in twenty years when Austin wouldn't care that his father was Jed Maitland.

*

The bastards had the gall to come to him on his own turf. Jed tossed back the last of the scotch in his glass. Not a smart move on their part. He'd actually given them more credit than to grant him the home field advantage, but the stupid SOB's had a mission and were determined to see it through.

To see him through, the way he looked at it.

Finito.

Done.

"Like hell."

In too foul a mood to enjoy the beauty of the Texas sunset turning the vast openness of the rugged land into a solid gold landscape, he stepped away from the double-story glass windows. Circling the bar, he tipped the bottle of Jim Beam into the crystal tumbler, then lifted the glass and drained it. The scotch burned his throat, fueling his anger. *The bastards.*

He was Jed Maitland, dammit. They couldn't do this to him. No one could force *him* out of the game. He'd been a winning quarterback since his rookie year and had three championship rings to back up the hype. Multi-million dollar contracts, the top four product endorsements and other perks had made him rich. Wise investments had made him obscenely wealthy. Not bad for a kid from the swamplands of Mississippi. Except now they wanted to force him out. Maitland the Maniac. A legend to rival Montana and Elway, Unitas and Staubach. Not chance.

Bastards.

He'd be damned if he'd accept what his agent, Bob Yorke, had termed as management's *generous* offer. Hell, he was firing the useless piece of shit tomorrow. No one treated Maitland the Maniac as if he were no better than a relief quarterback from a third rate team. He hadn't warmed the bench since he was ten years old, and he wasn't about to start now.

He refilled his glass with more Jim Beam and drained the bottle. "Generous my ass."

His shoulder hurt like a son-of-a-bitch and this was the thanks they gave him. Muttering a string of vile curses, he picked up his glass and headed toward the leather sofa. Bottles of painkillers sat on the glass end table. He picked one, snapped off the top with his thumb and shook three into his mouth, downing them with a healthy dose of his new best friend, Jim.

He glanced at the glass cocktail table where a football mounted on a marble base and protected by a Plexiglas covering stood proudly. His rookie year he'd led the Wranglers to the division championship game. They'd lost to San Francisco and had kissed the championship good-bye, but he'd played one hell of a game, coming up only six yards short of Joe Montana's passing record. As a rookie, he'd set his own, and no one had come close to taking his record, either.

Yet.

He set his glass on the table and took the Plexiglas off the football, which had been signed by the team. The pigskin was cold to the touch, but nothing fit his hands better than a regulation ball—except maybe a hot and willing woman.

He spun the ball in one hand. The pain in his shoulder didn't ease as quickly as he would have liked, reminding him of what *they* were saying he could no longer do for a living. God, he didn't know anything except the game.

He'd show them. The orthopedic specialists had said the surgery to repair his shoulder hadn't been the success they'd hoped for, that his competition days were over. What did they know? How could they judge based on a mere six weeks of recovery? Three months of intense physical therapy, and he'd be good as new. Maitland the Maniac would walk back onto the field for training camp, and it sure as fuck wouldn't be as an assistant coach or a third-rate chump.

For now, he planned to get drunk, good and drunk, for the entire weekend. And God help anyone stupid enough to cross his path. Namely the press. The bloodsuckers had falsely labeled him a bad boy, a renegade, and he hadn't bothered to correct them. He had his reasons. There were people to protect.

Might as well live up to the image.

He leaned back into the soft leather sofa. The feel of the ball failed to soothe him, nor did the reminder of what he once was, and would be again, if he had anything to say about it. The anger inside him peaked, and he gripped the ball hard. Thanks to the effects of the medication, he felt only the dulled edge of pain when he brought his arm back and took aim. With a curse to the pricks trying to ruin his career, he chucked the football across the room, shattering the glass and mirror shelves filled with crystal glassware behind the bar.

A sense of satisfaction, along with the misty haze of painkillers and alcohol, wove through him. He settled his head against the back of the sofa and closed his eyes, waiting for sweet oblivion to take hold.

TWO

GRIFFEN CLOSED THE floral-covered journal Dani had left for her son, a lump the size of a Texas melon lodged in her throat. She tugged the old worn cardigan tighter around her and wiped at a stray tear. Dani's words to Austin were filled with such love, Griffen had no choice but to give the journal to him. The fact that Dani hadn't mentioned Jed by name helped with her decision. Her sister, thankfully, omitted that little detail in the telling of how she'd met and fallen in love with Austin's father.

Along with her feelings and emotions of what she was going through during the last few months of her life, the journal spoke of her short relationship with Maitland. According to Dani, they'd loved a lifetime in the time they'd spent together.

Griffen doubted Maitland had returned Dani's feelings. His womanizing was legendary. He subscribed to a find 'em, fuck 'em and forget 'em philosophy, a serious character flaw which had gained him plenty of bad press over the years, not to mention a paternity suit he'd lost about five or six years ago.

She reached for her mug of tea and sipped, wincing when the cool liquid hit her tongue. She placed her mug inside the microwave and pressed the REHEAT button just as Austin sauntered into the kitchen.

"Whatcha doin', Mom?" he asked, heading straight for the refrigerator.

Austin leaned in and pulled out a gallon of milk. He stood

tall, the dark gray sweats hanging loose on his lanky body. Soon, he'd start filling out into the man he would one day become, and she wasn't ready for it.

His likeness to Maitland was uncanny and she couldn't believe she hadn't noticed the resemblance until now. Austin had a couple of posters of Maitland in his bedroom, along with other Wranglers' memorabilia. She kept telling herself she should have seen the likeness, but how could she have? Jed Maitland was the last person on earth she'd have ever believed to be her son's biological father.

"A glass, Slick," she reminded him when he opened the milk carton and prepared to chug.

He sighed, more of a show of teenage annoyance she'd become accustomed to the past few months since Ross had walked out on them. He poured his milk and set the carton on the counter. "Jim Packard's dad is taking him fishing Saturday and they invited me. Can I go?" His voice had begun to change. Her baby was growing up, whether she liked it or not.

The microwave dinged, so she retrieved her mug. "As long as your homework is all caught up."

Austin gave her an impatient glance, but quickly nodded his assent. She really was lucky. Austin was a good kid and he worked hard in school. He enjoyed competitive sports, but there was little question that football was his first love, something he'd been doing since he was eight years old.

Walking back to the round maple table, she set her mug on the rose chintz tablecloth. She picked up the journal and hugged it close to her chest. "Sit down, Austin."

He looked at her, curiously, but did as she asked. She took a deep breath and forced a smile. Whatever happened, she knew she had to believe she was doing the right thing. "I had a visitor at the store today."

Austin gulped his milk, then wiped the milk-moustache with the sleeve of his T-shirt. "Did they buy that Louis XIV?" he asked, hopeful.

Her smile softened. "No. Actually, he brought something. For you."

He looked at her, those deep brown eyes, his father's eyes. "What is it?"

God, why was this so hard suddenly? Because she'd be lying to her son by omission and she hated being anything less than honest with him. Good parenting meant you were an example to your children. What kind of example would she be setting if she lied to him?

"Your mother had a safety deposit box we didn't know existed. Someone at the bank recently learned she had passed away and I was listed as the beneficiary. The gentleman who came into the store delivered the contents, along with the balance in her savings account."

He set his cup on the table and reached for the plate of chocolate chip cookies in the center. "Cool. Are we rich?" he asked around the cookie in his mouth.

Despite the gravity of her heart, she managed a small smile. "Hardly."

She set the journal on the table in front of him. "She left something for you, too." Reaching into her bag, she retrieved the envelope addressed to him, bypassing the publicity photo of his father. "She wanted you to have these."

Austin stared at the journal as if afraid to touch it. "Have you read it?"

"Yes."

Nodding, but still not touching either item, he looked across the table at her. She saw the confusion and the flash of pain in his eyes. "Do I have to read it now, or can I take it to my room?"

She stood and circled the table, wrapping her arms around him. "It belongs to you, honey. You can read it whenever you feel you're ready. Or not at all." Another woman, her own sister, had given birth this beautiful boy, but he was *her* baby and always would be. No one, not even a legendary quarterback, could threaten her relationship with her son. She hoped.

"It's your decision."

"Okay." He stood, scooping up the journal and the letter.

He started out of the room, but stopped at the kitchen door. "I love you, Mom," he said, then dashed out of the room.

Her heart constricted. His footsteps pounded on the stairs as he took them two at a time. "I love you too, Slick," she whispered, silently praying she'd done the right thing.

Griffen shoved the checkbook aside in disgust. The money she'd received from Dani's bank in Mississippi hadn't gone far. After writing the checks for one of the mortgage payments on the house and her Jeep payment, her checkbook balance looked pitiful and small. She couldn't keep them going much longer at this rate. Her father had offered to help, he'd give her the sun and the moon if she asked for it, but she refused to go to her family for money. This was her mess, her problem, and she'd handle it on her own. Ross had made a lot of empty promises when he'd left, and she hadn't heard a word from him in the six months he'd been gone. Well, other than the complaint for divorce his lawyers had served on her two weeks after he'd left. He'd taken nothing, other than her money, leaving behind Austin, the credit card balances, the loan balances, and all the past-due notices.

In another few days, her divorce would be final and then she could unload the house. She and Austin didn't need the huge four thousand square foot, five bedroom home sitting on twelve acres of lakefront property on the outskirts of town. There was a smaller bungalow within the Hart city limits coming available, and she'd already made an informal arrangement with owner, Edith Henley, to purchase the cozy three bedroom house with the proceeds from the sale.

She turned on her iPad and made a list of things she needed to do the following day. First would be contacting the realtor in town to list her house. She'd contact an auctioneer and sell off her inventory from the shop which should raise some cash. Just unload it all. A clean break. If she could manage to sell the boat, jet skis and the other off-road toys to a private party, she'd make a lot more money. But time was at issue, almost as much as the cash, and she was short on both.

An hour later, she'd added updating her resume to the bottom of the list just as Austin walked into the family room. He stood in front of her desk. From the distressed look on his face, she figured he'd read Dani's journal.

"Who is he?" he demanded, a catch in his voice.

She set her iPad aside and looked over the Queen Anne desk to her son. His eyes were bright with unshed tears and his hand trembled as he set the letter and journal from Dani on the polished wood in front of her. "It doesn't matter," she said, keeping her tone even as she leaned back in her chair. "Your mother loved you. I love you."

Austin balled his hands into fists at his sides and gave her an angry frown. "Dad didn't. And neither did my real father."

What could she say about Ross to ease her son's pain over the rejection by the only father he'd ever known? Since he'd left, the two-timing bastard hadn't even bothered to call and talk to Austin. "Your Dad—"

"Is a jerk." He wiped at the tears sliding down his face.

Her heart broke. She wanted to hold him, to rock him as she had when he was little, to tell him that it didn't matter. But she sensed he didn't want her comfort now. He needed to be angry, to face the emotions so he could deal with them and begin to heal.

She wrapped her arms around her middle. "That's not fair."

"What he did to us wasn't fair." Austin dropped onto the sofa and gave her an intense stare, revealing a hardness she'd never seen from him before. "Who is he?"

"He doesn't know about you. He..." She couldn't lie to him and tell him the man who fathered him might have a family of his own like she wanted to. Things would be less complicated if she could lead him to believe that contacting his father could hurt others, but she couldn't do it. Instead, she opted for a fragment of the truth and hoped it was enough to satisfy him.

"It was your mother's choice and I think we should

respect her decision."

"You know and you won't tell me." He didn't question, he accused, and that hurt. She wanted to protect him, but she couldn't deny the truth. The best she could hope for was convincing him the identity of his father held little importance. "What good will it do if you know?"

He shrugged. "I have a right to know who my own father is."

She crossed the room to sit beside him on the sofa. Almost afraid that he'd pull away from her, she reached for his hands. They were strong, even for a boy so young, but she squeezed them between her own anyway. "I don't want you to get hurt."

"How will knowing who my father is hurt me?" he asked, his voice a hoarse whisper as he fought back more tears.

He didn't know what he was asking. He didn't understand that his knowing the truth scared the life out of her. "Austin, leave it alone. Please."

He jerked away and stood. "No." He stepped around the square table and stopped in the center of the large family room. "Who is he?" he demanded. "Do you know him? Have you met him?"

"No, I haven't."

"Tell me. Please, Mom."

"Austin, I can't do that."

He glared at her, and she felt his anger as if it were a tangible thing. Gone was the sweet boy she loved. He'd been replaced by a young man who could end up hating her if she didn't make the right decision.

"You can. You just won't," he said. "I'm not a baby."

She stood and came to stand in front of him, taking hold of his shoulders. "And you're not all grown up yet, either. I don't think—"

He shrugged away from her. "You don't want to tell me cuz you're afraid I'll want to leave you and go with him."

She sucked in a sharp breath at his accusation, at the direct hit to her heart. He was only thirteen. How could he know losing him was her greatest fear? What if Maitland wasn't really the creep the press made him out to be, but the gentle caring man her sister had loved? What if he wanted to take Austin away from her? She had adoption papers, she had a birth certificate that said "father unknown," but she also had a letter from her sister that told her the truth. And she had a son who could hate her if she kept that truth from him.

Austin took a tentative step toward her. "I'm sorry, Mom. I didn't mean it."

She held up a hand to stop him. "No, you're right. That is something that I'm afraid of. But that's not why I don't want to tell you."

"Then why?"

"He's not a very nice person."

"But you said you don't know him."

"I know *of* him."

Confusion filled his dark eyes. "I don't understand."

She pushed a lock of thick, dark hair off his forehead and kissed his cheek. "I love you, Austin. Very much."

"I know, Mom. I'm sorry."

"It's okay, honey." They'd been through so much together. They would weather this dust storm, as well. She hoped.

She took his hand and led him upstairs, stopping outside his bedroom door. "You really want to know who he is?"

He was quiet for a moment, as if weighing the consequences to the knowledge she was so reluctant to impart. "Yeah, I want to know."

She opened the door and stepped inside. A twin bed he'd just about outgrown was covered with a black and red Texas Wranglers comforter, school books and a sweatshirt were scattered over the top. On the wall above his bookcase was a poster of Jed Maitland in full gear, arm drawn back, ready to send the ball sailing across the field into the hands of a waiting receiver. The caption read *Maitland the Maniac, Four Thousand Yards to Glory*. Resting atop the bookcase was a series of framed sports magazine covers. Austin's prized Jed Maitland collection.

"Look around you, Austin."

His dark brows pulled together in a frown as he glanced around his room. "I don't get it."

She drew in a deep breath, then lifted one of the frames from the bookcase and handed it to him. "*This* is your father."

Austin stared at the *Sports Illustrated* cover. Disbelief danced across his features, chased by awe as he traced his finger over the protective glass.

"No way," he said. "Jed Maitland is *my* dad?"

"I'm afraid so." She moved to the bed, dodging his basketball uniform and a pair of grungy sneakers with dirty socks sticking out of the tops. She sat, not certain her legs would hold her much longer.

"Wow," he whispered. Excitement mingled with the wonder in voice. "I want to meet him."

Dread and panic filled her. "Uh-uh." She shook her head. "Not going to happen, Slick."

"Mom, I have to meet him." He looked back down at the picture in his hands. "Jed Maitland is *so* cool."

She came up off the bed and took the frame from him and set it back on the pine bookcase. "He's *not* cool, Austin. The public image may be, but in reality the man is a jerk."

"That's just stuff his publicity people make up. He's epic, Mom."

Yeah, he was epic, all right. An epic screw-up. Fast cars and even faster women flocking around him, anxious for any scrap of attention the hot shot jock would pay them. There was the paternity suit, which he'd settled out of court. And the time he'd been in an accident, wrapping his Ferrari around a telephone pole. He'd been charged with driving while intoxicated. A concussion had been the cover up, and miraculously, the charges were dropped amid a flurry of press coverage.

No. Jed Maitland was *not* the type of man she wanted influencing her son.

"He doesn't even know you exist," she said, trying to

remain calm. All she wanted to do was rant and rave, especially if it would keep Austin away from his natural father.

Austin shrugged and grinned. That killer *Maitland* grin. Her heart nearly stopped.

"So. We'll tell him."

She gaped at her son. "No, *we* won't." She'd had enough of this conversation and headed for the door. "I wouldn't even know how to get in touch with him."

Hoping that was the end of the discussion, she left the room. She needed tea. Something soothing, something to take away the fear and the panic. How could Austin even ask such a thing?

Easy. His father was a hero, a legend. Of course he'd want to meet him.

Screw tea. She needed vodka.

"I do," Austin said from behind her.

She stopped and gripped the railing. Slowly, she turned. "You do, what?"

"I know how to get in touch with him," Austin clarified, then ran back to his room.

She couldn't move. Her feet wouldn't carry her another inch. Slowly, she sank down until she was sitting on the top step. Austin's wanting to meet his father was one thing, but it was another matter altogether if he actually knew how to find him. How could she plead ignorance? How could she tell him it was simply too difficult for her to talk to the man, to tell him that she had adopted his son? An adoption Maitland could easily contest considering he'd never been informed he even had a son, let alone one who was given up for adoption without his consent.

A wave of defeat washed over her as she stared down the carpeted stairs to the imported marble-tiled entry. She mentally outlined the design, trying not to think. Crossing her arms, she settled them on top of her knees, then rested her chin on her forearms. Defeat. She'd been doing nothing but admitting defeat all day and she was tired. Tired of fighting, tired of losing, and too worn out emotionally to deal with this latest turn of events. How could she compete with the hero worship of a man who wasn't even worthy of the adoration?

She tilted her head as Austin rushed toward her, a dog-eared sports magazine in his hands. He skidded to a stop and plopped down beside her on the top step, shoving the magazine in front of her. "He has a spread out at Possum Kingdom Lake. They did this article on him with pictures and everything."

To emphasize his point, he tapped the picture of Maitland leaning nonchalantly against the railing on the deck of a monstrous home. The heather-gray *Property of Ole Miss Athletic Department* t-shirt he wore emphasized a finely tuned body she couldn't help but admire. The faded, ripped at the knee jeans hugging muscular thighs didn't hurt, either. Wind tousled dark hair and a killer smile softened his rough, angular features making him look almost boyishly innocent.

She knew better. There wasn't an innocent bone in Maitland's deliciously hot body.

"He's got this really awesome gym and everything in his basement. Nice, huh?"

The word "no" hovered on her lips, but she bit it back and instead took the magazine from Austin. *The Making of a Legend.* What would a legend want with a thirteen-year-old boy with stars in his eyes? "Do you realize what you're asking?"

"Yeah." He flashed her that smile again. "And I still want to meet him."

Griffen could just picture *that* meeting. Maitland would threaten to have them arrested for trespassing, toss them off his property, probably with the business end of a shotgun. Austin would be crushed.

She couldn't do it. Somehow, she had to make him realize this would lead to nothing but heartache for him.

"It's not a good idea. Think about it, Slick. He doesn't even know about you. Do you know what kind of shock this would be to him? To any man?"

"But if he knew..." He shrugged.

If he knew he'd probably tell her to call his lawyer and get in line.

"What if you tell him first?" he asked, hopeful.

"Me?"

"Yeah. You tell him and then when I see him it won't be such a shock. He'll be..." He hesitated, then snapped his fingers. "Forewarned."

She couldn't answer him. Hell, she couldn't look at him, so she kept her gaze on the imported tiles below, instead of the hope in her son's eyes.

He slipped his arm around her shoulders. "Please, Mom."

Oh God. "Let me think about it," she finally said. "I won't make you any promises, but I will think about it."

"Yes." He kissed her cheek, then wrapped both arms around her, nearly squeezing the life from her. "You could go Saturday when I'm fishing with Jim and Mr. Packard."

She headed down the stairs. "I'll think about it," she warned, but Austin had already disappeared into his room.

"That's all I'll be thinking about." That, and the heartbreak her son would suffer when Maitland told her to get lost.

THREE

AGAINST HER BETTER judgment, on Saturday morning Griffen made the long drive from Hart out to Possum Kingdom, an elite lakeside community far away from the city and in the middle of nowhere. Multi-million dollar homes dotted the landscape, occupied by people who lived a lifestyle that exceeded her Visa limit. While she hadn't exactly grown up poor, her family was more of the roast beef and potatoes crowd, not wagyu connoisseurs.

By the time she pulled her Jeep Cherokee into the long driveway of the Bluff Creek Point address, her stomach was in knots. As she pulled up alongside a black Cadillac Escalade complete with the vanity plate TCHDOWN parked in the driveway, her case of nerves had tripled. The Mediterranean-style home was lavish and picture perfect, and probably worth more than twelve city blocks in her hometown of Hart, founded by her great, great grandfather.

She half expected a swarm of Dobermans to come charging after her as she left the Jeep and headed up the flagstone steps to the enormous front door. She had no idea if Maitland was even in town. When a series of phone calls had failed to produce results, she'd promised Austin she'd at least try the

Possum Kingdom house. She had to see this through now, even if it meant disappointment for her son when the "legend" wanted nothing to do with him. While she wasn't exactly keen on the whole idea, her son was willing to take the risk. So, here she was, about to knock on a total stranger's door and tell him he had a son with her sister more than a decade ago.

She rang the bell. Her plan was simple. Tell Maitland who she was and why she was there, then leave and never see him again. Austin would be heartbroken, but he'd just have to get over it. She'd return to Hart, sell her business, and send out her resume. With luck, she and Austin would be settled within the next three months, and she'd have that nine-to-five job, a 401k and health insurance.

Simple.

Easy.

No complications.

Maybe she should have hired someone to perform the uncomfortable task in front of her. Now that would have been smart. They'd called her Smart Hart in high school. When had she become so damned stupid?

She rang the bell again and hefted her bag higher onto her shoulder. Inside, she carried copies of Dani's journal along with another copy of the letter addressed to her. The only items she had to prove Dani's claim of Maitland's paternity were thin at best, but without a DNA test, it was all she had to offer.

No sound drifted from inside the house. She tried the bell a third time and started counting. If she hit fifty and no one answered, she'd leave. She knew where he lived now. She'd just send him a letter.

Twelve, thirteen.

A simple plan.

Twenty-four, twenty-five.

An easier-to-execute plan.

Thirty-six, thirty-seven.

The least complicated plan.

Forty-one, forty-two.

27

Simple and easy flew out the proverbial window when Jed Maitland opened the door. "Yeah?" His voice was gravel hard and about as welcoming.

Griffen couldn't speak. She couldn't have found her voice with both hands and a road map. Lord he was tall, and she was far from petite. His hair was a mess, hanging in bloodshot, chocolate brown eyes, looking as if it hadn't seen the productive side of a comb in weeks. The green striped button-down shirt he wore hung open, revealing a massive chest with a light sprinkling of chest hair that arrowed down, disappearing into a pair of worn jeans he'd only managed to zip, not button.

She pulled in a deep breath and wrinkled her nose. Dear God, he reeked. This was the man her sister had fallen in love with? A man who smelled like the bottom of a whisky bottle?

Her fears fled. So did her worry about competing with her son's hero. This over-the-hill, past his prime "legend" was nothing but a used up excuse for a man. She almost wished Austin *could* see him right now. Surely the sight in front of her would take down her son's hero worship faster than a sacked quarterback.

"Mr. Maitland?"

He narrowed his bloodshot eyes and leaned against the door jam, impervious to the chilled breeze against his exposed skin. "Who are you?" he asked.

"Griffen Somerfield. Griffen *Hart* Somerfield. I'm Dani Hart's sister."

He gripped the door and stared at her. She waited for him to slam it in her face. Instead, he shocked her clear to her toes by straightening and stepping back, pushing the door wide in silent invitation.

This was it. She sucked in a breath and took that fatal step onto a rough, brick floor. Her place wasn't small by any stretch of the imagination, but Maitland's foyer was at least the size of her formal dining room, if not larger. He strode past her, leaving her no choice but to follow or remain in the foyer alone.

She walked to the edge of the den, her high heeled boots

clicking over the brick flooring. She took the four steps down and followed him across the expansive room to an old fashioned mahogany bar, complete with a brass foot rung. Behind the bar a mirror, or what had once been a mirror, lay shattered. Atop the counter below the mirror and on the floor behind the bar lay an inordinate amount of broken glass. She stepped over newspapers littering the carpet and moved toward a white leather sofa. The toe of her boot clipped an empty bottle of Johnny Walker Black.

"Drink?" he asked, not looking at her.

"No. Thank you," she said, continuing her perusal of the room while she set her bag on the arm of the sofa. She righted a nearly empty bottle of Jack Daniels and set it on the coffee table next to an empty bottle of Jim Beam. The interior walls were rounded log, but that didn't prevent Maitland from displaying awards and trophies of his professional career. "Mr. Maitland, I'm sorry to disturb you like this."

Jed turned to face the woman with a husky voice that more than bordered on sexy. So this was Griffen. The middle of the three Hart sisters. He hadn't recognized the family resemblance to Dani at first, but it was there in her eyes and in the way she carried herself.

And he needed a drink. He downed a shot of José, then poured himself another, not yet ready to deal with the past.

He turned back to the bar and splashed another two fingers worth of tequila in the glass, halted, then topped it off. He had a bad feeling. The churning in his gut had nothing to do with the mother of all hangovers, and everything to do with the purpose of Griffen Hart's surprise visit. "The name's Jed."

He faced her, raising his glass in mock salute. She didn't say anything, just looked at him with those big green eyes that brought back memories he didn't care to recall. He took a long swallow of booze to keep them at bay.

"Very well. Jed." She perched her curvy behind on the arm of his sofa. Her long, jean clad legs easily reached the floor. She wore her auburn hair, a shade or two richer than Dani's, in a long, wavy cut that just about brushed her shoulder blades.

The woman had Irish written all over her, and he'd bet she had a temper to match her don't-fuck-with-me attitude.

"You had an affair with my sister fourteen years ago, correct?"

The disdain in her voice irritated him. "Fifteen, not that it's any of your business." He wasn't in any mood to travel down memory lane, especially with a woman who looked down her straight and perfect nose at him.

She moved her bag to the seat of the sofa and adjusted her position on the arm. "I'm afraid it is, Mr. Maitland. Dani had a son."

The anger never far from the surface started to rear its head. "So what does that have to do with me? Dani and I split up a long time ago, *Sister*."

She sighed and reached for her bag. "I knew I shouldn't have come here."

"Then why did you?" He couldn't keep the memories away and silently damned Griffen Hart straight to hell for making him remember.

She stopped and turned back to face him. He took another sip of whisky. Yup, she had a temper, all right. Her eyes nearly sparkled with it, and if he was in a better frame of mind, he might have found her interesting. Too bad he was in a shitty mood.

"I'm here because it's the right thing to do," she said, the sharp, clipped tone of her voice matching the anger simmering in her gaze. "An investigator came to see me a few days ago and delivered the contents of Dani's safety deposit box. She passed away nine years ago and the bank only recently confirmed her death."

He set the glass on the bar with a snap and moved to the windows to stare out at the lake. Dani was gone. She'd been out of his life for a long time, but he couldn't believe she was really gone. It wasn't as if he'd hoped she'd come back to him, but the news of her death still touched him in a place he'd long ago forgotten about—his heart.

Not bothering to turn around, he asked, "How?"

"According to the investigator—"

"No." He shoved both hands through his hair. "How did she die?"

"It doesn't matter." The anger had left her voice. "What—"

He spun around to face her. "How the fuck did she die?" Regardless of what this woman thought about him and his relationship with her sister, he'd loved Dani, had planned to marry her, but she'd disappeared from his life. And it had damned near torn out his heart.

To her credit, she didn't flinch. "When Dani was sixteen, she was diagnosed with Leukemia. She'd been in remission for a number of years. Then all of a sudden, she came home from college, pregnant and almost immediately suffered a relapse after Austin was born. Having him was just too much for her."

He hadn't even known she was ill. All the time he'd spent with her, he hadn't even known she'd been sick. Okay, so she'd been in remission, but why had she kept something like that from him?

Apparently she'd kept a lot of things from him.

"Austin," he repeated. Dani had named her son after his grandfather, the man who'd raised him. The man responsible for where he was today. He'd been ten and heading for trouble fast, but his grandfather had signed him up for a youth football program in the small, backwater Mississippi town where he'd gone to live after his parents had been killed in an accident.

"Where's this kid of hers now?" he asked, telling himself he was merely curious. Dani had never contacted him again after she'd disappeared. What were the chances the kid was even his?

"My ex-husband and I adopted him before we lost Dani."

"Then why are you here?" Was she looking for a handout? Had the kid gotten to be too much for her and she was planning to dump him on his doorstep? She could forget it. He had his own problems.

"He's your kid, *Sister*. Obviously you've got adoption papers that say so."

The look she gave him could have fried the balls off a

swamp full of gaters. She shoved a lock of silky looking hair behind her ear, then tossed her bag back on the sofa in show of obvious frustration or anger. He was guessing anger.

"I'm here, *Mr.* Maitland because I just learned that you are Austin's biological father. Unfortunately, my son is a huge fan, and as nauseating as I find it, *you* are his idol. I'm sure even you could imagine what that kind news would do for a thirteen-year-old boy."

He braced his feet apart and crossed his arms over his chest. "So what do you want me to do about it? You here for an autograph?" Yeah, he was being a bastard and he knew it. But it kept people away, kept them from getting too close.

"I'm here because I promised my son I would come." Her hands landed on her gently rounded hips and she gave him a look filled with disgust. "I don't expect, or want, anything from you, but Austin does. He's going to be disappointed for a while." She picked up her bag again and slung it over her shoulder. "But don't let it worry you. He'll get over it."

She opened the canvas bag and withdrew a thick manila envelope, tossing it on the glass table. "For your reading pleasure," she said before turning on her heel and storming out of his house, and hopefully his life.

Jed heard her car start and pull out of his driveway. He stood by the window, staring at the envelope for a long time. The past was a place he didn't want to travel. Too many bitter memories awaited him at the end of the road.

He crossed the room, picked up the envelope then hit the switch to ignite the logs in the fireplace. Dani had walked out of his life fourteen years ago. He wasn't about to let her back in now.

The split logs caught, and he waited until a healthy fire blazed, then tossed the envelope inside. The edges turned black and curled until the package was fully engulfed in flames.

Satisfied, he picked up a fresh bottle of Jack Daniels and made his way to the sofa. He flipped on the big screen television. A rowing competition played on ESPN. He hit the mute button and stared at the screen as the four man rowing team from Cal State Northridge took the lead.

With the bottle resting comfortably between his legs, he popped three more painkillers into his mouth, then tipped the bottle and chugged. In another twenty minutes, he wouldn't care who won the rowing competition. Better yet, he wouldn't give a fuck about anyone or anything, not even the resurrected memories of a past best forgotten.

And that was just fine with him.

Jed rolled over with a groan and turned off the ringer on his cell phone. No way was he taking that call. Dr. Robick's secretary had a high-pitched, nasally tone that grated on the nerves, especially when combined with the continual hangover he'd been waking up with since the weekend. He didn't need a wake-up call. He knew he'd missed another appointment.

Did they think he was stupid?

He squinted at the screen on his phone. Wednesday? What the hell happened to Monday and Tuesday?

He ignored the icon indicating he had more than a dozen voice mails waiting to be retrieved. No doubt more calls from his agent and the head coach. Calls he had no intention of returning. He scrolled through the missed call log. Even his publicist had picked up the torch to hassle him.

He was sick and tired of being badgered by the people who'd gotten rich off his name. Now that there was a chance he'd no longer have what it took to increase their wealth, the vultures wouldn't leave him alone. He'd expected the opposite, but as his agent had pointed out, they were only protecting their investment.

"Meal ticket is more like it," he muttered, swinging his legs over the side of the king-sized bed.

He stretched his arms over his head, but his shoulder caught, sending sharp pain shooting down his arm into the numb fingers of his right hand. Ignoring the painkillers and the half empty bottle of scotch on the nightstand, he headed for the shower and hopefully salvation from the pounding in his head.

He stripped and stepped beneath the jets, letting the steaming water pound against him, wondering what to do next. Maybe he should find a new orthopedist and get a second opinion.

A second opinion? Or someone to tell you your career isn't over?

He grimaced at the thought of his career being at an end. He was only thirty-five years old, far from over the hill. Or was he? Linc Monroe, his best friend and one of the greatest wide receivers to ever grace the field, had warned him long ago the game would suck him dry, use and abuse him until there was nothing left to give. And Linc had known, because he'd been there once himself until...

With a vile curse, Jed dipped his head beneath the spray. No. He wouldn't go there. Besides, over the hill wasn't for Maitland the Maniac. He had his entire life in front of him. *Has-been* wasn't in his vocabulary. And he was not about to crawl off somewhere to lick his wounds and cry about a lousy injury that could keep him off the field. He'd never whined like a spoiled brat and he wasn't about to start now. So what if they said the surgery hadn't had the results they'd been hoping for? Who were they to tell him his career was over? No one was going to tell him what he could or couldn't do with his life.

God, he was tired of everyone wanting a piece of him.

Visions of a long legged, auburn-haired beauty with fire in her eyes traipsed through his mind. He might have had the hangover from hell when Dani's sister had arrived on his doorstep, but that hadn't meant he couldn't appreciate her sweet ass or the subtle lilac scent that had remained in his house long after she'd gone. Even she'd wanted a piece of him, he decided, cultivating his foul and rebellious mood. Not for herself, but for her kid.

His kid.

His *and* Dani's kid.

He cast that thought aside and reached for the shampoo.

Minutes later and feeling somewhat more human, he stepped from the shower. The pounding headache hadn't eased up enough, so he opened the medicine chest for the bottle of plain, old-fashioned aspirin. With a flick of his thumb, he snapped open the cap, shook two into his mouth and swallowed.

With a towel draped his waist, he strode back into the bedroom just as his cell phone started vibrating across the nightstand. He had to get out of there. Find a place where no one knew him, where no one expected anything of him or from him. A place where his agent, lawyer or publicist couldn't badger him into something he wanted no part of—retirement from the only thing he knew.

Retire?

Him?

Now that was the laugh of the season. He wasn't about to become a locker room joke. He'd worked too fucking hard for that to happen.

He dressed quickly in jeans, a black t-shirt and a pair of scuffed boots, then dragged a comb through his hair. "Over the hill, my ass," he said to his reflection.

He tossed the comb onto the dresser, then grabbed a duffle bag from the walk-in closet and threw in a few essentials. A pair of aviator sunglasses rested on top of the dresser, and he slipped them on, purposely ignoring the Wranglers ball cap resting nearby. Instead, he grabbed the black and gold Pittsburgh one and shoved it on his head. Jed Maitland was getting the hell out of Dodge for a while.

Where he was going, he couldn't say, and he really didn't give a rat's ass.

FOUR

ONCE UPON A time, Griffen and her sisters, Dani and Mattie, had found an old lantern in their Grandpa Caulfield's barn. They'd been young and silly and had pretended it was a magic lamp, making wishes that had never come true. She carefully set the old lantern on the counter, moving it away from the collectibles she'd pulled from the top display shelves for the going out of business sale scheduled for the following day. The lantern held no monetary value, but no way was she parting with it.

She climbed back up the ladder and started hauling down the antique china tea sets. They were elegant and delicate, but slow movers, so she marked them down to half price, even if it would cut into her profit margin.

"What profit margin?" she muttered, reaching for a red-patterned Homer Laughlin cup and saucer set with a pretty pink rose in the center. By the time she was finished, she'd be lucky to clear enough to pay off even one of the past due business loans.

As she swiped two month's worth of dust from the china, she cursed Ross for putting her in such a precarious financial position. She never should've listened to him, but followed her instincts instead and kept the business solely in her name. Allowing him to cloud her judgment, listening to his lies about their partnership being one of love and business, had been more than stupid, it was proving fatal.

Things would return to normal soon. She had to believe that, despite evidence to the contrary. When she'd placed a call to the mayor's wife to discuss the Louis XIV table last week, Mrs. Carter had finally agreed to buy. Although she was clearing only a fraction of what she'd originally paid for the antique, she was glad to be rid of the pricey item.

The bell over the door jangled and she looked up, smiling when her sister, Mattie, walked through the door. "You're just in time," Griffen said as she climbed down the ladder balancing a teal, rose-patterned teapot. "I'm marking these down and I know you've been wanting this Royal Albert tea service."

Mattie returned the grin as she kicked off her heels and wiggled her toes into the thick carpet in front of the counter. "How much?" she asked. "You know I'm too cheap to pay full price."

Griffen dusted her hands on her jeans. "Fifty percent off," she said, delighted when her sister's eyes sparkled greedily. "But for you, seventy-five."

"Sold." Mattie picked up a delicate china cup and admired it, gently tracing her finger over the scalloped edge. "Set it aside for me. I didn't bring my checkbook."

Griffen pulled several sheets of tissue from beneath the counter and started wrapping the set. "What are you still doing in town?" Other than attending classes every day at Hart High School where Mattie taught Home Economics, she rarely ventured far from home. Mattie was a creature of habit, or rather, had become one since her late husband, Ford Grayson's death five years ago.

Mattie rubbed her flat tummy that Griffen knew held not even a single stretch mark from the birth of her daughter five years before. "It's Thursday. That means Goldie's fried chicken special." An anticipated gleam entered her sister's eyes. "And the hot fudge sundaes for desert are on me."

Griffen's stomach growled. Lunch had consisted of a cup of instant noodle soup, half a container of yogurt and iced tea, no sugar. "Can't. I've got a ton to do before for the sale tomorrow."

Mattie sighed and flipped her long, dark hair over her shoulder before leaning on the glass case. "You're no fun. How can I convince you to let go for once and gorge yourself on Goldie's homemade hot fudge?"

Griffen smiled at her younger sister. "One bite is a lifetime on my ass." She picked up the soft cloth she'd been using and wiped down a pink china cup. "Forget it. I'm not like you. I have to watch what I eat."

Mattie straightened. "I watch what I eat."

Mattie could eat a Big Mac and fries for breakfast, lunch and dinner and never gain an ounce. Life just wasn't fair. "Sure you do," Griffen teased. "You watch it disappear from your plate."

"Is it my fault I was born with a great metabolism?" Mattie pushed away from the counter and strolled around the store. "So you're really selling out, huh?"

Griffen dropped the cleaning rag on the counter. "I have to, Matt." As much as she didn't want to lose her business, the books, and the bank, were both telling her otherwise. Since she'd made the decision, she hadn't looked back. No regrets, she'd decided. Step into the future and embrace it with both hands. At least that's what she kept telling herself whenever her confidence started to slip.

Mattie traced her hand along the back of a one-hundred-year-old tapestry sofa. "Dad told me you've got an interview with your old firm in Dallas next week."

"Not exactly an interview," Griffen said. "I made an appointment to meet with Greg Coulter. Hopefully he'll have a job for me."

"No luck with the banks in town, huh?"

"None." Keith Shelton had been kind and understanding, but empty-handed. Joe Gibson, the realtor, had already shown her home to a couple from Dallas looking to relocate to a smaller town to raise their children, but so far, they hadn't made an offer. The real estate market hadn't quite recovered, but with the auction coming up, she could afford to be patient, for at least a little while longer.

Mattie sat on the sofa, her bright green eyes filled with compassion. "I'm really sorry, Griff."

Griffen shrugged. "I'm not looking forward to that drive every day, but I need to make a decent living. Want some iced tea?"

Mattie shook her head and wrinkled her nose in response. Her sister was a diehard Coke drinker. "I wish I could help."

"Don't worry about it," she said. "Just promise you'll come to the auction with me."

"You shouldn't go. Let the auctioneer handle it and deliver the proceeds to you when it's over."

"You're probably right," she said, but knew she'd attend anyway. She couldn't help herself. Obviously, she was a glutton for punishment.

She hefted a milk crate filled with 78s and carried it to the sofa. She needed to catalogue and separate the old records for the auctioneer, so she might as well stop putting it off. There wasn't much of a demand for old records, but she was spending the money to advertise in newspapers from the surrounding communities in hopes there might be a collector or two looking for Eddie Arnold, Rosemary Clooney or Dean Martin.

She set an empty box next to Mattie, then pulled a stack from the box and handed them to her sister. "Help me sort." She hauled over another crate. Hoping to steer the conversation toward a more pleasant topic, she asked, "So where's my niece?"

"The she-devil Phoebzilla?" Mattie asked with a grin that made Griffen laugh. Phoebe was no she-devil, she was just her mother's daughter.

Mattie started sorting the old records. "She wanted to stay with Dad and Austin. They were watching an old movie when

I left. I'm betting by the time I pick her up, she'll have connived them into the three hundred and forty-third showing of *Beauty and the Beast* or *Mulan*."

Griffen and her sister worked companionably for the next thirty minutes. As they separated the records by artist, Mattie shared more tales of Phoebe's exploits.

"She's such a little monster." Mattie laughed as she wiped dust from her hands. "If she's this much of a handful at five, what's she going to be like at fifteen? Hannah Richards, the elementary school principal, pulled me from my class the other day because Phoebe wouldn't let Lewis Nettles out of the cloakroom until he apologized for pulling Denise Fitch's braids."

Griffen stifled a grin. "Who does that sound like?"

"Ford."

"No, you."

Mattie gave her a narrow-eyed glare. "I was nothing like Phoebe."

Griffen laughed. "Remember what you did to Jason McDougall in the fourth grade?"

"That was the fourth grade, not kindergarten," Mattie said. "Besides, Jason deserved having his face painted green. He put a spider in my desk."

Griffen moved the empty crate to the floor and stood. "A plastic spider," she reminded her sister before she went to the office for her iPad.

"He still scared me," Mattie called after her.

With her digital tablet in hand, Griffen returned to the showroom. The sunlight was fading, but at least the days were growing longer.

A sparkle on Mattie's ring finger suddenly caught Griffen's attention. "What on earth is this?" she asked, reaching for her sister's hand. A beautifully cut, three-step diamond and emerald engagement ring, occupied Mattie's left hand. "Oh Matt, it's so beautiful."

Her sister smiled shyly. "Trenton proposed."

"I can see that." Tears blurred her vision as she reached for

Mattie and gave her a hug. She couldn't be more thrilled that her little sister had found happiness again. For years Mattie had mourned Ford, who'd been shot down over the Mediterranean Sea during the war with Afghanistan.

Mattie and Ford had been high school sweethearts. Against both of their families' advice, they'd married right after graduation and together they'd headed to Waco to attend Baylor. Then Ford had joined the Navy, went to Officer Candidate School, then flight school followed by SEAL training. Mattie had eventually joined Ford in San Diego, California. When he'd been assigned another top secret mission during Mattie's ninth month of pregnancy, he'd insisted she come back to Texas to be with her family for the birth.

The night they'd learned Ford's plane had been shot down, Mattie went into labor and delivered Phoebe. She'd been so devastated by Ford's death, it'd taken her two months before she'd even held her daughter.

Griffen held Mattie's hand up for a closer look at her engagement ring. "Wow," she said, smiling at her sister. "Trenton has excellent taste."

Mattie eased her hand out of Griffen's grasp. "Hmmm," she murmured. "I suppose he does."

Griffen frowned. "When did he propose?"

"Last weekend."

"When were you planning to tell me?"

"Over fried chicken and Goldie's awesome gravy," Mattie said. "I would've told you sooner, but I've been getting used to the idea. Besides, you've had a lot on your own plate lately."

She had no intention of talking about her problems. "Have you set a date?"

"Fourth of July."

Griffen tried not to look so surprised, but couldn't help herself. "That's barely three months away. That ring doesn't exactly scream elopement, Matt. It's a few hundred guests, frilly veil and a four tiered wedding cake kind of ring."

"I know." Mattie sounded worried. "I don't want a big

41

wedding, Griff. I'd be happy running off to Vegas."

"But..."

"I've been married before. I don't think a big wedding is appropriate."

"Bullshit," Griffen said and stood. She snagged her iPad from the cushion then went to sit on the floor next to the stacks of records. "You can have any kind of wedding you want. And if you really want to run off to Vegas, then do it."

"Trenton has partners and important clients of the law firm that he wants to impress."

"Did he say that?"

"No, but I know he does. Appearances are important to him."

And they weren't to her sister. Her gaze slid to the old lantern still on the counter. Mattie Elizabeth Hart Grayson, the high school economics teacher who wanted nothing more out of life than to marry her high school sweetheart and raise a house full of his babies. Mattie preferred simple and elegant, not over-the-top and showy.

"We can talk wedding plans later. How's Austin holding up?" Mattie asked. "He seemed a little quieter than usual this afternoon."

Griffen sighed, her heart hurting all over again. "He needs time to deal." Austin had been disappointed when she'd returned from Maitland's ridiculously expensive lake house in Possum Kingdom five days ago. The dejection in her son's eyes had just about torn her heart to shreds. She'd hated telling him, but he'd needed to know Maitland wasn't interested in playing daddy, no matter how painful.

"That's pretty much how he's been all week." Leaning back on her hands, the tablet forgotten on her lap, Griffen let out a long breath. "He was so upset Maitland didn't want anything to do with him. I think I could kill that lousy bastard."

Mattie leaned forward, resting her forearms over her knees. "Why did you tell him? Do you think he might have been better off not knowing at all?"

"I know he would've been." Of course her son would've

been better off not being rejected by another man in his life. But she also believed she'd done what her sister had wanted her to do, even if Dani's wishes hadn't coincided with her own.

"It's what Dani wanted." And that's all she was going to say on the subject. She had done the right thing, and now her son had been hurt. Maitland was morally compromised and a jerk. What did he know about the feelings of a young boy? She could have kept quiet about the entire situation, but, no, morally *un*compromising as she was, she'd been honest. For once she should have done what her heart told her and kept the identity of Austin's father to herself.

"Hey, I remember this." Mattie stood and pulled the old lantern from the counter. She lifted it toward the light, a grin tugging the corners of her mouth. "You're not selling this are you?"

"No." She entered a few more names into the inventory program on her tablet. "Looks like it wasn't a magic lamp after all. None of our wishes came true."

Mattie picked up the dust cloth and wiped at the relic. "Maybe we just weren't specific enough."

"I wanted to be successful, remember?"

Mattie set the lamp on the low table near the sofa. "You are successful."

Griffen stared at her sister in astonishment. "Look around you, Matt. I'm losing my business. One step ahead of bankruptcy doesn't exactly scream success."

Mattie crouched on the floor in front of her, a conspiratorial light in her eyes. "I don't buy that. You can still turn this around."

"And I'm sure you're going to tell me how. What pearls of wisdom do you have for pulling a miracle out of this mess Ross left me?"

"You don't have to sell out. Dad can loan—"

"No." Griffen stood, stepping around the records and her sister. She dragged her hands through her hair. "I won't do that. It's my problem and I'll handle it."

Frustration lit her sister's eyes. "Why do you have to be so stubborn?"

Griffen glared back at Mattie. She wasn't being stubborn, she was being responsible. There was Austin to think of, and his future. She wouldn't allow her son to go without just so she could follow through on some silly dream to own her own business. As much as she hated losing Antiquities, she was being practical, as usual.

Mattie crossed the room to stand in front of her. Compassion, understanding and love chased across her sister's features. "I just hate to see you lose your dreams," she said in a low voice. "I lost mine once. I know what that's like."

Griffen blinked back an unexpected rush of tears. She took her sister's hand and squeezed. "A failed business doesn't even compare to losing your husband, Matt."

Mattie's smoky lashes swept closed and she pulled in a deep breath. When she opened them, she offered a shaky grin. "Let's get out of here," she said. "Goldie's fried chicken and gravy is waiting. I feel the need to celebrate my engagement with carbs."

"I can't," Griffen answered regretfully. She ducked behind the counter, pulling out the gift box with the Royal Albert tea service. "Here. Take it."

"You sure? I know you need the money."

"Not that much," Griffen lied. "Consider it an engagement present."

Mattie took the box. "Thank you," she said. "Come on. Come with me, Griff. You need to eat."

"I'll pass. I've got tons to do here before tomorrow. Austin is staying with Dad so I can work late."

"All work and no play will make you a very boring girl."

Shaking her head, she ushered her sister out the door. "Say hi to Goldie for me," she said, then flipped the sign to Closed. She'd had enough excitement the past few months to last her a lifetime. Boring was just fine by her.

*

After spending two nights in small towns that held little nightlife other than local taverns, Jed still hadn't decided where he was headed. All he knew was the freedom felt amazing and he was in no hurry to return to the vultures waiting to peck over his remains. So far, no one had recognized him. He'd even enjoyed a few games of eight ball with the locals in the last town. He could get used to this. Maybe he should become a drifter, just float from one town to the next, take in the sights, the atmosphere and just enjoy the hell out of life for a change. No pressures, no worries, surviving on his wits rather than his name.

But by Friday afternoon, his wits had deserted him when he steered his SUV off the highway to the secondary road that would take him to Hart, Texas. Maybe it was a morbid sense of curiosity or something more he wasn't quite ready to face, but as he neared the main drag of the charming little town, answers still evaded him.

He pulled up to the stop sign in the center of town. A group of boys ran across the street, backpacks and book bags bouncing as they darted across the street into a place called Goldie's. They looked to be around twelve or thirteen. Perhaps Austin was one of them. Not that he cared. Mere curiosity, nothing more.

He continued to cruise down Main Street, then flipped-a-bitch at the edge of town to circle back. He hadn't eaten since breakfast and his stomach had started growling thirty miles ago.

He parked in front of the diner and killed the engine. A warm wind blew in from the west as he left the Escalade, signaling the heat of summer would be arriving much sooner than the calendar dictated. Green still covered the countryside, but it wouldn't be much longer before the blazing heat of the Texas sun would burn nearly everything it touched, turning the landscape varying shades of brown. Local ranchers would gather in town diners, complaining about the low return on beef and rising operation costs in general. School would let out for summer break and the local hot spot would make a mint from video arcades and soda sales.

The small town of Hart wasn't much different than the swampy, southern town where he'd been raised by his grandparents. A part of him missed those days, he realized with a pang of longing. Back then, no one had expected anything from him, other than a decent report card and a somewhat clean bedroom.

He gaze wandered over the sleepy little town. A tavern sat on the corner, a neon beer sign flashing in the window. He stood by the front of the Escalade, staring at the entrance to The Hangout, thinking the taste of scotch could soothe his appetite just as well as anything on Goldie's menu.

Deciding he'd be better off with a solid meal rather than a liquid one, he crossed the sidewalk and stepped into the diner. This late in the afternoon, only a few patrons occupied the booths, one with the group of boys he'd spotted earlier. Their raucous laughter filled the restaurant, competing with the Carrie Underwood tune playing on the jukebox in the corner.

He took a seat at the counter and reached for the red plastic menu. The fare was classic diner—burgers, fries and a variety of deep fried dinners with enough cholesterol to clog the arteries of an elephant. An insert boasted a fish platter as the Friday special.

"What'll it be?"

Jed looked up and grinned at the silver-haired waitress with Goldie embroidered on her more-gray-than-blue uniform. "How's the special?"

She pulled a pencil from behind her ear and looked at him over the rim of her bifocals. "Good. Everything we have is good." She didn't bother to return his grin.

"I'll try my luck with the special."

"Coffee with that?"

"Sweet tea." He gave her another grin. "And a piece of that peach cobbler you've got cooling over there for desert."

She grinned then, the lines in her face deepening. "Got yourself a good nose." She reached behind the counter and set a glass filled with ice in front of him.

"My grandmother used to feed it to me when I brought home A's," he said, pouring on the Maitland charm. He wasn't above bribery when it came to peach cobbler, especially one that smelled as good as the one cooling behind the counter.

She poured the tea from a pitcher, then spun away, hanging the ticket with his order on a metal ring. "Buck! Order!"

She returned with clean silverware. "Don't look the type to bring home too many of them A's, if you ask me."

He leaned back when she set silverware in front of him. "I managed my fair share."

Goldie grunted, only he wasn't sure if it was from disbelief or approval. She turned her attention to the booth filled with boys, lowered her bifocals to the edge of her nose and had more than a hint of stern lecture creeping into her hazel eyes.

As he waited for Buck to dish up the daily special, he listened to Brad Paisley on the jukebox and just enjoyed the relative peace of the place. Maybe he *should* retire, he thought. Return to his hometown, back to the house his grandfather had left him when he'd passed away. He still had a degree in history he'd managed to earn from Ole Miss, and enough money to last him ten lifetimes. Maybe he should disappear into the state school system. His grin turned caustic. Bet that would tick off the vultures.

Buck screeched for Goldie when his order was ready. She grumbled something Jed couldn't quite make out, then placed a steaming platter of fried cod, fries and a side of greens in front of him.

"You're not from around here."

He kept his attention on the food. "Nope." Now he remembered what it was about small towns that made him uncomfortable. Curiosity. He should have hit the tavern.

She wiped down the counter. "Passing through?"

Was he? Or was he going to do something he'd probably regret for the rest of his life? Two days of anonymity and not drinking himself into a drunken stupor had him realizing he'd been on a collision course for far too long.

He slathered a pat of butter on the greens. "Visiting an old friend," he said, feeling regret creep into his soul. "Can you tell me where Griffen Hart lives these days?"

Goldie's eyes narrowed over the rim of her bifocals. "You an old friend of Griffen's, huh?"

"You could say that," he hedged, then popped a ketchup soaked fry into his mouth.

"You could, huh?" She planted her hands on the counter, her narrowed gaze becoming a hostile glare. "Seems if you was any kind of friend, you'd know where she lives."

"It's been a while." He reached for the tea and downed the contents, then offered up his empty glass for a refill. Goldie took the hint and went for the pitcher.

"Where she living these days?" he asked, after she topped off his glass.

Goldie set the pitcher back under the counter and started filling salt and pepper shakers. "Still in that fancy house on the lake," she said. "But you can probably find her at the antique store 'bout now."

"Oh, yeah?"

"Antiquities. A block down," she indicated with a nod of her head. "Big sale going on today and tomorrow." She screwed the tops on the filled shakers, then delivered them to the booths.

When he finished his meal, Goldie dished him up a heaping serving of the still-warm cobbler with a scoop of vanilla ice cream on the side. His hunger finally satisfied, he dropped enough cash on the counter to cover the bill and a generous tip, then left the diner.

Well, hell. He was here. In Hart. Although he still hadn't figured out *why* he'd come, he might as well pay a visit to Griffen.

He headed in the direction Goldie had told him to go, passed the barbershop, the post office and Hart Savings and Loan, then crossed the deserted street to Antiquities. A red and white sign with bold blue letters indicated a going out of business sale.

Interesting. Maybe he hadn't been wrong in thinking she'd

come to him for a handout. Hit up the rich guy and claim that an adopted kid was his. He wondered how much she would demand to keep the news away from the media? But that didn't make much sense. Considering he hadn't heard word one from her since she'd walked out of his house a week ago.

Curious, he pushed open the door to the shop. Some sale. The place was deserted. He closed the door and the bell jangled as he looked around. Traffic patterns were established by strategically arranged furniture. Bowls, vases and Victorian lamps all doubled as display and decoration. To his left sat a country style dining room, complete with a pine hutch filled with dishware similar to those his grandmother had owned. A heavy pottery bowl laden with waxed fruit sat atop a white lace table runner, flanked by matching candle holders with blue and white drip candles.

He stepped deeper into the shop, around a vintage hi-fi with a stack of old Dean Martin records arranged in organized confusion on the top. A table he suspected to be Chippendale sat off to the side, an array of perfume bottles and a silver backed comb and brush set were perched on top of an oval mirrored tray. He caught sight of the price tag for the Chippendale and did a double take. Pretty stiff for a close-out sale.

Turning, he caught the scent of lilacs. Griffen's scent.

A lace curtain separating the showroom from the office was pulled back and tied with a blue velvet bow, giving him a perfect view of her profile. She stood, bent over a roll top desk, her attention engrossed in whatever she was reading. Her auburn hair was swept up in an elegant style that showed off the slim column of her neck. The urge to press his lips to the skin at her nape, to breathe in her sweet scent, unnerved him.

"I'll be right with you," she called, not taking her eyes from the paperwork in front of her.

He didn't say anything. He didn't think he could. The woman wearing the white sleeveless blouse and slim navy, linen skirt that stopped mid-thigh, couldn't have been the same spitfire who'd come to his lake house last weekend. While that woman had stirred his temper, this elegant, sexy-as-sin vision stirred his libido.

She shut a journal of some sort and turned to face him, a pleasant smile lighting her face. "Can I help..."

Recognition flashed in her eyes. The sweet smile curving her lips disappeared into a tight, thin line. The spitfire was back. For some reason, that thought pleased him.

He hitched his elbow on a display case and leaned casually against the glass. "Hello, Sister," he said, deciding this was going to be a whole lot more fun than emptying a fresh bottle of scotch.

FIVE

GRIFFEN STARED IN utter shock at Jed Maitland.

Why was he here? In her store? Curiosity? Or something else? Something that could threaten the mess her life had become. She had enough to cope with right now without having to add dealing with him to her growing list of problems. Oh God. What if Austin heard his *father* was in Hart.

"What are you doing here?" she demanded.

He straightened and strolled across the gray and blue pile carpeting to the framed reproduction print of a Picasso abstract hanging above a round gilt table. "Heard you were having a sale."

She skirted behind the counter. Drunk, obnoxious and surly, Maitland could easily be overlooked as a threat. Instinct told her sober was another matter altogether and she'd better keep her guard up around him. "You heard wrong. We're closed."

He kept his back to her. "Sign says you don't close until six."

Against her will, her gaze slid to his faded-denim-clad ass.

He inclined his head toward the Picasso reproduction. "Nice copy."

Nice ass.

"I never did understand his blue period though," he said with a shrug of his wide shoulders.

"No one does." She forced her eyes anywhere but on him and the way his shoulders filled out the shirt he wore or the way the denim covered that mighty fine backside. She moved the business card holder in front of the till, then pushed it back to where she'd had it. "I'm closing early."

He turned to face her and smiled, the corners of his dark eyes crinkling. If she didn't fear his presence could hurt her son, she might, *might*, have found that killer grin appealing. If he wasn't Jed Maitland with a reputation to make Casanova blush, she might even find him relatively attractive. Only she didn't find him attractive, relative or otherwise. The man wasn't even likable. Not one iota. The only thing he meant to her was one more complication in her life she didn't need, one she couldn't run away from, no matter how tempting the thought.

He moved to the tapestry sofa and sat, propping one scuffed boot on his knee and stretching his arms along the back. "Guess that's why you're going out of business, huh?" He just smiled at her, a lazy, comfortable smile that had her gritting her teeth.

Her nerves were shot, and he wasn't helping much with his I-have-all-the-time-in-the-world attitude. Bad news came in threes, and Maitland's appearance was her third for the day. The shop had been open since ten. Little more than a dozen customers had bothered to venture in to browse all day. Her final divorce decree had arrived from the courthouse in the morning mail, declaring her officially single. While the thought of divorce from Ross didn't exactly break her heart, that one document reminded her of one more failure in her life. And now Maitland was lounging around as if he had nothing better to do. Her icing on the cake. "What do you want, Mr. Maitland?"

He shrugged, then winced, reminding her of the reports of his injured shoulder. "I was passing through."

She braced her hands on the counter and tried to ignore the churning in her stomach. "And?"

"And nothing."

"I find that hard to believe."

His eyes narrowed and that square jaw of his hardened for an instant before he resumed his relaxed pose. "Believe what you want, Sister. I'm passing through."

She wasn't about to play mouse to his cat. "Then I suggest you continue passing through." She pushed away from the counter and headed toward the office. "Good day, Mr. Maitland."

Tea. Tea would help settle her stomach. She filled a mug with water and zapped it in the microwave, listening for the bells over the door to signal his departure. The bell on the microwave dinged and she jumped.

Get a grip. She retrieved the mug and dipped an Earl Grey tea bag into the steaming water to steep. The man couldn't hurt them if she didn't give him the power to do so. She'd ignore him and he'd leave. If he didn't, she'd—

"I'd like to meet him."

She flinched, then spun around, her hand shooting to her throat. "There's a sign over the door that says 'private,' or can't you read?" Rudeness wasn't her typical style, but he was crowding her, not just physically, but emotionally. His presence was making her face what frightened her most and she wasn't prepared. Going to his place in Possum Kingdom, she'd been ready. Finding him on her turf wasn't something she'd ever dreamed would happen, and she didn't like it one bit.

"I'd like to meet my son," he said again, his deep, rough voice hard.

She lowered her hand and turned back to her tea, adding a packet of sweetener to her mug. His rich chocolate colored eyes weren't bloodshot this time, but clear and, she realized, held a hint of danger. "Last time we spoke, you didn't have a son. I have adoption papers that say he's my son, remember?" Hoping to come off more confident than she was feeling, she sipped her tea as if *she* had all the time in the world.

53

He shoved a hand through his thick, dark hair, and gave her a crooked smile. "You caught me at a bad time. I apologize."

She lifted a brow at the curving of his lips, a smile she considered more cocksure confidence than contrition, then lowered her mug. "From what I know about you, it's never a good time. Oh, wait. I take that back. You always have a good time, don't you, Mr. Maitland?"

She needed to get away from him. He stood too close. Close enough for her to catch the spicy scent of his aftershave. Stepping around him wasn't easy since he was so big, and she brushed against him on her way back into the showroom.

He followed her. "Now wait just a freaking minute."

Why wouldn't he go away? Why did he have to keep dogging her, standing too close and making her nervous? She snatched an atomizer from the Chippendale and wiped at dust that wasn't there. "Is that what you had with my sister, Mr. Maitland? A good time?"

"You're a real piece of work, you know that?"

She caught his reflection in the ornate mirror hanging on the wall in front of her. His eyes were hard, as was the firm jaw he was busy clenching. Arms crossed over his wide chest pulled the black graphic t-shirt tight, emphasizing his massive size. She'd seen that gloriously wide chest bared only a week ago. Then, he hadn't affected her. Now, he intimidated her, and she wasn't used to being intimidated.

With more calm than she believed herself capable of possessing in the face of such a huge, angry man, she gently returned the atomizer to the Chippendale. Turning to face him, she smiled, a smile meant to infuriate him so he'd get out her life. "And you're an ass," she said sweetly. "So I guess that makes us even."

She took a step, but he blocked her path and glared down at her. "I said I was sorry about last week."

"Apology accepted." She moved again, but he moved with her. She realized she knew nothing about him, other than various press reports and entries in Dani's journal, both sources of information conflicting. One depicted him as sweet, kind and gentle, while the other declared his motto as live hard, play harder, and leave a good-looking corpse.

"Please leave." Who was the real Jed Maitland?

"Not happening." He shook his head. "Not until we resolve this."

She tipped her head back until she could see his eyes. The determination in them made her sorry she'd bothered. "What's to resolve? You made your position perfectly clear."

"I want to meet the kid." He didn't shout, but there was a frustrated edge in his voice.

"He's not your responsibility." Anger sparked from her own mounting irritation, making her voice rise.

He moved then, stepped back and dragged his hand down his face. "Then why did you come out to see me if you're not looking for someone to take responsibility for him?"

He didn't know, she realized. He had no idea why she'd done the single most difficult thing in her life. "You didn't read it, did you?" She dropped the dust rag on the display case. "You didn't even bother to read Dani's journal, did you?"

Jed vaguely recalled throwing a package into the fire after Griffen had left his place. He'd had no idea what it contained. At the time, he hadn't cared.

She wrapped her arms around her slim waist. The aversion in her eyes disappeared, replaced by a serenity he didn't understand. Or maybe it was acceptance?

"Dani left the journal for Austin," she said, her husky voice calm. "She told him about her relationship with his unnamed father. But he knows you're his father now. The same father who rejected him, so I would appreciate it if you would please leave before he learns you're here. I won't have my son hurt by you again."

So much for acceptance. Maybe she was right. Maybe he should just head out of town. "I don't want to hurt him. I just don't know what you expect me to do. Why did you even tell me about him?"

For an instant, fear clouded her expressive jade eyes, until she blinked and it was gone. "I came to you because my son asked me to at least tell you about him."

Her arms dropped to her sides and she moved toward him, her steps slow and measured. Okay, so maybe that wasn't fear in her eyes after all.

"You're his idol." Her voice held an odd tightness in spite of the calm, even tone. "Ever since he knew what a football was, he's been a fan of Maitland the Maniac." She continued forward until she was standing a foot away from him. The scent of lilac and woman swirled around him making him uncomfortably aware of her femininity.

He looked down at her, not the least surprised by the pure anger now firing in her gaze. *Concentrate on the anger, Jed ol' boy. This one is too much. Even for you.*

"Do you have a clue what that means to a kid like Austin?" She placed her hands on her hips, drawing his attention to the material of her blouse outlining very full breasts.

His hands itched to test their weight.

Aw, hell.

She narrowed her gaze and advanced another step. "To him, you're a dream come true, only it's too bad you turned out to be such a nightmare. If I hadn't come to you, Austin would have found a way, so don't tell me I shouldn't have told him the truth."

He raised his hands, as if she held a loaded gun to his head. "Hey. Calm down, Sister."

She took another step toward him and poked a finger at his chest. "What would you have done if a thirteen-year-old boy had come to you out of the blue and said he was your son? You would have crushed his dreams and gone on to the next game without a backward glance. *That* is what you would have done."

He grabbed her hand before she drilled a hole in his chest. Bad move. Her velvety soft skin had him thinking some very inappropriate thoughts about Griffen Somerfield.

"Didn't you realize the complications?" he asked, concentrating on the issue instead of the reckless surge of awareness making his dick twitch. "You should have left well enough alone."

She yanked her hand from his and looked up at him, her eyes filled with fury. Damn, but this woman was exciting. And far different from his usual type.

Back off, old boy.

She had *white picket fence, kids and a pair of Golden Retrievers* written all over her. With little effort, he could see the dog hair and Crayon-coloring on the walls now. She was the type who believed in forever, but none of that stopped his blood pressure from hiking a few degrees.

Her breath hitched in her throat and a sheen of moisture brightened her eyes. Damn, he hoped she wasn't going to start bawling. He'd hate that.

"I did what I had to do to protect Austin. I figured you'd throw me out and that would be the end of it. Austin would be hurt for a while, but he'd get over it. I never expected you to come waltzing into Hart."

How dare she lay the blame wholly on him. He wasn't the one who had popped up out of nowhere with a wild story about a kid from a lost love.

"Well, I'm here," he said in a well-modulated voice that warned most people they were treading on very thin ice. "What great plan do you have now, Sister?"

"Mom? Mom, are you all right?"

"Ah, hell," he muttered. Any plans for an unnoticed escape were out of the question now. They'd been busted cold.

The look in Griffen's eyes was nothing short of pure anguish. She glanced at the boy, then back at him, her arms wrapping around her middle again as if she feared she'd fall apart if she didn't hold herself together.

She slowly brought a hand to her son's shoulder, and Jed couldn't help noticing how her fingers trembled or how the color had drained from her cheeks. If the woman hadn't just bitten off his head and spit down his throat, he would have thought she'd looked ready to faint.

"I...I didn't hear you come in," she said.

"Are you all right?" the boy asked again, shooting Jed a

hostile look.

Jed stared at the boy. Dani's son. *His* son. There would be no denying the truth. The kid had Maitland all over him, from the tall lanky frame to the thick dark hair and the same deep colored eyes inherited from his own grandmother Maitland. Looking at Austin was like looking at his old junior high school yearbook photo.

"I'm fine," she whispered.

She didn't look fine. She looked as if a stiff wind would break her in half. Hell, he wasn't feeling real stable at the moment himself.

Griffen cleared her throat and fought desperately to regain her composure. Comparing Austin's looks to the posters of Maitland in his room hadn't come close to seeing the two of them standing together. The resemblance was more than uncanny, it was downright spooky.

"Austin," she managed past the lump in her throat. "This is—"

His eyes narrowed in Jed's direction. "I know who he is," he said, his tone insolent.

Jed extended his hand to Austin, but her son stood beside her, protective, and refused to accept the invitation. She watched him closely, could see the hesitation in his eyes, the war between wanting to have his father accept him and fearing another rejection.

"I was explaining to your mom how she, uh...caught me at a bad time last weekend," Jed said.

Austin remained silent, but he glanced in her direction. God, she hated this. A nod, any indication whatsoever, and she knew Austin would accept whatever Maitland was offering. This wasn't fair, and she wanted to scream with frustration. Maitland could shake Austin's hand and walk out, rejecting, then crushing his own son. And it would be her fault.

Jed extended his hand again. "It's a pleasure to meet you, Austin."

Austin's eyes clouded with hesitation and something else— hope.

Her heart twisted so hard she couldn't breathe. *Why?* she cried in a silent plea for understanding. With a slight nod of her head, she closed her eyes, unable to bear the sight of Austin accepting what little attention his father was willing to toss his way.

She moved quietly aside, stopping at the display case where she rested her hand on the glass. With her free hand, she rubbed at the knot of tension gathering in the back of her neck. She could hear the drone of their voices, the stilted conversation between them, but she couldn't concentrate on what they were saying. All she could think about was what Austin had wanted so desperately—the chance to meet his father. She prayed her son could withstand the disappointment once Maitland's curiosity was satisfied and he left Hart as quickly as he'd breezed into town in the first place. And she hoped that was exactly what he planned to do.

"Why are you here?" Austin asked, the hope in his voice adding to her anxiety.

Good question. Why was he here? He'd said he wanted to meet "the kid," but surely he had to have another motive.

"I guess I wanted to see you for myself," Jed answered.

Anger, mingled with an overwhelming sense of helplessness, shook her. The high emotion and strain she'd been under before Austin walked in on them returned, bringing with it a sudden, reckless urge to physically remove Maitland from her presence. Not just now, but forever. She wanted him eradicated before he became too entwined in their lives. The urge was so strong, it totally unnerved her.

"You've seen him, you can leave now."

"Mom, it's okay," Austin said.

Sure, he thought it was fine that Maitland had come dancing through his life. His dream come true, his idol, the man he'd worshiped for years, was standing in front of him, telling him what a pleasure it was to meet him. What kid wouldn't lap up that kind of star-spangled attention like a starved puppy? Well, her son was no pitiful puppy to be patted on the head.

"Are you staying?" Austin asked.

She'd heard enough. More than enough. She crossed the showroom to Austin's side. "No, he's not." She ignored the mortification on her son's face. Better he suffer the disappointment now. She could just imagine the hurt Austin would face if Maitland thought he'd hang around for a while to play daddy only to run out when the dull, day-to-day routine bored him.

"I don't have any immediate plans," Jed said with a smile.

"I have a basketball game tomorrow night. Will you come?"

"No, he won't," she said. Austin and Jed ignored her, infuriating her until she was certain her blood pressure would shoot through the roof.

"I'd like that." Jed clamped his big hand on *her* son's shoulder. The boy practically beamed.

"Great. See you there." Austin spun and planted a kiss on her cheek. "I promised Granddad I'd help him build that bookcase for Phoebe's room. You'll pick me up?"

Before she could find her voice, Austin raced out of the store. The bells jangling when the door slammed closed in his wake.

Her anger in full bloom, she turned on Jed. The smile on his handsome face was relaxed and warm, adding fuel to her already burning fire. "How dare you?"

He cocked a dark, arrogant brow at her and she bristled even more. "God help you if you hurt my son, Maitland." Taking a step toward him, she poked him in the chest again, gaining an ounce of satisfaction when he winced. "Because I'll personally make sure there won't be anything left for the doctors to put back together if you do."

By the time Griffen had picked up Austin from her father's house, she'd calmed considerably. She couldn't remember the last time she'd lost her temper. In fact, she didn't think she'd ever been so angry. Not even her ex had managed to stir up that much emotion in her.

Was that why her marriage had failed?

When Ross walked out and took her bank accounts with him, she'd been upset, hurt, that he could do something so low, but she'd coped. When the unpaid bills he'd kept from her started showing up in droves, she'd dealt with them one at a time. Even when she'd received the original notice of default on the business, she'd been disappointed, more in her own failures than with what Ross had done. But today, she didn't doubt for a second she could have single-handedly strangled Jed Maitland. And passionately enjoyed every second of it.

She took a deep breath, refusing to give the anger and frustration more fuel. The night held a chill, so she set a couple of logs in the fireplace and managed to get a decent fire blazing in the hearth. After turning on her iPod in the docking station and setting it to a pop playlist, she headed to the fridge for an opened bottle of blackberry merlot. Austin had been in bed for a couple of hours already. She should be drained after her emotional outburst this afternoon, but she was too restless to sleep. With luck, the wine would do the trick.

She'd talked to Austin when they'd gotten home from her father's, but her fears about him becoming too attached to the idea of Jed being his father were far from put to rest. Although he'd promised to *play it cool*, she wasn't all that convinced. There wasn't playing anything with a guy like Jed.

A quiet knock on the kitchen door startled her. A sense of dread filled her when she peeked out the curtain. Looked like she wasn't the only one who couldn't sleep. She tugged open the door. "What?"

"Can I come in?" Jed asked, unfazed by her uncharitable welcome.

His hair was mussed, as if he'd been running his hands through it half the night. She didn't question how he'd found her. Hart was a small town and all he had to do was ask where she lived. Anyone would give him directions.

"Will you go away if I close the door?" she asked, hopeful.

His soft chuckle made her skin tingle. "No."

She stepped back and opened the door wide. "Then I guess

you can come in," she said, already regretting her decision. "Can I get you something to drink? I was about to have a glass of wine."

He rolled his shoulders and winced. "Coffee, if it's not too much trouble."

That surprised her. He leaned against the soapstone counter with his arms crossed and said nothing, just watched her as she made the coffee. He didn't smile, he didn't move. He just stood there looking at her, making her nervous as hell.

When she finished with the coffee maker, she pulled an oversized mug from the cabinet since he didn't exactly look like the delicate china type. "Do you take anything in it?"

"Black." He shifted and rubbed at his shadowed jaw. "I really am sorry about the way I treated you last weekend."

She shrugged and moved to the refrigerator where she pulled out the leftover cheesecake Austin had brought home from her dad's. "Think nothing of it. I don't."

He pulled out a chair, spun it around and straddled it. A sexy smile flirted around the corners of his mouth. "You're not a very good liar, Sister."

She turned her back on a grin that was already becoming familiar to her and opened the silverware drawer. "Yeah, I'm rusty. Not much practice."

What was she doing? Joking with him? He was the enemy and now she was feeding him her sister's heaven-on-a-plate cheesecake and making coffee for him. If she wasn't careful, she'd be smiling at the bastard before much longer.

She set a fork and knife on the table beside a desert plate. The coffee maker gurgled in the background as Adele's husky tones drifted into the room with them. As much as she hated the thought, he *was* Austin's father. Because of her own misguided sense of righteousness, they were going to become a part of each other's lives. How large a role he planned to play, she didn't know. But for Austin's sake, she needed to make the best of a bad situation.

Despite herself, she returned that killer grin of his with a shaky-at-best one of her own. *For Austin's sake.* "The name is

Griffen."

"Call me Jed?"

She pushed her hair behind her ear. *Please don't let this be a mistake.* "Okay. Jed."

He rested his arms over the back of the chair and smiled up at her. "We shouldn't be fighting all the time. I don't want to take your son away from you."

She poured herself a glass of merlot before answering him. The man had a point. Instead of pushing away the source of her irritation, she could end up alienating her son. *That* she couldn't allow to happen. When Jed left, it would be because he'd grown tired of playing daddy, not because she'd driven him away.

She sat at the table, then sliced him a piece of cheesecake. "Then why are you here?" she asked, setting the dessert in front of him.

He spun the chair around. "I needed to get away for a while."

So he was hiding from something. Things get tough and Maitland cuts and runs. Her confidence in her decision grew and she wondered how long it would take for him to run out on Austin. "And you decided to come to Hart?"

"An unconscious decision."

She didn't say anything, just sipped her wine as he cleaned his plate in record time. She sliced him another piece and he graced her with that killer grin before devouring the second helping with equal enthusiasm. When he wasn't drunk or rude, she supposed he really could be considered attractive. On the outside, there was no doubt he was one hot piece of man-flesh. From what she'd heard about him, he was a hot mess. Still, she found it difficult to believe Dani's words of praise.

He took another drink of his coffee, then looked over his mug at her, his dark brows creasing into a frown. "What?"

"Just trying to see what Dani saw in you," she said as she set her glass on the table.

He chuckled, a low rumbling that sounded warm and friendly. And nice. "Gee, thanks."

There she went again, smiling back at the bastard. "I'm sorry, I didn't mean that the way it sounded. It's just that you're so different from the man Dani described in her journal. She really loved you."

A hard look altered his features. Obviously her sister was not a welcome topic. "It was a long time ago." He carried his dishes to the sink and stood looking out her kitchen window.

"So it was." She drained her glass and wondered again what someone like him had seen in her sweet, loving sister, and why he clammed up anytime Dani's name was mentioned?

"I should get out of here," he said, turning. "Thanks for the coffee and dessert."

She stood and faced him. "You're welcome. But you didn't come here for a late night snack."

He shoved his hands in the front pockets of his jeans and leaned against the counter. "No."

"Then why?" She tugged her ancient sweater tighter around her. The coldness in Jed's eyes chilled her. If given the chance to get to know him a little better, would she discover Dani's interpretation of him was the true man? The thought spooked her for reasons she didn't fully understand.

She really didn't see her and Maitland ever becoming friends. He was Austin's natural father and she his adopted mother. They were natural enemies. She was afraid to let him too close, and he'd resent her interference, just as she resented his very presence. They were stuck in a no-win situation regardless of any supposed truce.

"I'm not sure why I stopped by." He looked around her kitchen, taking in the white curtains, the antique Coca-Cola memorabilia, the shelves cluttered with old tins. When he looked back at her, uncertainty changed his expression. "Austin's a good kid."

Why did he have to do this? Why did he suddenly have to look so uncomfortable, so vulnerable, and sound so damned sincere? She preferred his arrogance. *That* she could handle. "You spent five minutes with him."

He shrugged. "I'm a pretty good judge of character."

"I didn't realize you were ever sober long enough to get a lasting impression." She'd been right, they could only be adversaries where Austin was concerned. They couldn't be in the same room together for twenty minutes without her biting off his head. She felt like a cornered animal, snapping at anyone who came near her or her young.

His eyes narrowed and he took a step toward her. "I'm not the bad guy."

She held her ground, determined to show him she wasn't intimidated by him. Here, in her kitchen, he was just a man. No legends allowed.

"You are if you're going to end up hurting Austin. The novelty of having a son will wear off eventually."

"You think I'm that shallow?" His mouth tightened with disapproval.

She sighed. "Don't take this personally, but yes, I do."

"You don't know me."

She tugged on her sweater again. Nope, she wasn't intimidated by him. "I know *about* you."

He advanced another step toward her. "Believe everything you read in the grocery store rags, eh?"

She *wasn't* intimidated. Nope, not really. Still, she backed up anyway. She caught a scent, the same spicy aftershave she'd noticed earlier. God, he smelled good.

"I know you already have a kid you're paying for and never see," she said. "Austin doesn't need your money. In case you're wondering, I can support my son. I don't want him hurt."

"But it's my fault he got hurt anyway, isn't it?"

"My expectations were lower than Austin's." The flash of anguish in his eyes had her moving away and turning on the tap to rinse the dishes. "Sometimes things don't work out like we hope they will," she said, opening the dishwasher.

"Like my being here. That didn't work out like you hoped, did it?" There was a tightness to his voice and a determination on his face that should have warned her to drop the subject.

Instead, she set the plate in the dishwasher. "Since we're being honest, no it didn't." Fear made her more bold than wise. "I never expected someone like you to care about a boy you fathered fourteen years ago."

His hands were shoved into the pockets of his jeans, drawing her attention to his long, athletic legs. "You don't know me."

"So you've said." She closed the dishwasher. "But I know enough to know I don't like you very much."

"Like I said, Sister, you don't know me." A smug grin tipped his mouth. "But you will."

He walked out. But she knew his departure was only temporary.

She stayed in the kitchen, wondering why a man she didn't even know could evoke such intense emotion from her. He'd issued a challenge, and, God help her, for the first time in months, she actually felt alive.

Jed headed straight for The Hangout in search of a bottle of blessed numbness. He was crazy, that was the only logical explanation for the stupid stunt he'd just pulled.

What the fuck was he thinking?

He wasn't, that was the problem.

He walked into the bar and stood by the door, waiting for his eyes to adjust to the dimness. As soon as he could make out the shape of the long bar, he strode across the smoke-filled room. Other than a couple of older guys at the end, the place was deserted for a Friday night. They looked at him curiously, and he nodded, then pulled up a stool on the opposite end of the bar.

The bartender, a burly, gray-haired guy, with a towel slung over his shoulder, sauntered toward him and placed both hands on the bar. "What'll it be?"

"Scotch. Double," Jed ordered. "Straight up."

"Sorry, buddy. All we serve here is beer."

"Fuck," he muttered under his breath. What the hell kind of bar didn't serve alcohol? Real alcohol? No wonder the place was practically empty. "Then make it a six pack of Corona.

And make sure they're cold."

The bartender reached into a cooler and set six tall bottles in front of him. Jed tossed a fifty on the bar and reached for the first beer. He took a long pull, draining over half the bottle.

He had no business sticking around this one horse town that didn't even have a traffic light. He'd finish his beers, then leave. The kid would be disappointed, but, as Griffen had said, he'd get over it. Better to cut out now before the kid started thinking he planned on...what? Being a father to him?

He downed the rest of the first bottle and reached for the second. No matter how much or how fast he drank, the beer couldn't wash down the past that had slammed home when the kid had looked at him with adoration in eyes too much like his own. He flexed his shoulders to shake off the tension. It didn't work. Nothing could alleviate the edginess he was feeling.

The bartender slapped his change on the bar, then reached into a tub of soapy water. "Don't think I've seen you around these parts. Name's Eldridge," he said.

Jed stood and gave the guy a hard look. "Well, Eldridge, when this six pack is gone, bring me another. And eighty-six the conversation. I'm not in the mood for chit-chat."

He picked up his beers and moved to a booth in the corner. The place was too quiet for his liking, so he left the bottles on the table and headed for the jukebox. He pushed buttons at random, not really caring what music played, just something to shut out the condescending voice in his head chiding him for his momentary lapse of reason.

Okay, so maybe he did owe it to Dani to get to know his son. He'd already figured out that much. But, now he'd have to deal with Griffen, an over-protective, hot-tempered, long legged, sexy-as-sin beauty who didn't think very highly of him.

Satisfied when an older George Strait tune filled the quiet, he returned to the table and downed the next beer. He hadn't rubbed up against a woman like Griffen in a long time. She wasn't impressed by his wealth or his status. Even as a man he didn't impress her, she'd made that abundantly clear.

Not that any of it mattered. Before the sun rose in the

morning, he'd be long gone. And Griffen Somerfield with her fiery green eyes and gentle curves would be nothing but another memory washed away by copious quantities of alcohol.

SIX

JED SAT ON the edge of the queen-sized bed, his elbows braced on his knees, staring down at the worn beige carpeting of the Lakeside Motel. For the third day in a row, he woke up feeling human. His head didn't pound, his eyes didn't burn. Even after the six pack of Corona he'd downed at The Hangout last night, his mouth didn't taste like the Mojave Desert. There were no empty bottles of Jim, Jack or José littering the bedside table. No prescription bottles lie within easy reach to alleviate the pain in his shoulder or to help erase a past he'd worked hard to forget. Thanks to Griffen, that past had come back to haunt him, in the eyes of his own son.

He hadn't thought about Dani in a long time. He'd accepted the fact that she'd left him without a word. No bad reasons, no lame excuses, no false lines about how they should stay friends. No, when Dani Hart had walked out of his life she'd done it with style, practically leaving him at the altar. He'd dealt with it, gone on with his life, but he'd learned never to let anyone that close to him again. He'd had women since. Plenty of them. But nothing serious because he'd made sure he called the shots.

He knew what he wanted to do—contact his lawyer and let him handle the situation. Steve Rafferty would make a formal, albeit quiet, acknowledgment of Austin as a Maitland, all neat and tidy and legal, with a generous monthly child support payment. He'd make sure the kid had all the advantages his money could offer, but that would be the end of his involvement. He wouldn't make any demands. There would be no legalities to change Austin's name from Somerfield to Maitland. His acknowledgment of Austin would eliminate a potentially messy paternity battle or a feeding frenzy for the press.

Quick. Easy. No hassles.

Just the way he liked it.

He reached for his cell phone and hesitated. He was already paying for a kid, and she wasn't even his. He'd seen her when she was born, then again on her first birthday. He figured the little girl was around five or six years old by now. His lawyer made certain she was provided for, but that was all. Any other involvement was too painful a reminder of his responsibility for Linc's death.

No one except Steve understood why he hadn't fought the paternity suit and offered to settle before the case went to family court. Unfortunately, the pre-trial settlement hadn't satisfied the press. They'd crucified him, claiming his easy capitulation was merely a sign of liability. He was guilty, but not the kind of guilt the press had implied.

He turned on his cell. No sense putting off the inevitable. He didn't need an affiliation proceeding or even a DNA test to prove Austin was his son. All he had to do was look at the kid and see the truth for himself. He and Dani had created a child together. And as far as he was concerned, that was enough for him.

On the second ring, he swore, then disconnected the call. Did he really want to reduce the child they'd brought into the world to a monthly check and a college fund? It didn't matter that he wasn't father material. It didn't matter that the kid deserved better than what he had to offer. There was no question in his mind how he'd felt about Dani. Did he really want to blow off her son? Their son?

He'd promised the kid he'd show up at his basketball game tonight. If he kept his promise, what kind of message was he sending? That he was willing to be his father?

Making decisions wasn't something he usually had to worry about. He paid others to do that for him. There were lawyers to handle legal issues, an agent to handle product endorsements and contract negotiations, and a publicist to run damage control with the media. Decisions left to him usually were made within a split second on the football field.

He stood and yanked an Ole Miss t-shirt over his head. His shoulder caught, sending sharp, searing pain through his body. He swore again, vividly, then waited for the pain to ease to a dull ache. The truth of the matter was simple—he didn't have a clue how to handle this.

What if news that he had another illegitimate child was leaked to the press? The media would eat Austin and Griffen alive, and he didn't want that to happen, either. They didn't deserve the kind of attention his name and nefarious, if inaccurate, reputation would bring them.

He should just slip out of town as easily as he'd arrived. Last night he'd considered doing it, too—for all of the time it took him to wipe out a six pack. Dani would have expected more from him, but he wasn't that guy any longer. He hardly resembled the same guy she'd claimed to love. The years had changed him. Hardened him.

He shoved his feet into his scuffed boots. What would cause the boy more pain? If he left without a word, Austin would be disappointed. But what if he stuck around for a while? What if he really wanted to become a part of the boy's life?

Jed slipped his jacket off the hanger and carefully shrugged into it. He knew what would happen. His son would discover his father wasn't the hero he believed him to be.

"We still haven't heard from you, Griffen," Nell Whitmore said, lifting the box with the Holly Hobby tea pot she'd just purchased. "Are you going to enter the quilting competition again this year?"

"I really haven't had the time." Because she was too busy treading water so she and Austin wouldn't drown in the flood of debt. She didn't say that to Nell, or Nosey Nell, as she was called her behind her broad back. "I'm going to have to pass this year." She tallied a silver comb and brush set Ina Dickerson had purchased for her daughter-in-law and gave her the total.

"That's a shame." Ina pulled out her checkbook. "Didn't you take third place last year?"

"Second." Griffen placed the check in the till. "Maybe next year," she added with a smile.

Ina and Nell continued gossiping, while Griffen excused herself to see if she could assist Hanna Richards in making a decision about the pottery bowl she'd been fingering for the past ten minutes.

As she explained the origins of the pottery to Hanna, the bells over the door jangled. Griffen glanced over her shoulder and her greeting smile wavered.

Jed.

She didn't say anything, because her brain ceased to function. Instead, she stood next to the turn of the century dining room furniture, holding the pottery bowl, staring at him. He wore the same scuffed boots and a pair of jeans that fit him to perfection. A black Ole Miss t-shirt clung to his wide chest, the sleeves emphasizing tanned, corded biceps. He carried his leather jacket carelessly over one shoulder. Jed's professional career may be over the hill, but the man definitely had a lot going for him—too much.

Awareness rippled through her when he smiled at her. Her physical reaction to him caught her off guard. This was not good.

"Hi," he said, his deep voice warm and intimate. His gaze slid over her from head to toe, as if they'd shared some secret liaison.

Her cheeks heated. "I'll be with you in a minute." Dear

God, she hoped he didn't notice her blushing. But a guy like him was probably used to such silliness. Problem was, she wasn't.

She handed the bowl back to Hanna and concentrated on making the sale. She didn't have to look to know Jed had moved deeper into the shop. She heard his polite greeting to Nell and Ina at the counter, quickly followed by the elder ladies' whispers. Great. Couldn't he have waited another twenty minutes before arriving?

He'd surprised her when he'd called earlier to tell her he'd pick her up for the game. At the time, she knew she was making a mistake by agreeing, but instead managed to convince herself she was making the best of a bad situation for Austin's sake. That knowledge did nothing to alleviate the added anxiety once the potential gossip started running rampant. She'd been divorced little more than twenty-four hours. How unseemly for her to appear in public with a man, let alone one oozing sex appeal from his pores like Jed. She could just imagine how quickly the tongues would wag once the town took a good look at Jed with Austin.

Everyone in Hart knew she and Ross had adopted her sister's child. Hushed whispers, and some not so hushed, had circulated regarding the paternity of Dani Hart's illegitimate son. In less than an hour, anyone with two good eyes in their head would know what she'd learned only a week ago.

Hanna Richards ran her hand over the rim of the pottery bowl. "If you'll discount this by another ten percent, I'll take it."

"Wonderful." Griffen forced a smile and picked up a matching set of pottery candlesticks. "I'll let you have these at the same discount."

Hanna bit her lip. "I really shouldn't."

"You know you'll never find another pair that matches so perfectly."

"Okay." Hanna nodded. "You talked me into it."

Pleased, Griffen led Hanna to the register and wrapped up her purchases. Nosey Nell and Ina still chatted about the planning committee for the annual Fourth of July carnival, all the while sending curious looks Jed's way. To his credit, he paid them no attention, looking as if he was considering the purchase of the curio cabinet in the corner.

When Hanna said her good-byes and left the shop, the pottery set under her arm, Griffen rubbed her moist palms down her black trousers then turned to Nell and Ina. "Is there something else I can show you ladies?" she asked, hoping they'd take the hint and leave.

"Oh, no, dear, you go right ahead," Nell said, her eagle eyes filled with curiosity. "We're just catching up on our gossip."

Griffen smiled and nodded, then headed across the showroom to Jed. As much as she wanted to, she couldn't ignore him. That would only fuel Nell's interest. "See anything you like?" she asked, coming up beside him. He smelled of spice again, and man.

She drew in another deep breath. Playing with fire wasn't her style, but damn, he smelled nice.

He turned his attention to her, that killer grin tilting the corners of his mouth making him look even more devastating and hot. "Maybe."

She frowned at him. "Don't flirt with me, Jed," she warned, telling herself she was merely concerned with the gossip, not because of her sudden, stupid reaction to him. Forget the fact that she wasn't even in the market for a man, he just wasn't her type. If and when she found herself attracted to another man, it would be with someone who shared her values. Someone who put his family's needs before his own selfish desires. If there ever was another man in her life, she'd make damn sure he was the kind who wouldn't run at the first sign of trouble. Someone who would be around for the long haul, someone nothing like her ex-husband.

Or Jed.

"You think about entering the quilting competition, now," Ina called on her way out of the shop.

Griffen turned to see Ina dragging Nell with her. She nearly groaned when Nell craned her neck for another look at Jed.

"Who was that?" he asked with an inclination of his head toward the front door.

Griffen stepped away from him. She needed to close out the till. "Nell Whitmore, town gossip." She punched a series of buttons on the register, then began to slip the cash and checks from their compartments while the till tallied her sales for the day. "Trust me, nothing ever gets past that woman."

"We had one like her in my hometown," he said, crossing the room to the counter. He leaned his elbow on the glass, bringing him down to eye level. His eyes shone with an intelligence she couldn't help admiring.

She slipped a rubber band around the cash and checks, then slid them inside the cash bag. "Doesn't every small town have at least one?" The register tape stopped running, so she tore it off and started folding, scanning the totals as she went. Not bad, but not good enough.

"The old biddy got me into more trouble," he recalled with a deep chuckle.

She looked up and found him smiling again and returned his grin. "Somehow I doubt it was her fault you got into trouble." After she slipped the register tape in the bag, she headed toward the back room.

Jed followed her. "No," he said, a trace of humor still lacing his voice. "But it was her fault I got caught."

She hadn't really thought of him as a child. All she knew was the man who'd come into her life because she'd been foolish enough to invite him. Imagining him as a boy wasn't all that difficult. She had her own replica of him in the form of her son. His son. "That sounds more like the Jed I know."

He propped his shoulder against the door jamb. She could feel his eyes on her as she bent to place the cash bag in the safe. What could someone like Jed, a man who was pretty much indiscriminate in his choice of women, possibly see when he looked at her? Would he see the adopted mother of his child, or would he see a woman?

A woman who hadn't gotten laid in almost a year.

"Getting to know me, Sister?"

She hated when he called her that. After closing the safe, she spun the dial with a flick of her wrist. Too bad she couldn't snap off the uncomfortable avenue her thoughts had taken just as easily. "We need to leave."

She stood, but she didn't look at him for fear he'd see her wayward thoughts mirrored in her eyes. Mattie called her the pragmatic one. Practical Griffen. Smart Hart. She'd never been the one to inspire a man's fantasies like Mattie. She'd never be the sweet and gentle one like Dani had been, either. She'd always done what was right, what was expected of her. She tackled problems head on, solved them, then moved on to the next crisis regardless of what she really wanted to do.

No. Someone like her would never inspire a man like Jed. He no doubt liked his women warm and willing. And barely legal. At thirty-two, she was practically over the hill in his eyes.

By the time she made sure the store was locked up, she'd regained her equilibrium. The truth of the matter was simple. Jed was a flirt. A gorgeous one, but a flirt nonetheless. She might find him attractive, but it was nothing more than an appreciation for a hot guy with a bad boy reputation. She'd do well to remember that when dealing with him while he was in town. Which wouldn't be long. Once his curiosity was satisfied, he'd leave. Of that, at least, she was absolutely confident.

Jed was happy to let Griffen do the driving to the gymnasium since his shoulder had been bothering him for the better part of the day. The aspirin he'd taken before leaving his motel room had helped to ease the throbbing, leaving behind a constant ache he was getting used to feeling. Funny the things a guy noticed when sober.

He leaned back into the passenger seat and glanced at Griffen. She kept her attention on the road, her thumb tapping the steering wheel. A nervous habit.

He stifled a grin. He'd been surprised by her blush-filled greeting, but thought she'd looked adorable with color creeping into her cheeks. Who would have figured her as the blushing type? The thought made him smile and wonder where else she might blush.

His imagination ran a little wild and he shifted uncomfortably on the seat before putting a halt to those thoughts. He'd never be elected to sainthood, but he couldn't deny his attraction to her. She had the kind of legs that he liked, long and shapely. He'd bet they were smooth and silky, too. When she'd bent over the safe earlier, he'd stared at her ass. His temperature hadn't been the only thing to rise when he'd imagined cupping her sweet little bottom in his hands.

She had the kind of body to drive a man to his knees, long, slim and curvy in all the right places. But he liked her eyes the best. They were expressive and revealed exactly what she was thinking. He couldn't remember ever meeting anyone like her, or at least he'd never cared enough to remember.

She pulled into the parking lot and found an empty space behind a school bus. After she killed the engine, she sat staring out the windshield to the fading sunset. "My dad will be here," she finally said.

Realization dawned quickly. The angry father, seeking redemption for the wrong done to his daughter. "I take it he knows then."

She nodded and her long, wavy auburn hair swayed gently. "He knows."

"Are you warning me because I'll have to contend with an outraged father?"

She turned to face him, a slight smile curving her peach-tinted lips. "My father has never been outraged in his entire life, so I seriously doubt it. I just thought you should know."

He didn't say anything. By the way her forehead puckered, he suspected something else was on her mind.

"Jed, I'm not prepared to answer questions about you."

He thought about that for a moment and understood what she was trying to say. Hart was small town, and small town folk loved gossip, especially something as scandalous as his presence.

She drew in a deep breath and slipped a stray strand of hair behind her ear. "All anyone has to do is see you and Austin together to know the truth." She unfastened her seatbelt and turned in her seat to look at him. "Austin and I live here, Jed. This is our home."

"You afraid I'll embarrass you?" What did she think he was going to do? Get roaring drunk and break up the place? Screw anything in a skirt that came within ten feet of him? She had a pretty low opinion of him, and he didn't like it.

"No." She settled her hand on his arm. Her touch may have been innocent and meant as reassuring, but all he could think about was the feel of her skin sliding over his.

Her lips parted and she let out a breath.

He stared at her mouth. God, he wanted to kiss her.

"This isn't coming out the way I'd hoped," she said. "You coming here is going to mean to these people that you're acknowledging Austin as your son."

Yeah, he got it. Once he walked into that gym, there'd be no turning back. Word would spread like wildfire that Austin Somerfield's real father had come to town. The local diner would buzz with the gossip that Dani Hart had an affair with someone like him. Hushed whispers and speculation would fill the local laundromat or the baby food aisle in the town's one and only grocery store. Someone with a reputation, someone the press had labeled a bad boy had brought a smirch to their quiet, cozy little town. A man who shirked his responsibility to the town doctor's daughter and left her alone and dying with a child to raise. The gossip, he was sure, would be anything but kind, and once again, miles from the truth.

He placed his hand over hers and gave her fingers a gentle squeeze. In all honesty, he had no idea how long he planned to remain in town, but he didn't think it'd be more than a few days. He wouldn't be around to protect her or Austin from the gossip. Once he left, people would find some other grist for their rumor mill. His life was elsewhere. He belonged elsewhere.

"I knew that when I agreed to come." He knew, yet he was

still determined to keep his promise.

She closed her eyes and he had the wild urge to reassure her it wouldn't be as bad as she was obviously imagining, but he couldn't. He knew better.

She opened her eyes and he saw her concern. There was little he could do to alleviate it short of leaving. He was between the proverbial rock and hard place. If he left, he'd disappoint his kid. If he stayed, then his son would have to face the rumors. Fate had brought them together. What choice did he have but to face it one crisis at a time? His life was too screwed up to do much else at the moment.

"Are you ready?" she asked.

"If you are."

He'd only meant to give her hand another squeeze, hoping to convey that for now, he'd remain by her and Austin's side. The last thing he'd meant to do was give a slight tug on her hand to pull her closer, but he did. Telling himself pushing that wayward lock of hair behind her ear had been his only intention was nothing but a big, fat lie. Especially when he slid his fingers along her jaw to cup the back of her head in his hand and draw her in to share in his insanity.

"Jed?"

He ignored the confusion in her voice, concentrating instead on how her eyes darkened with desire. Her lashes fluttered closed as he brought their mouths closer together. The instant their lips touched, he knew he was screwed. One kiss from this woman would never be enough. When her lips parted, he swept his tongue inside, tasting, tempting, taking.

His body throbbed with anticipation. Despite their location, he deepened the kiss. She made a sound, a sexy little purr that spiked his libido. God, he wanted her.

The sound of a car door slamming brought him crashing back to reality. She scrambled away from him so quickly, his pride took a hit. Rationally, he understood, but he wasn't feeling rational. He was horny and for about five seconds, he'd bet she'd been willing.

She dug into her purse, then pulled down the visor and

checked her reflection in the mirror. "We should go," she said, reapplying her peach lip gloss with her finger.

He might have bought her cool, unfazed response if it weren't for the fact that her eyes were still simmering with awareness. "You know this isn't over."

She reached for the door handle. "Of course it is," she said, then exited the Jeep.

He chuckled. No, it wasn't. Not by a long shot.

Griffen's insides were trembling by the time Jed pulled open the heavy door leading to the gymnasium and not just out of fear of what lie inside when people saw Jed and Austin together. He'd kissed her. And she'd let him. Worse, she'd liked it. A lot.

The squeak of tennis shoes on the gym floor, the shouts of the boys and their coaches as they warmed up for the game met her, along with the face splitting grin of her son when he spotted them. She scanned the crowd already gathered for the last regular season game and located her father center court. He stood and waved, and she waved back before heading in his direction.

"Here we go," she muttered under her breath, when they climbed the bleachers to the fifth row where her father waited for them.

Jed took her elbow and guided her up the bleachers. "It'll be fine."

The sound of his low, sexy voice sent a shiver rippling down her spine. She struggled to ignore that little sensation of pleasure and concentrated instead on not falling on her face.

Griffen stiffened when her father stood. He kissed her cheek in greeting, then looked pointedly at Jed. She chanced a look over her shoulder. Jed's expression was blank, unreadable, and she'd have given anything to know what he was thinking.

"Dad, this is Jed Maitland."

Jed extended his hand toward her father. "Dr. Hart," he said, his deep voice strong and confident.

Griffen held her breath as she waited for her father to make the next move. She should have called him and warned him Jed was coming to the game. But she'd figured Austin would've told him, so she hadn't bothered and realized her mistake too late. This couldn't be easy for her father.

Thomas grasped Jed's hand. "Jed. Glad you could make it. Austin's been talking about nothing else all day."

Griffen expelled the breath she'd been holding and sat. "Austin stays with Dad on Saturdays while I'm at the store," she said, mortified to discover her voice was as unsteady as the rest of her. Her heart pounded, and she chastised herself for being ridiculous.

She really needed to pull herself together. This had nothing to do with Jed meeting her dad, and she knew it. Thomas Hart was not the type of man to cause a scene in public. It wasn't like he and Jed would scrap it out right there in the middle of the gym.

No, she was a wreck because Jed had kissed her and, for the space of those few moments, she'd lost every ounce of common sense she possessed. There'd been nothing pragmatic about her response to Jed's kiss. Her body had come wholly and vibrantly alive and it scared the hell out of her.

For Pete's sake, get a grip.

Feeling more than silly, she took several deep, slow breaths in hopes of regaining her composure. Parents and students filtered into the gym and she nodded to those she knew, ignoring their curious glances as they spotted Jed beside her. Brian Packard, Austin's buddy's dad, approached them and sat beside her father. With nothing more than a nod to her and Jed, Brian began talking to her father about the upcoming tournament the following weekend.

Griffen cast a glance at Jed. He sat with his arms braced on his knees, his attention on the court. Would he be proud of her son? Would he congratulate him on a game well played, or would he only point out the mistakes as Ross had done the few times he'd bothered to come to any of Austin's games?

The referee blew the whistle and she turned her attention to the court as the teams took their places. Austin, as center, stood in the middle of the circle with the opposing team's center while the referee held the ball over their heads. The ref tossed the ball high and Austin leapt for it, pushing the ball toward the home team's basket.

Jed didn't move, his jean clad thigh pressing against her as he watched the game. While Austin charged agilely up and down the court, Jed said nothing, but his leg tensed against hers every time Austin attempted a basket. By the time the buzzer sounded the end of the first half, the Hart Stallions held a ten point lead.

As the boys filed off the court to their respective locker rooms for a half time break, Jed straightened and looked at her. The smile on his face and the pride shining in his eyes warmed her heart.

"He's good," he said with enthusiasm.

Never once in all the years she'd been married to Ross had he expressed pride in Austin's accomplishments. He'd never commented on Austin's natural athletic ability, and he'd never beamed like Jed was doing right now. Now that she thought about it, Ross was so self-serving he only bothered to attend functions that might have helped him impress his clients. Instead of going to one of Austin's games to support their son, he'd done so to show people that he was a great family man. What a crock of crap. Ross may have been the only father Austin had ever known, but in twenty minutes, Jed, the very last man on earth she'd ever expected, was more of a father than Ross had ever been.

"He must get it from his father," she whispered, her throat too choked with emotion to manage much else.

A tear escaped and slid down her cheek. Jed slowly lifted his hand and cupped her cheek in his palm, the pad of his thumb wiping the moisture away. "Why the tears?" he asked, his voice a low, intimate sound that scraped against her emotions.

She couldn't speak, the gentleness in his tone, the warmth of his touch, unnerved her. She shook her head and pulled away when all she wanted to do was lean into him and kiss him again. But she didn't. How could she when she couldn't even tell him her fears were coming to fruition? That he wasn't the worthless prick she'd initially believed?

She turned her attention to the court and pretended to watch the Stallion cheerleaders' half-time routine, wondering how to tell him that if he was willing to be a father to Austin, she wouldn't stand in his way. Oh, she'd fight him to the end if he ever tried to take her son from her, but deep in her heart, she believed Jed had the capability to be good for Austin. This Jed, the proud father, not the man who drank too much or played too hard and would only be a bad influence on her impressionable son.

"Excuse me." A young man approached them. "Aren't you Jed Maitland?"

"Yeah," he said and looked at the teenage boy.

"Could I have your autograph, Sir?" he asked, thrusting a pen and paper napkin in front of Jed.

"Sure. What's your name?" he asked the boy.

Griffen looked away. What was she thinking? As the kid praised Jed, telling him how much he admired him, she realized she had to be out of her mind to even think of him as good enough to be anything but a bad influence to Austin. Jed Maitland was not father material. He was a celebrity, a professional football player with the morals of a starved mongrel. Even if he did want to play a role in Austin's life, what kind of role would that be? Give his son season passes and see him only when he managed to be competing locally?

"Sorry about that," Jed said when the boy hurried off to show his friends. "It goes with the territory."

"I imagine it does," she replied. Jed didn't say a word about her snippy tone, so she kept her attention on the court as the boys filed back into the gym.

The crowd cheered when the Stallions returned, and Jed cheered right along with them. She wanted to yell at him to stop. This was a one-time shot for him. He wasn't going to come to Austin's games in the future. He wouldn't be there to

JAMIE DENTON

help Austin when he took ninth grade algebra next year or the following year when he studied U.S. history and biology. He wouldn't be around to fix flat bike tires or give driving lessons. And while it might be his area of expertise, he certainly wouldn't be around to offer his son advice when it came to the opposite sex.

She kept silent for the remainder of the game, but no less aware of Jed beside her. By the time the game ended, her mood hadn't improved. The Stallions lost by a basket, but since this was the last regular season game, a celebration was still in order.

"The team's going for pizza," she told Jed as she stood. "I'll take you back to your car."

From his seat on the bleachers, he looked up at her. "Mind if I tag along?"

Of course she minded. "I'm not sure you'll enjoy it. It's noisy and crowded. Kids running all over—"

"I remember what it's like." Jed stood. "I'd like to come."

With the intent to dissuade him, she narrowed her eyes and frowned at him. "I really think you'd be better off—"

"I'm coming," he said, his tone firm and maybe a little antagonistic and arrogant.

Refusing to acknowledge his determination, she turned her back on him, pasted a smile on her face and looked to her father. "Dad, you coming?"

"Not tonight, honey," Thomas said, pulling on his coat. "I've got plans."

"Plans?" Her father never had plans. How could he desert her and leave her alone with Jed?

He chuckled and kissed her forehead. "Plans," he repeated firmly, then shook Jed's hand. "Hope to see you for Sunday dinner tomorrow, Jed."

"I'm not sure of my schedule yet," he answered.

"Dinner's at five. My daughter, Mattie, is an excellent cook." Thomas moved down the bleachers to the stairs where he stopped to talk to an old patient.

Maybe her luck was changing and Jed would leave. He said

he wasn't sure of his schedule. Perhaps she could convince him he wasn't wanted. Yeah, right. Like Jed would go away simply because she wished it.

She headed toward the door with the rest of the crowd. Jed moved beside her, his hand resting against the small of her back as he guided her through the crush of parents and students. That tingle of awareness shot up her spine again, and as much as she wanted to, she couldn't ignore it, or him.

And that, she realized, was only the beginning of her problems.

SEVEN

JED KEPT HIS attention on his conversation with Austin as Griffen drove to the pizza joint. Something had happened in the gym during half-time. He wasn't sure exactly what, but it didn't take a genius to know she was ticked at him. For what now, he could only guess.

Maybe because he'd gone and kissed her. Problem was, he wanted to do it again. That, and a hell of a lot more.

When she pulled into the parking lot, Austin unsnapped his seat belt, reached for the door, then hesitated. "Thanks for coming to my game."

The look in his son's eyes chipped away at the stone wall surrounding the location of his heart. This was getting dangerous. "I enjoyed it."

Jed turned in time to see Griffen give him a looked filled with irritation, but she quietly slipped from the Jeep and closed the door. Austin darted toward the front door of Porky's Pizza Palace while Jed waited for Griffen to circle the vehicle. "Is something wrong?" He fell in step beside her.

She wouldn't look at him, just kept walking across the lot toward the entrance, her steps clipped and hurried. "What makes you think there's something wrong?"

He grabbed hold of her arm. As appealing as he found the view of her ass as she walked away from him, he wanted, needed, to see her expressive eyes. She looked up at him and he released his hold on her arm. Irritation and frustration filled her gaze. "You're awfully moody tonight."

A perfectly arched brow shot skyward. "You don't know me well enough to gauge my moods, Mr. Maitland."

He blew out a harsh breath, his own frustration mounting. "Are we back to that again?"

Her lashes fluttered closed and she backed up a step. "I'm sorry," she apologized, then looked at him again. "I'm just having a difficult time coping with all this."

"All what?"

"With..."

Her words died when he narrowed the distance between them. Obviously, he had a death wish because he leaned toward her and breathed in, taking in that faint scent of lilacs along with something more elemental that held a dangerous attraction. Surrounding her with his presence, he pushed the advantage and lowered his head until her sweet breath fanned his lips. To her credit, she didn't flinch, she didn't back away, just looked at him, her eyes filled with an awareness that had his blood pumping hard.

He didn't give a rat's ass that they were standing in the middle of a parking lot, he kissed her. Again. Her lips were sweet and soft, and he couldn't get enough.

"You guys coming or what?" Austin called from the door. "Everyone's already inside."

Jed ended the kiss and straightened, not sure whether to be grateful for Austin's interruption or to have a serious talk with the kid about timing. Griffen turned away, but not before he caught sight of the blush warming her cheeks.

Oh yeah. She's interested.

What he planned to do with that knowledge, he didn't know. Before Griffen, he couldn't remember the last time he'd made a woman blush.

He followed Austin and Griffen into Porky's, then led the way toward the back to a corner booth as far away from the crowd as he could manage. He waited until Griffen sat before he slid into the booth opposite her. Austin climbed in beside him and grinned, sticking his open palm on the table in front of his mother.

She sighed, then opened her bag and pulled out her wallet.

"I got this," he said, digging into his pocket. He plucked a fifty out of his wallet and handed it to Austin.

"Jed, don't," she said, her voice a harsh whisper.

"Be quiet," he told her with a grin as he handed off the bill to the kid.

"Wow. Thanks." Austin scooted out of the booth and shot across the crowded restaurant to the video game room.

Griffen frowned at Jed. She suspected he didn't mean any harm in giving Austin what probably seemed like a fortune to a thirteen-year-old, but that didn't mean she wanted him giving her son money. The sooner she established some ground rules for the time he would be around, the better. "I would appreciate it if you wouldn't do that."

He leaned forward, his arms resting on the plastic red and white checkered table covering. "You're being over-protective."

Dropping her wallet into her bag, she gave him a level stare. "No, I'm not. I don't want him spoiled. I can't—" She folded her hands on the table in front of her. How could she say this without sounding pathetic?

"Can't what?" he prompted.

She moistened her bottom lip. "I can't compete." She hated admitting weakness to this man. And it didn't help that he affected her, made her wonder about things she had no business thinking about. Like how it would feel to be held by those strong arms or cuddled against that wide chest. Or what his body would feel like pressed up against hers, skin to skin, man to woman.

He reached across the table, his large, strong hands sliding over hers. Her imagination kicked into overdrive as she wondered what his hands would feel like on the rest of her, skimming over her, holding her against him as he sank into her.

Oh, hell. Something was seriously wrong with her.

"Griffen, look at me."

She didn't want to, fearful he'd see the erotic fantasy in her eyes. But when he tugged gently, she did as he asked.

His gaze held a sincerity she would have thought impossible for a man like him. "This isn't a competition." His voice was as gentle as the expression in his dark eyes. "He's my son, Griffen. I don't know yet where all this is going to lead, but I'm not going to take him away from you. I promise you that."

She nodded, because she couldn't speak. He'd voiced her greatest fear and painstakingly put it to rest with gentle and infinite care. Now all she had to do was get over herself and believe him.

"Thank you," she finally managed on a hushed whisper.

The waitress stopped by their table to take their order, then returned with a pitcher of Coke and three glasses. With a minor fortune in her son's pocket, chances were they wouldn't see him again for at least an hour.

She poured them each a glass of Coke. "So tell me..." She handed him a red plastic glass. "Who is the real Jed Maitland? And I don't want the publicity version, either."

Who was the man who'd kissed her? The one she couldn't stop thinking about in terms of sweat drenched bodies and tangled sheets.

He leaned back in the booth. "Not much to tell. My parents died when I was ten and I was raised by my old man's folks."

She knew the pain of losing a parent. Three years ago, her own mother had passed, and she'd been devastated. She could only imagine what it had been like for a child to lose both parents. "I'm sorry," she said. "That must have been very difficult for you."

He grinned, and her heart nearly stopped. Would she ever get used to that killer Maitland grin? For the life of her, she didn't think so.

He lifted his glass and took a long drink. "For my grandparents, it sure was," he said. "I wasn't an easy kid to like at first."

She gave him a teasingly shocked expression. "I find that so hard to believe."

He laughed, the sound running along her nerve endings and settling into a warm glow in the pit of her stomach. "Very funny," he said in a wry tone.

"So you went to live with your grandparents," she prompted, anxious to keep the conversation going. She needed to keep her attention on something other than the way he was affecting her. Or how much she wanted to kiss him again. For starters.

"I was pretty rotten." He braced his arms on the table, the sleeves of his t-shirt tightening against his thick corded arms. "My granddad was ex-military, but he was a good man who took his responsibility seriously. If I'd had to live with anyone else, who knows where I would've ended up—probably as a permanent resident in a ten-by-ten with a roommate named Big Bubba."

"Jail? Really?" She'd spent so much time thinking the worst of him, she shouldn't have been surprised. Except the more she got to know him, the more she believed that perhaps she'd been wrong about him. Maybe everything printed about Jed wasn't true. Maybe Dani had known the real man behind the legend, after all.

"I was a wild one." He chugged down the last of his drink then refilled his glass and topped off hers, as well.

"From what I've heard about you, you haven't changed much."

He lifted a dark eyebrow and gave her a tolerant look. "I keep to legal activities these days."

"I don't know about that," she said, feeling a tad guilty for being so hard on him. She propped her elbow on the table and cupped her chin in her hand. "What about that high dollar sports car you wrapped around a telephone pole? Weren't you charged with possession?"

"Not quite." He swirled the ice in his glass. "It was legally prescribed medication."

She straightened when the waitress brought their salads. "But still drugs," she said once they were alone again.

He picked up the fork and stabbed a cherry tomato. "I was taking Naprosyn for a knee injury, hardly a controlled substance. I had an allergic reaction and passed out." He popped the tomato into his mouth.

Was she so narrow-minded she actually believed the less than sterling reports about him? "Seriously?"

"I told you not to believe everything you read in those grocery store rags."

She set her fork aside and leaned forward. "I don't read rags. I told you, Austin's a fan. You're a pretty familiar topic at the dinner table. Now, what about that bar in San Diego? The one they say you destroyed in a bar fight."

"It was no big deal." He shrugged, concentrating on his salad.

"Trashing a bar sounds like a big deal to me," she said. "Especially when it ended in thousands of dollars' worth of damage."

He set down his fork and looked at her, the laughter disappearing from his eyes, replaced by a deep anger she didn't understand. "Some jacka—some jerk smacked his date around because she'd had too much to drink and was coming on to one of my friends."

"So you beat the crap out of the guy?"

Jed shrugged again. "I never said I was a saint."

"You destroyed a bar. And did some serious damage to another human being."

"A man who hits a woman doesn't qualify as human." His expression hard. "The bastard had it coming."

Okay, so maybe the guy did have it coming. Only she wasn't used to that kind of violence, and never would.

She picked up her fork again and dug into her own salad. "That's quite a temper, Maitland."

The waitress returned with their sandwiches and a pizza for Austin. "I don't like men who hit women," he said.

No, she didn't either, but she wasn't sure she could justify his violent reaction. She pushed the thought aside and looked past his shoulder to see Austin walking toward them. He slid into the booth beside her.

"This for me?" he asked, dragging a slice onto his plate.

"He had manners," she said to Jed. "I just don't know what he's done with them tonight."

"Sorry, Mom." He grinned sheepishly and started to reach across her, but she stopped him. Sighing, she handed him the shaker of Parmesan cheese.

Jed stifled a grin at Griffen's gentle reprimand. He remembered his grandmother doing pretty much the same, constantly reminding him that he wasn't a godforsaken heathen. "Good game tonight."

"Up until we lost." Austin said. "I missed a couple of blocks and it cost us."

Jed shrugged, not wanting to place a lot of emphasis on the mistakes, but rather what Austin had done right. His granddad would be proud of him. He'd had a good role model. "Did you learn anything?"

Austin's dark eyebrows puckered as he chewed. "Whaddya mean?" he asked, before taking another bite of pizza.

"You said you missed a couple of blocks. Did you learn anything?"

Understanding dawned in Austin's eyes. "I went for the ball, not the player."

Jed looked from Austin to Griffen. Worry lined her features. He could just imagine what she was thinking, and it annoyed the crap out of him. What the hell did she think he was going to do? Rip the kid a new one for screwing up on the court?

He focused on Austin. "Then you learn from it and move on."

"I don't get it. I fu...I messed up," he said, then shot a quick glance in Griffen's direction.

Jed shook his head. "The point is to learn from your mistakes. Next time, you'll go for the player and not the ball."

Austin sat up straight. "Really?" he asked, his voice

cracking.

Ah, puberty. Jed smothered a grin. "Really."

"Cool."

"Yes, cool," Griffen said, relief evident in her voice. She handed her son a napkin. "Now wipe your chin."

Austin swiped at the glob of pizza sauce on his chin, then helped himself to another slice. "I'm gonna go play some more video games."

Griffen couldn't help but be pleased her son seemed so happy for a change, more like his old self. Too bad it would only last for as long as Jed was in town, but she quickly squelched that hope. No sense borrowing trouble.

Austin slid from the booth. "Thanks for the pizza."

She grabbed his hand before he could shoot off like a rocket toward the video game room again. "Thirty minutes, Slick."

Austin shook off her grasp. "Screw that," he said, his voice filled with impatience. "It's Saturday night."

"Hey, you always talk to your mother that way?" Jed asked.

Griffen held her breath when Austin lifted his chin a notch, a glint of determination flashing in his eyes. "No."

Jed gave Austin a level stare. "I didn't think so," was all he said, but the warning in his tone was unmistakable.

Austin's eyes narrowed slightly, but when he returned his attention to her, contrition replaced hostility. "Sorry, Mom," he said, then took off at a more sedate pace toward the game room.

Griffen turned her attention back to Jed. Maybe he did have what it took to be a father. He certainly didn't have a problem calling Austin on behavior he considered out of line.

"He's usually not so rude," she said, feeling the need to defend her son. Life hadn't been as good to Austin as she would have liked. He'd lost his mother at a young age. The only father he'd ever known had walked out on him and never looked back. And now he was getting acquainted with his biological father, a superstar athlete. Surely a little rudeness was understandable given the situation.

She mopped up the crumbs Austin left behind. "It's just the excitement of the past week," she added.

Jed set his empty plate on the edge of the table. "If I'd spoken to my grandmother that way, my granddad would've had his boot up my ass before I could blink."

She moved her own half eaten sandwich to the platter with the pizza remnants, then looked at him. "You handled him well tonight."

He sat watching her, his expression curious. "Did you think I'd tear into him for a few mistakes?"

She sighed. "No. It's just—" Just that Ross would have, and that truth bothered her. Her ex-husband expected perfection, little boys included. He'd never been cruel, he just hadn't been supportive.

"Just..." Jed prompted.

"Ross was never very interested in Austin." She doubted he appreciated hearing the man who'd raised his son had been less than the ideal parent, but Ross simply wasn't fond of children. He couldn't relate to them...like Jed, she thought and frowned.

"Is that the PC way to say he ignored the kid?" A hardness crept into his voice.

"Not quite. He just didn't take much interest in him or the things he enjoyed."

"And what does Austin enjoy?"

"Football," she said on a dramatic sigh and shook her head. She hated feeding his oversized ego, but if he did stick around long enough, he'd discover the truth eventually. She easily imagined him bursting with his damned male pride if he ever saw Austin on the gridiron. The boy had a gift, but at least now she understood where that natural ability came from—his father. "According to Austin, other sports were made to pass the time until football practice starts up again."

Jed smiled, one of those proud papa smiles again and her heart beat just a little faster. Why? Why was it that the man Austin held biological ties with, the man who hadn't even known of his existence until a week ago, showed more interest than Ross, who'd raised Austin? She just didn't understand.

"I guess it's in the genes." His grin never faltered.

She couldn't help herself. She smiled back. "I suppose it is."

The way Jed figured it, Austin would be busy in the game room with his buddies for a while yet. He didn't mind. For the first time in a very long time, he was enjoying an intelligent conversation with a beautiful woman, and he liked it. The women he usually dated weren't exactly Mensa candidates.

"Coffee?" At her nod, he signaled for the waitress and placed the order. "So why'd you leave your ex?"

"I didn't. He left me," she said without an ounce of bitterness in her voice.

Her bland tone took him by surprise. He'd been dumped— once, and it had pissed him off big time. He hadn't allowed it to happen again, either. There'd never been anyone serious since. Any affairs had been on his terms, just the way he liked it. "How long were you married?"

"Close to eleven years."

"Were you happy?" he asked after the waitress returned with a couple mugs of coffee.

She added a dollop of cream to her coffee and stirred. "I thought so at the time," she said. "I don't know any longer. We never really fought, we just..."

"Drifted apart?"

"Co-existed." A melancholy smile canted her lips, now devoid of that tempting peach lip gloss. Damn, but he wanted to kiss her again.

"I was still in college when we got married, for one thing," she continued. "I'd barely had my first real job when Dani relapsed. I took a leave of absence and we moved back here so I could take care of her and Austin, but Ross commuted back and forth to Dallas. Once Dani passed, I did go back to work for a while, but it was just too hard on Austin. He'd just lost his mother and here I was, leaving him every day. It was too much, so I quit and eventually opened Antiquities. I was able to take care Austin and I liked having my own business. There were a lot of times I thought Ross was jealous of the time I spent with Austin."

Bastard. "Is that why you never had any kids of your own?" Because her ex was a selfish prick?

She sipped her coffee and looked at him over the rim of her mug. "He never wanted children."

"But you did."

She set her mug on the table and issued a light chuckle. "Boy did I. Ross was horrified."

"I think your ex is a jackass." What kind of dumb son-of-a-bitch wouldn't want to give a good woman like Griffen a house full of babies?

That thought had some interesting images filling his mind. Bodies slick with sweat, tangled limbs.

Austin returned to their table and slid into the booth next to Griffen, forcing Jed's baser thoughts back into a holding pattern. God help him, he didn't feel an ounce of guilt for lusting after the kid's mom.

Griffen brushed a lock of dark hair from Austin's forehead. "You look tired, Slick."

Austin scooted close to his mom, then rested his head against her shoulder. Jed watched them and sipped his coffee, feeling an odd sense of peace. He waited for the panic to set in, for the flight instinct to take over, but it never happened.

Austin didn't bother to stifle his yawn. Jed had seen so many facets to his son in the past twenty-four hours, he was having a hard time keeping track. First, he'd been confronted by an angry youth who looked ready to take his head off. Tonight he'd watched the athlete on the court, his movements and ability pure magic. He'd seen a hungry teen devour half a pizza in less than ten minutes, and now he caught a glimpse of the little boy looking to his mama for comfort. He saw things he'd missed by not knowing about Austin's existence, and that bothered him. But he knew enough about himself to know he wasn't cut out for the day-to-day parenting. Thankfully, Austin had Griffen, who would see to his needs before her own, and who would offer him guidance and support and love.

She slipped her arm around Austin's shoulder and kissed the top of his dark head. She spoke to him, her voice low and soothing.

Austin rolled his eyes and sat up, as if he remembered he was in public where his friends might catch him being cuddled by his mother. "Did I thank you for coming to my game?" he asked.

Jed finished off his coffee and signaled the waitress for the bill. No matter how much he hated for the evening to end, Austin was tired and so was Griffen by the look of her.

"You did. Thank you for inviting me."

Austin shifted in his seat. He looked at his mother, then back at him, a frown creasing his brow. "Okay, here's the deal. Everyone's asking me why you're here with my mom and me. What should I tell them?"

Jed looked to Griffen for support, hoping she had one of those ready-made, parent-type answers. Considering where his thoughts had been wandering all night, he didn't want to touch this one.

Griffen smiled at her son. "The truth is always best, and the least complicated."

His brown eyes rounded in surprise. "I can tell everyone that Jed Maitland is my dad?"

When Austin turned his attention to Jed, he tried not to wince. Griffen had warned him when he'd walked into that gym tonight that his presence would be construed as a full-blown acknowledgment. This was it. No half-truths, no avoidance, no running away from his responsibility.

No turning back.

"Your mom's right," he said. "The truth is best."

Austin beamed at him, a smile so blinding and bright Jed refused to regret his answer. Except he had one question— what exactly had he done now?

EIGHT

"PLANS, DAD? REALLY?" A mixture of humor and skepticism filled Mattie's voice. She checked the meat thermometer inside the beef roast before setting it on the counter to rest. "What is that? Senior citizen code for hooking up?"

"I was being discreet," their father called out from the back porch. Dr. Thomas Hart and Trenton Avery, Mattie's fiancé, were deep into a game of chess, pretending to keep an eye on Austin and Phoebe while they played in the back yard with Jessie, her father's ten-year-old Border Collie.

Griffen leaned over the sink to the open kitchen window so she could see her father and Trenton. "Don't put this on me. You go all cryptic and then think I'm not going to discuss it with Matt? Come on, Dad. You know us better than that."

"Trenton, you're a lawyer," Thomas pleaded. "Help me out here."

"Sorry, Doc," Trenton said with a chuff of laughter. "I have to go with conflict of interest on this one."

Mattie slid a baking sheet with oven-roasted Brussels sprouts and onions smothered in olive oil from the second oven. "Oooh," she said, "you hear that, Griff. A *smart* man."

"You say that like it's a rare thing," Trenton said, his grin filled with affection.

"Isn't it?" Mattie countered playfully, as she set the dinner rolls to bake.

Griffen pushed away from the sink and headed to the dining room and the china cabinet for the dishware to set the table. She was thrilled her sister and Trenton were getting married. For far too long Mattie had mourned Ford's death, and it was good to see her happy again. Trenton was a good man, very nice looking, hard-working and on the verge of making partner in his Dallas law firm. But more importantly, he obviously adored her sister and Phoebe.

A moment later Mattie came into the dining room carrying the storage case with the silver cutlery and a stack of ivory cloth napkins and fancy napkins rings. Sunday supper was a tradition in the Hart household, one that had continued even after their mother's death three years ago. Just as their mom had done, their father still insisted on using what he called the "fancy dishes." There were a few sets of dishware to choose from—her parents' anniversary china, two different sets passed down through the generations on both sides of the family, and the Christmas dishware.

Mattie set the silver flatware case on the buffet and lifted the lid. "I hear Dad's not the only one withholding vital information."

"Are you kidding me?" Griffen nearly dropped the salad bowls from her Grandmother Caulfield's dinnerware set. Seriously? Two kisses and she was the subject of gossip? "What have you heard?"

"Not a word." Mattie laughed. "But you are now *so* busted."

She went back for the matching dessert plates. "I really don't want to talk about it."

"Yes, you do," Mattie argued. "Griff, I know you. You've been stewing ever since you walked in the door."

"I do not stew." She set the dessert plates on the table and went back to the cabinet for the crystal stemware. "I'm just worried Jed is going to hurt Austin, that's all."

"So..." Mattie prompted. "Do you like him?"

Griffen let out a long, slow breath and met her sister's gaze over the dining room table. "I don't want to like him, Matt. He's..." *All wrong for me.* "He's just so..."

"Hot?"

Griffen tried not to smile, but she couldn't help herself. "Oh my God, you have no idea."

Mattie bit her bottom lip and checked to make sure they were still alone. "Have you slept with him?" she asked, keeping her voice low.

"Mattie," Griffen exclaimed in a harsh whisper. "Really? Do you know nothing about me?"

"The man is sex on a stick. What do you expect me to think?" Mattie folded the napkins and slid them into the holders. "But you at least kissed him, right?"

"Twice," Griffen admitted reluctantly, as she started setting out the placemats.

"And..."

"Oh my God, you have no idea," Griffen repeated, then giggled like a teenager. "He has this way of making you forget everything except him. It's like every ounce of reason I possess just disappears." She clutched a dinner plate to her chest. "I've never felt anything like it."

"Really?" Mattie's dark eyebrows arched upward. "Not even with Ross?"

"Not even with Ross," Griffen said. "How sad is that?"

"Well, you know what they say...you can't miss what you never had in the first place."

Griffen frowned. That wasn't fair. "I loved Ross."

"Of course, you did."

"Don't be condescending, Matt. We might not have had the same kind of passion as you and Ford had, but we loved each other." For a while, at least.

"That's crap and you know it. Ross was safe. He didn't make you think too much or feel too much. Jed Maitland does both and you've only just met the guy."

"He's Austin's father."

"He's a man, Griff. A very hot, sexually magnetic man, who obviously finds you attractive."

"I have a pulse. For a guy like him, that's the only requirement." She started arranging the place settings. "Besides, how weird is it that he and Dani were lovers?"

"Stop making excuses," Mattie chastised as she helped set the table. "It's not like you're stealing your sister's boyfriend."

Mattie had a point, but the thought had crossed her mind. And she had Austin to consider, as well. Jed wasn't the forever type. What would they do when whatever it was that was happening between them fizzled? She couldn't let her attraction for Jed color her judgment, especially because of Austin.

"Nothing happened," she said abruptly. "We kissed. Twice. It's not a big deal."

Her sister gave her a sly grin. "You're such a bad liar."

Griffen sighed, but was saved from having to respond because her father walked into the dining room.

Mattie immediately crossed her arms and gave him a level stare. "So, Dad. Are you going to tell us who she is?"

"You're not going to let this go, are you?"

"Sue me. I'm diligent."

"You're a pain," Thomas said with a laugh. "Fine. If you must know, I had plans last night to spend the evening with a lady friend."

"Oh my God," Mattie said. "It *was* a hook up."

Thomas's expression turned stern. "I do not hook up, young lady."

Griffen set the last place setting. "Who's the lady friend, Dad?"

"That, my dear," he said in a gentle, but firm tone, "is none of your concern."

"You know we'll find out eventually." Mattie slid her arm around her father's waist. "You should've just invited her to supper."

"Speaking of which," Thomas said. "I have two hungry grandchildren running poor Jessie ragged out there. How much longer?"

How much longer are we going to wait for Jed? He didn't have to say it, because Griffen knew. She'd been thinking the same thing for the past fifteen minutes.

Damn him. Because Jed couldn't be bothered to keep his word, Austin was going to be hurt, and that made her angry. "Ten more minutes?"

Griffen waited until her father left before turning to Mattie. "This is why I'll never sleep with Jed Maitland," she told her. "He's an irresponsible, undependable, narcissistic—"

"Hot piece of man-candy," Mattie said as they headed back into the kitchen to finish putting supper on the table.

"You're not helping," Griffen retrieved the salad from the fridge. "He can't do this to..."

"You?"

"Austin," she said as she began scooping the mashed potatoes from the crock pot. "He's going to be crushed when he finds out Jed is a no-show."

Mattie pulled the rolls from the oven. "Maybe you can cut the guy just a little slack. You do realize that this can't be easy for him, either, right? I mean, he just found out he has a thirteen-year-old son. That's gotta take some adjustment."

Maybe Mattie had a point. But then again, maybe Jed was exactly what she'd accused him of being when he'd waltzed into Antiquities two days ago—only interested in having a good time.

Jed paced the motel room and glanced again at the digital clock on the bedside table for the third time in the past five minutes. He was already an hour late. Griffen's family would be waiting for him. Austin would be waiting for him.

Shit.

He easily pictured Austin looking repeatedly at the gold watch Griffen wore on her delicate wrist, his shoulders slumping with disappointment as each minute passed and Jed didn't appear. And it was damned easy to picture the tight line of Griffen's lips.

Fuck it.

He couldn't face them. He'd tried, but he just couldn't bring himself to walk into that house tonight and announce he was ready to be a father to Austin.

Time for a reality check.

He paced to the window. The sun hung in the west, but wouldn't be dipping behind the horizon for at least another hour. His life was a shambles and he was adding to the carnage, turning confusion into pure mayhem. He'd left his place in Possum Kingdom to escape the vultures picking over his flesh and had stumbled into something far worse. A woman, when she wasn't biting his head off, who turned him on to the point of discomfort. Hell, who was he kidding? Even when she was spitting mad at him he found her far more tempting than any of the women he'd ever had the pleasure of bedding in recent years.

And while he was at it, he couldn't forget the kid. *His* kid. Griffen had warned him Austin would eat up whatever scrap of attention he was willing to toss his way. He should've listened to her.

Dammit, he couldn't do it.

He *wouldn't* do it.

The best thing for all of them was for him to leave. Now. Get the hell out of town and save his sanity while he still had the chance.

He dragged his duffle from the closet, then opened the dresser drawers, and started shoving his clothes into the bag. In the bathroom, he grabbed his shaving kit and grumbled about expectations and disappointments, and how they'd just have to get the fuck over them.

He reached for the aspirin bottle on the night table, popped two, then checked the clock again. He sure as hell hoped they didn't hold dinner for him, because the goddamn guest of honor wasn't showing.

The aspirin stuck in his throat, so he chugged the remnants in the orange juice carton he'd bought from the convenience store earlier. From across the room, he hurled the empty carton at the waste bin, missed, then swore again.

The sweet call of freedom beckoned. He slapped the room key on the dresser, picked up his duffle and headed for the door. As he reached for the doorknob, his cell phone buzzed.

Griffen.

Yeah, he was out of there. Edgy, caged in, trapped. He didn't need this shit. For too long he'd been tied down by the one thing he'd loved the most. Four quarters of glory every season for thirteen years. Linc had warned him the game would bleed him dry, use him up and toss him aside like yesterday's garbage. Linc had almost gotten free, had been ready to start a new life, until his dreams of freedom had been tragically shattered.

By him.

With a ripe curse, he stepped through the door and slammed it behind him.

His phone dinged, signaling the arrival of a text message. He unlocked the SUV and climbed inside. The sooner he got out of this one horse town, the better he'd feel.

He turned left and headed in the opposite direction, avoiding downtown and Main Street. Dragging in a deep breath did little to calm the anger and frustration burning just below the surface.

Or was it fear?

"Fuck that." He floored it.

What the hell had he been thinking yesterday? He'd let things go too far. A couple of relatively tame kisses and his curiosity had nearly been the end of him. One night with a woman, talking of all things, and he'd started thinking in terms of family and kids. She'd wanted a house full of babies. If she'd asked, for reasons that spooked him nearly blind, he'd have been more than willing to provide them for her. Well, it was a good thing he came to his senses before he did something really stupid.

Family? That was a laugh. He didn't have room in his life for family. He didn't want a family. Fine. He had a kid. But that kid was living with his adopted mother who was doing a good job of raising him. Didn't they know they'd be better off without him in their lives?

He drove past the lake and took the turn-off toward the highway. With his arm slung over the steering wheel, he gunned the truck again, shooting him dangerously over the speed limit.

He crested a hill. The sun glinted off the windshield, and he shielded his eyes as he reached for his sunglasses. The SUV swerved, but he righted it, then slammed on the brakes.

The Escalade shuddered in protest at the abuse, then skidded to a halt, spinning until he was facing east. He checked his rearview mirror, then pulled over to the side of the road, tossed the sunglasses back on the dash and swore a blue streak.

Turning off the ignition, he pocketed the keys. His boots hit gravel as he followed the short dirt path toward the cemetery.

The gate was iron and rusty and probably one hundred years old. When he pushed on it, the hinges creaked but it swung wide enough for him to pass through. Marble headstones of varying size sprung from the ground, some elaborate, others simplistic. Jed moved among the headstones, monuments and simple ground plaques. He passed family plots until he found what he was looking for tucked in the far eastern corner beneath the heavy branches of a live oak to protect the Hart family plot from the sun.

Danielle Lily Hart had only been twenty-five years old when she'd passed. Had either of them ever been that young? He'd been twenty when Dani had come into his life. For so long he'd convinced himself he'd been a little more than a kid, but standing at her grave site, he admitted the truth—what he'd shared with Dani had been real.

A sharp pain twisted in his chest as he looked at the rose-colored marble. He read the inscription chiseled into the stone. *Beloved Daughter, Sister, Mother.*

He'd loved Dani, truly loved her with a man's heart, not the boy's fantasy he'd been telling himself all these years since she'd left him. They'd planned on marrying right after the draft, but then she'd disappeared from his life. And she'd taken his child with her, a child he'd never known existed.

He stepped over the stone border and approached the headstone where he took a knee. "You should have told me I had a son." He touched the stone, wincing at the cold hardness, his fingers lightly grazing over the word mother.

"He was my son, too, Dani. You should have told me."

Had she thought he wouldn't have loved Austin? Had she believed he wasn't capable of taking care of his own child? If she'd told him the truth, that she was sick, that she was pregnant with his child, if she'd given him half a chance, maybe his life would have turned out differently. He certainly wouldn't have been so goddamn reckless if he'd had someone who depended on him.

He didn't know how much time had passed when he finally stood. The sun was quickly disappearing from the sky as dusk settled around him. He didn't know if he had what it took to take care of his son now, but for reasons he didn't question, he'd been given a chance. He'd been given an opportunity, and what was he about to do? Run. At the first sign of emotional commitment, he was ready to turn tail and run as fast and as far away as he possibly could.

He made a sound, more like a grunt of pain than the self-deprecating laugh he'd intended. Perhaps Dani really had known him better than he knew himself.

But he *had* been given a chance to know his son, and something told him he'd never have another opportunity again. If he left now, not only would Griffen turn against him, so would his son. Dani's son. Didn't he owe it to her memory, and to Austin, to at least attempt to do the right thing? For once in his sorry-assed life, he couldn't think about only himself.

He turned away from the headstone and returned to his vehicle. His hand shook as he reached for the handle. Never in his life had he ever been afraid of anything. Now, the thought of being a real father to his son scared the absolute living hell out him.

Griffen snapped off the television, unable to concentrate on the program. She could hear Austin moving around upstairs in his room. Regardless of the brave front he'd shown tonight, she knew her son was beyond disappointed. He was hurt. All through dinner, he'd been silent. Afterward, while she and Mattie had cleaned up, Austin had sat quietly in the living room in front of the television. In the two hours since they'd come home, he hadn't left his bedroom.

"Screw you, Jed," she whispered to the silent room.

To be perfectly honest, Austin wasn't the only one feeling the letdown of Jed's abrupt disappearance. She'd been wavering between disappointment and disillusionment all evening. It didn't matter that she'd tried to convince herself she was merely worried about Austin. The truth wasn't quite so neat and tidy. As many times as she'd replayed the previous day through her mind, she'd come to one solid conclusion. She couldn't stop thinking about Jed Maitland in ways that had zilch to do with shared custody.

The discovery of a different side to him, one far removed from the public persona and bad boy image, didn't really astonish her. Her reluctant admission that he wasn't the scourge of the earth, did, however. She so desperately wanted to despise him, wanted to believe he was nothing more than a hot piece of man candy. But how could she when she'd encountered an intelligent and charming man who'd shown compassion and tenderness when dealing with his son? And her? She hadn't been prepared, not for that side of him. Nor had she been prepared for those kisses—or that she'd *wanted* him to kiss her. When she peeled away her layers of defense, one simple fact remained. Despite her fears that Jed might replace her in Austin's heart, she harbored a dangerous attraction for him that could only lead straight to disaster.

She pushed her hair off her forehead, then let out a long, slow breath and tried to rationalize the situation. Her curiosity had been piqued, nothing more.

Nothing more than a few moments of pleasure when he kissed you.

Yeah, well. There was *that*.

A pair of headlights flashed through the huge picture window. She tugged on the long front ends of her plum-colored cardigan, then rubbed her palms on her plaid pajama bottoms before heading to the front door. She peered out the curtain on the side glass panel into the darkness. Parked in her driveway was a black Cadillac Escalade.

Jed.

God, she really didn't want to deal with this crap. Austin had been hurt and his feelings had to be her first priority. She refused to allow Jed to keep pulling her son along on an emotional roller coaster.

With an angry yank, she opened the door and stalked across the lawn toward him. She refused to allow him to keep hurting hurt her son. As far as she was concerned, he was four hours too late.

He rolled the window down, but kept his gaze forward, staring at the doors to the three car garage. "Is Austin upset?" he asked, his tone reserved.

He looked miserable. *Good.* Annoyance with him and frustration with herself for caring, warred inside her. "Why should he be upset?" Her sarcasm boarded more on anger. "It's not like he can depend on you."

He faced her then. The moonlight cast an eerie shadow over his angular features, making him look hard and uncompromising, giving her the distinct impression that *he* was angry.

He was angry? She was a hissy fit waiting to happen.

"Come on, Griffen," he said in a voice that matched that hard expression, "cut me a break. I really don't need to hear a lecture right now." He raked a hand through his hair and let out a rough breath. "Look, I'm sorry."

A heavy layer of dew clung to the ground, adding a chill to the night air. She tugged the ends of her cardi tighter around her. "I'm not the one you should be apologizing to."

He rolled up the window. For a single heartbeat she thought he might leave. Until he opened the door and stepped from the interior. She spied a duffle bag on the seat and couldn't keep the wishful thought that he'd come to say good-bye from springing through her mind. She had enough to deal with, and he was just one more complication in her already complicated life.

He closed the door and pocketed the keys before turning to face her. The eerie cast disappeared and she saw him clearly. Something had happened, but what, she didn't have a clue. There was a determination in his gaze and a tension in his body she didn't think she wanted to face.

"I'm going to apologize to Austin," he said, "then you and I need to talk."

She didn't want to hear anything he had to say. To be honest, she wasn't even entirely certain she wanted him near Austin.

"I have an early day tomorrow." She was grasping, but didn't care. "Some other time."

"This can't wait," he said and took off toward the house.

By the time Jed reached the top of the staircase, his resolve wavered. No, he had to see this through. He'd made up his mind, and no matter how much he wanted to skip out, he couldn't do it. Not this time. He'd spent too many years of his life running from his past.

A light shone under the door to his left. He crossed the landing and knocked softly before he changed his mind and slipped into the familiar, habitual pattern of avoidance.

"Come in," Austin called.

Jed opened the door and stepped inside. A brass lamp cast the room in a soft, buttery glow. His son sat at a wooden desk, his finger holding a space in an open book, while he scribbled notes in a spiral notebook. The room wasn't much different than Jed's own when he'd been a boy. Sitting on shelves above the desk were model cars and airplanes he assumed Austin had built. Pictures of race cars and football memorabilia, from pennants to posters, cluttered the walls.

Griffen had told him Austin had a serious case of hero worship where he was concerned, but he hadn't really believed her. He spied a series of frames on the bookcase. Covers of various sports magazines featuring himself on the cover were carefully arranged. For an instant Jed considered autographing them for Austin, but squelched that thought. He was determined to have a real father-son connection with Austin, not one based on a hyped-up legend.

"Austin?" He closed the door and stepped more fully into the room, shoving his sweaty palms into the pockets of his pants. His brows rose when he spied a poster of the latest supermodel, wearing a Texas Wranglers' jersey and a pouty-lipped smile, hanging on the backside of the closed door. Jed wondered if Griffen knew Austin had the poster. Somehow, he didn't think so.

The boy sat up straight and slowly set his pencil on the notebook. He didn't turn around, just sat looking forward to the low shelf cluttered with old copies of *Sports Illustrated*, as if he couldn't bear to face him.

Jed didn't blame him. What he'd done tonight was pretty low. "I'd like to apologize for not coming to your granddad's tonight."

Austin stiffened, then shrugged his shoulders, before picking up his pencil again. His dark head bent over the desk as he scribbled more notes.

Jed wasn't about to be put off by the kid's dismissal. He didn't expect Austin to make this apology easy for him. While the kid might not be Griffen's biological son, they shared the same stubborn streak.

"I don't have an excuse to give you. Only the truth. And the truth is that I was afraid."

Austin dropped his pencil and twisted in the chair to face him. His Maitland eyes held a spark of disbelief mingled with distrust. "What do you have to be scared about?"

Jed looked down at the carpet, then back at his son. The disbelief shifted, leaving behind only distrust that chipped another layer of stone away from his heart. "Of being your dad," he said.

The thought of being a father to Austin, a real father, scared the hell of out him. In all the years with his grandfather, the one thing that stuck most in his mind were the lectures about the value of honesty. Maybe it was time he finally listened and started to practice what the old man had preached.

Austin's eyes narrowed. "It's real easy. You hang around for a while, then you split. I think you got that part figured out."

Jed crossed the room and sat on the edge of the bed. "That's not the kind of father I want to be." He wasn't certain what kind of father he planned on being, either, but it was time to stop running. The reality was that he had a son with Dani. A son she'd loved enough to make sure he'd been taken care of by her sister when she'd died. The fact that she hadn't trusted him enough to raise his own kid hurt.

"Yeah, then. What kind?" The wariness in Austin's eyes belied the insolent tone. Show a brave front and don't let the bastards know you're afraid. He and Austin had that much in common.

He was treading on some very thin ice. One wrong move, one misplaced step, and he'd sink faster than a lead weight. Split second strategy on the gridiron wasn't shit compared to handling his son's fragile trust.

"I don't know." He braced his elbows on his knees and leaned forward, keeping his gaze on Austin. "I was hoping we could find out together."

"I haven't had a real good selection of role models," Austin admitted, his tone softening.

Jed didn't think the boy wanted sympathy. If anything, Austin was proud. Like him.

"I know what you mean," he said. "My old man died when I was ten."

"You had your granddad," Austin said, quoting common knowledge.

"I did. But it wasn't the same." He clasped his hands together and gave Austin a level look. "I'm going to make mistakes. I've never done this kind of thing before. So be patient, okay?"

The shy beginnings of a grin tugged at Austin's lips. "I've never been Jed Maitland's son before, either."

He smiled. "I wish my job were as simple."

Austin's grin faded as quickly as it formed. "Does this mean we'll spend time together? You know, do stuff once in a while."

Jed stood, surprised when he wasn't struck by a desire to slither from the room and out of the kid's life. Austin wasn't asking him for a commitment, nothing long term, just something once in a while. Standing by Dani's grave, he'd sworn he'd do the right thing for once in his life. And if that meant keeping promises he made to his son, then by God he was willing to commit. "You bet."

An odd sense of calm swept over him, when he'd expected panic instead. "I need to talk to your mom, but I'll stop by tomorrow. We'll talk more and figure out what we're doing as we go, okay?"

At Austin's nod, Jed headed for the door. "Goodnight," he said, then reached for the knob.

Austin nodded again and then picked up his pencil. He muttered something Jed couldn't quite make out as he stepped through the door, closing it softly behind him. By the time he reached the stairs, Austin's words registered, hitting him like a ton of bricks.

"Goodnight...Dad."

NINE

GRIFFEN DUCKED BACK into the family room the second she spied the light from Austin's room spilling onto the landing. For the past thirty minutes she hadn't moved, holding vigil at the base of the stairs, waiting for any sound that might indicate her son needed her. Her pride took a major hit when he hadn't.

As she dodged a box with the carefully wrapped Hummel and Lladro figurines in preparation for the move to the bungalow in town, Jed appeared in the archway of the great room. He looked haggard, a little worn around the edges, and more than a bit shaken. Part of her was dying to ask what had happened. Curiosity, nothing more. Not because she felt any sympathy toward him. If Austin read him the riot act, who was she to complain if it meant Jed wouldn't be hanging around upsetting her status quo.

He walked over to the sofa and sat, slinging his good arm over the back as if he belonged there. A dark blue, button down shirt outlined every dip and valley on his torso. It took every ounce of her self-control not to drool.

"I spoke to Austin," he said, his voice calm, his gaze clear and steady. A direct contrast to the wild beating of her heart.

She moved an empty carton off the recliner and sat on the edge, facing him. "Okay..." What that meant exactly, she wasn't sure. She just wished he'd get to the point because the anxiety was killing her.

"We're going to give this father and son thing a shot," he said evenly.

Her heart dropped into her stomach. She'd tried to prepare herself for this moment, knowing that once she'd gone to tell him about his son, their lives could change. Never in a million years had she expected anything to come from her visit. But now it had, and their lives were being altered once again.

She stared at Jed, still unable to believe what she was hearing. The worst of it was, she was absolutely powerless to prevent him from seeing Austin.

Panic crashed in and took hold. "No," she said, shaking her head. "That's not a good idea." Her voice shook in perfect concert with her insides. How long would it be before he took her son away from her? All he had to do was file a petition for custody with the court, and she could lose Austin. Jed was high profile, no doubt with friends in the right places. He had more money than God, and he was Austin's natural father. All she had going for her was an adoption decree. Considering his rights had been involuntarily terminated without proper notice, he had all the power.

"I'm bound to screw up now and then." The determination in his gaze transferred to his voice, bringing back that hard edge she didn't appreciate. "But we'll figure it out."

"Screw up now and then? Who are you trying to convince this is a good idea? You? Me?" She smacked her hands on her knees. "No offense, Jed, but your life has been nothing but a succession of screw ups."

"Now wait a minute."

"Exactly how do you plan on being a father to my son?" She thought of her own father. His gentleness. His caring. His always sound advice. "Good God. I can only imagine the words of wisdom you'd impart."

She shot off the chair. Blind panic caused every protective instinct she possessed to flow to the surface, bringing with it an intense ferocity that had her trembling as she faced him. "There is no 'we,' in this scenario, Maitland." She kept her voice low, striving for a calm she didn't feel. "It's me and

Austin. Just the two of us. Got that?"

He stood and circled the table until he was towering above her. She tipped her head back to see the furrows between his brows deepen. The message he relayed with his eyes was unmistakable. She'd pushed him too far this time.

"What I've got is a son." His low voice vibrated with suppressed anger.

She didn't give a damn about his anger. She didn't want to care about him, period. All she knew was she had to keep him from destroying their lives. She hadn't spent the past six months picking up the pieces of the disaster Ross had left behind only to allow Jed to finish what little semblance of order she'd managed to cling to.

"No," she cried, then brushed passed him. She needed to think, and she couldn't do that with Maitland occupying her airspace. His very presence was a threat to all she had left—her son.

She took off for the stairs and ran up to her bedroom before the tears started, quietly closing the door so Austin wouldn't hear her. Because once those tears fell, there'd be no calling them back, and she'd be damned if she'd cry in front of Jed.

She covered her mouth with her hand as the flood gate crashed open. Somehow her legs carried her to the bed where she fell across the turquoise and brown patterned comforter. Curling into a ball, she wept.

She cried for the past and for the unknown tomorrows she had yet to battle. She cried as if she'd never stop. When Ross had left her, she'd barely shed a tear. It hadn't taken her long to realize that whatever they'd once shared had died long before he'd started chasing skirts behind her back. She'd hardly blinked when she'd been served with divorce papers. And when the overdue notices and threatening letters had started arriving, indicating Ross hadn't paid the bills in months, she'd simply gone numb.

Making the decision to give up her beloved antique store and return to Corporate America hadn't brought her as much pain as she'd imagined, only a sense of unfettered relief. She couldn't remember the last time she'd indulged in a fit of tears, at least nothing that compared to the pain wrenching her heart now, a pain so fierce she feared she might break in two.

Austin was all she had left. Of all her dreams, of all her hopes, her son was the only thing she had that remained for her to hold on to, and she was losing him to the man who'd fathered him.

"Griffen?" Jed's voice drifted to her. She'd been so full of self-pity, she hadn't even heard him come into her bedroom.

"Go away," she said, her voice muffled by the turquoise accent pillow she clutched to her chest. "Please, just go away."

The bed dipped as he sat beside her. "You know I can't do that."

Somehow she knew he wasn't talking about leaving her alone. He wasn't leaving. Period.

She shoved the pillow aside, then wiped the moisture from her face before rolling onto her back. "What do you want from me?" She stared at the ceiling because she couldn't bear to look at his face. If she saw pity in his eyes, she'd start bawling again.

Jed thought he could handle anything, until he'd seen Griffen cry. God, he hated when women cried, but Griffen's sobs tore at his heart. He reached for her hand and tugged until she swung her purple fuzzy flip-flops to the floor and sat beside him.

"I want the truth." He brushed a lock of hair from her face, tucking it behind her ear. "What are you so afraid of?"

She looked at him, her eyes bright with the threat of another onslaught of tears. She sniffled and looked away. "You."

Her answer, and honesty, surprised him, mainly because he couldn't imagine Griffen admitting to anything remotely close to fear. He took hold of her slender shoulders and turned her to face him. When she still refused to look at him, he gently lifted her chin until he could see her eyes. Those expressive eyes that revealed more than she knew.

"Why would you be afraid of me?" he asked gently. He

kept his hand beneath her chin. Not because she'd look away, but because he liked the feel of her soft skin. "I told you I'd never take Austin away from you. He's your son, too, Griffen, just as much as he is mine. Hell, if not more so. You're the one who's been there for him all these years."

She shook her head. A tear hovered on her lash, then slid slowly down her cheek. With the pad of his thumb, he wiped it away, then traced the outline of her lower lip. She had full lips, sensuous lips and he had a sudden, wild desire to taste them.

"Give us a chance to get to know each other," he said when she continued to look at him with those teary eyes. "I can't do this without your help."

She laughed, a caustic, tear-filled sound and pulled away from him. Pushing herself off the bed, she turned to face him, her hands settling on her hips. The fire was back in her eyes, and he couldn't help the jolt of desire that pulsed through his veins.

"You don't need my help, Jed. You've had an in with Austin long before he even knew you were his father."

"That's an image. It isn't me." He came off the bed to stand in front of her. Her scent filled his senses. Damn, but she turned him on, made him want things he had no business wanting—her. "I can't change who I am."

She looked at him as if he'd lost his mind. He couldn't refute the possibility.

"Okay then," she said, "for how long? How long until you're bored with the routine? It isn't all hero worship, you know."

"I realize that." He kept his arms at his sides. An effort, when he really wanted to put them around her and draw her close. He wanted to chase her fears away, to kiss her senseless so she'd stop arguing with him. He needed her to accept that he was going to be a part of his son's life. One way or another.

Griffen moved away, putting some much needed space between them. She couldn't concentrate with him standing so close. Especially with a bed nearby.

"Being a parent is more than just showing up on weekends

when you're in town." She dropped onto the chaise in the far corner of the room and looked up at him. "It's communicating so he can understand you and what you expect from him. There are parent/teacher conferences at the worst possible time, late nights in the ER when he's sick. Making sure he gets his homework done. Washing his clothes. Taking him to the dentist. Making sure he doesn't get involved with the wrong crowd. It's knowing when to say yes and when to trust your instincts and say no. Dammit, Jed," she said coming off the chaise, "you're not a peanut butter and jelly kind of guy. You're...you're fresh lobster and five hundred dollar champagne."

He crossed his arms over his chest and braced his feet apart, his stance filled with a determination that unnerved her. Every inch of him was male. Delicious, hard male. She saw it in the darkness of his eyes and the arrogant tilt of his head. He was sex, primal and raw, and God help her, she wanted him. He made her feel alive for the first time in ages. It didn't matter she fighting for her way of life, she still wanted him in the worst possible way.

"You're not even willing to give me a chance."

His voice jarred her out of her temporary, sex-riddled stupor. She refocused. "Parenting isn't easy," she told him. "Our lives here are boring and simple. Little league, PTA meetings, ice cream socials, the summer carnival, homecoming and the winter festival. Hart is small town, not fast lane. We're a long way from the bright lights of a football stadium. There aren't any screaming fans here, either. How could that possibly appeal to someone like you?"

"The truth?" He rubbed the side of his five-o'clock-shadowed jaw in contemplation. "I don't know," he finally answered.

"Well, I'll be damned if Austin and I are going to be an experiment for you. We aren't a pair of shoes you get to try on to see if you like the fit." Her frustration mounted and she welcomed the emotion, preferring it to fear any day of the week.

She circled the bed and came to stand in front of him. "Dammit, I need to know." She poked him in the chest, but this time he didn't wince. The jerk had the gall to grin. "You'd better figure it out fast, pal, because I won't let you..." hurt me, but she stopped herself before she said the words. Letting him know she found him attractive was one thing, but no way was she going to let on that she...what? Cared for him?

As much as she worried about his relationship with Austin, she also feared that she could come to care for Jed. A lot. He wasn't all rough edges. There was a tenderness, a gentleness in him that called to her. When he'd found her crying, the careful way he'd treated her had softened her.

His grin faded and something lit his eyes that made her heart beat a wild rhythm. Her mouth went dry as dust when she recognized the emotion. Desire.

"Won't let me what, Griffen?" His low voice vibrated with it, causing heat to coil low in her belly.

She backed up a step.

He advanced.

"I won't let you make promises you can't keep."

"But I do keep my promises." He taunted her. He continued to move toward her, his steps slow and measured. For each step he took forward, she took one back, until she brushed up against the wall. He kept his gaze locked with hers, and the heat in them simmered. "I'll make you a promise right now."

She couldn't have spoken if her life depended on it. A sinking suspicion crept through her mind that her sanity was riding on the use of her vocal cords, but she couldn't utter a sound. No man had ever looked at her as Jed was at this moment, with fierce determination and a desire that burned hot. He held her transfixed with those mesmerizing eyes. The tips of his boots brushed the edge of her fuzzy flip-flops.

"I promise," he said as he slowly drew his hands up her arms to settle on her shoulders, "that I'm going to kiss you."

Her vocal cords still refused to cooperate, so she shook her head.

"No? I'm a man of my word, Griffen. That is something you can always count on with me."

With that, he dipped his head. His lips hovered near hers and he waited. Giving her a chance to object?

Not a chance. She held her breath, afraid to move, afraid to breathe, afraid he'd turn and walk away.

He brushed his mouth against hers, and she let out a sigh. Slow and gentle, he traced the outline of her bottom lip with his tongue. But it wasn't enough so she parted her lips, inviting him inside. He took the hint and deepened the kiss, bathing her mouth with swift, penetrating strokes. She shivered in response. Whatever resolve she might have possessed, crumbled.

Jed slid his hands from her shoulders to her neck, then cupped her face in his palms. When she trembled beneath his touch, his temperature shot up ten degrees.

"Griffen," he groaned, then slanted his mouth over hers again, unable to deny the fierce need she fired inside him. He tasted the salt of her earlier tears and something uniquely Griffen. When she slipped her arms around his neck and sighed, a sexy little sound deep in the back of her throat, male satisfaction ripped through him. He sensed a change in their relationship, a connection that went above and beyond their bond to Austin.

And it changed everything.

Using the wall to his advantage, he surrounded her, with his body and his heat. The feel of her soft, full breasts pressing intimately against his chest nearly drove him mad. She responded with an openness that had made him crazy. Good God, he wanted her, wanted her beneath him, hot and wet with need. He wanted to hear his name on her lips when he filled her, wanted to see her eyes darken with intense pleasure. Pleasure he would give her again and again.

She rubbed her sweet body against him and he nearly came out of his skin. His control was slipping, fast. He wanted to make love to her, ride her so hard that she'd cry out from the force of her orgasms. He wanted her exhausted and pliant, willing to do anything he asked.

Griffen couldn't help herself, she kissed him back and loved every second of it. Jed overwhelmed her, turned her brain to mush, and she didn't care. The man was pure masculine power, and if she wasn't careful, she'd be lost forever. Right now, it didn't matter. She couldn't find the strength to fight it, or him for the simple reason she never wanted his drugging, bone-melting kisses to end.

All she could think about was the need building inside her and how much she wanted him. He shifted their bodies, then lifted her, using the wall to support her back. As if she'd done it a thousand times before, she wrapped her legs around his waist. Even through his khakis, the hard ridge of his desire pressed against her as if the thin fabric of her pajama bottoms didn't exist. She moaned and rolled her hips.

He deepened the kiss as she moved against him. His hips rocked forward in an erotic dance that pushed her dangerously close to the edge. She wanted more. Needed more.

His kisses were breath-stealing and insistent. The man was lethal, but at the moment, all she could concentrate on were the sweeps of his tongue and the feel of his erection pressed against her heated center. He slipped his hand under the hem of her shirt to cup her breast. When he dragged his thumb over her nipple, she moaned and arched toward him, wanting, needing more. Running her own hands over his wide shoulders, she reveled in the feel of rock hard muscle beneath her fingertips. She told herself she had to stop, but returned his kisses instead.

It'd been so long since she'd been held like this. Kissed like this. Aroused like this. When he pushed his hands into her pj bottoms, his hands against her skin, she thought for sure she'd explode. He made her squirm with a fierce desire to seek completion. She wanted so much more, the intimate contact of flesh against flesh. She wanted everything he could give her.

When he found her hot, slick folds and teased her clit with the pad of his thumb, she flew apart. He swallowed her cries as powerful shockwaves of pleasure pulsed through her. She couldn't breathe, she could only feel, and the incredible sensations turning her world upside down only made her hungry for more.

He dragged his mouth from hers and kissed her jaw, nuzzled her neck. She clung to him and tried to catch her breath.

"You're amazing," he said, his voice a harsh husky whisper tight with desire. He rested his forehead against hers and smiled.

That killer Maitland grin. A wicked smile designed to melt hearts and charm his way into the closest pair of damp panties. And that made her no better than some cheap gridiron groupie.

She went cold. What the hell was she doing? Inviting the enemy into her camp was one thing, screwing him in her bedroom was quite another. Yet, she couldn't deny that right this very moment, she still wanted him so much she ached.

"We can't do this," she said and reached her feet to the floor.

"Griffen..." His voice sounded as ragged as her emotions.

"Let me go, Jed."

Regret flashed through his eyes, but whether it was for what they'd just done or because she'd stopped him, she couldn't be sure. She didn't care to know. When he released her, she moved away from him because if she allowed herself to give into the emotions rippling through her, when he left, it would hurt. A lot.

He stood with his arms braced against the wall and kept his head down. She couldn't help feeling a tad guilty for leaving him hanging.

Her desire dimmed, replaced by shame. She'd kissed him, let him pleasure her. Hell, she'd essentially made love to him. "God, why did you have to come back?" she muttered, more to herself than him.

He pushed off the wall and turned to face her. His eyes were a shade darker, hot with a fire that had nothing to do with passion. "I had every intention of leaving and wish to hell I had."

"Don't let me stop you," she shot back.

A cocky grin tugged at the corners of his mouth. "Sweetheart, up until a few minutes ago, you wouldn't have stopped me."

Her eyes narrowed. What was she supposed to do? Thank him? God, she wanted to smack that smug expression off face. "Go to hell, Maitland."

"I've already been there," he said, then shoved his hand through his hair in agitation. "I was headed back to the PK and ended up at the cemetery outside of town."

"You went to see Dani?"

"Why does that surprise you?" Irritation lined his words.

She shrugged. "I don't know, it's just..." Just that she'd never understand the attraction between Jed and her sister. Especially the Jed she'd just clung to like a sex-starved buckle bunny. Dani had been sweet, fragile and Jed was her polar opposite. He was strong, powerful, the kind to go skidding sideways into the grave at the end of his life shouting, "Great fucking ride."

"Just that you don't see me as a sentimental kind of guy?" he finished for her.

She regarded him for a moment before answering. Sentimental was hardly an adjective she'd use in conjunction with Jed. "Not really."

"I'm damned sentimental." Annoyance crossed his too handsome features. "Dani meant a lot to me, more than you'll ever realize. If you had half the..."

"Half the what? Don't stop while you're on a roll." Her voice dripped with sarcasm to hide the hurt. The callous comparison to her older sister stung. "If I was what? Half the woman my sister was? Well, I'm not. So don't expect me to let you walk all over me then quietly slip out of your life before the boredom sets in."

"That's not—"

"I've never been any man's flavor of the month, and I'm not about to start now."

"You are impossible," he ground out in frustration. "I never meant..." He faltered, and regarded her quizzically. Then his eyebrows shot up as if he'd just been given a great revelation. "You're not afraid of Austin getting hurt. You're afraid you'll get hurt."

Smart bastard. "Like hell." She aimed for nonchalance and failed.

He advanced, closing the distance between them until she either had to look up or stare at his wide chest, the same chest she'd been rubbing up against earlier. Not willing to slink down that road again, she opted for his eyes.

He leaned in, crowding her, making her acutely aware of every square inch of his rock hard body. "If I kissed you now, you'd kiss me back." His voice dipped low and husky and filled with sex.

"Not a chance," she lied.

"I bet you're still wet."

She bit her bottom lip. Well, she was now, thank-you-very-much. And he hadn't so much as touched her.

"You know why?"

She opened her mouth to fire off a smart ass comment, but her vocal chords stopped working again.

"Because you want me. You want me to fuck you."

Yeah, he kinda had her there. And if she didn't get the hell away from him, that's exactly what they'd be doing.

She scooted a safe distance away. "Wow, that's some ego you've got there, Maitland."

He chuckled, the sound scraping her awakened nerve endings. "This isn't over yet."

"Wanna bet?" she shot over her shoulder.

He came up behind her, slipping his warm hands over her shoulders, down her arms until he entwined their fingers together. Leaning close, his breath fanned her neck. It took every ounce of willpower for her not to lean back and just give in to whatever it was that was happening between them.

"Don't you know better than to bet against a sure thing? Odds are you'll lose."

A shiver raced down her spine and she forced herself to move away from him and his over-blown ego. "The odds say when hell freezes over, Maitland. I think it's time you leave." She couldn't think when he touched her. No, that wasn't exactly true. She couldn't think of anything but sex when he touched her.

"I'm leaving, but I'll be back tomorrow. For dinner." He reached for the door and flashed her his lethal grin. "We'll see what we can come up with for dessert."

She stood staring at the closed door, waiting until she heard him backing out of her driveway before she collapsed on the bed. Somehow in the last hour, the battlefield had changed. They were no longer fighting about Austin. No, that issue had been somewhat resolved. She wasn't exactly certain how, but it had.

This was a battle with higher stakes. One she knew she had no hope in winning, either. Jed was absolutely right. She wanted him. She wanted him with an intense need she hadn't even known existed.

Her only salvation was knowing that need and desire did not equal love. And loving Jed Maitland wasn't something she'd never have to worry about happening to her. Because not even she was *that* stupid.

TEN

THE COLD SHOWER did squat to alleviate the pain in Jed's shoulder but it did manage to cool his out-of-control libido. He couldn't remember when a woman had set him on fire as much as Griffen, so much that he couldn't eradicate her from of his mind. With his luck, she'd probably haunt him until he had her, really had her. Once he made love to her, his fascination would wane. Soon she'd become a blur like all the rest. Griffen Somerfield would be no different.

And he was a liar.

Griffen was different, and that bothered him almost as how much he wanted her. She'd never agree to a casual fling. Not a chance. Griffen was a forever kind of woman, the romance and candlelight type. He'd be wise to steer clear of her regardless of how much he ached to have her. The thought did give him a little comfort emotionally. Physically, he was still in serious trouble.

Ignoring his discomfort, he reached across the bed to grab his cell phone off the bedside table. Now that he'd made his decision to be a part of Austin's life, there were details to be worked out, or rather, his lawyer had details to work out on his behalf.

The glowing red numbers on the digital clock read quarter

after one. When he'd arrived back at the Lakeside Motel an hour ago, the irritated clerk had frowned when he'd explained he'd left his key in the room, not bothering to enlighten her to the fact he'd originally left it behind because he hadn't planned on coming back.

He called his attorney at home. For the hefty sum he paid to keep Steve Rafferty on retainer, Jed figured Steve owed him a few late night calls. A woman's husky voice answered, probably Steve's wife, and Jed gave his name.

"Jed? Where the hell are you?" Steve barked in a familiar, sandpapery voice. "Everyone has been looking for you."

He didn't doubt that for a second. "I've got some business I need you to take care of for me."

"Tell me where you are first."

The last thing he wanted was for the hounds to come sniffing around Hart, Texas. "Later." Jed clicked the remote and the flat screen flickered to life. He hit the mute button. "I want a trust fund set up. I also want an initial payment and a separate monthly stipend sent to Griffen Somerfield."

Steve sighed, the sound long and drawn. "What have you done now?"

"It's complicated."

"With you it usually is," Steve said dryly. "Why should this time be any different?"

"I've got a kid."

"Another one?" Steve didn't sound the least surprised by the news.

"Cut the crap, Rafferty," Jed growled. He pulled in a deep breath and counted to ten. Ripping his attorney a new one wouldn't accomplish anything. The guy loved a good fight, but tonight Jed wasn't in the mood. "This time it's legit. He's mine."

Silence. Jed waited for the declaration to settle. Steve knew the truth about Linc Monroe. While he'd advised Jed against it, Jed had been adamant that Linc's unborn child be taken care of for the rest of her life, even if the cost had been his reputation over a phony paternity action.

127

"You're kidding," the attorney finally said.

His grip on his cell phone tightened. "Do I sound like I'm kidding?" He was fed up with everyone always trying to second guess him. Why couldn't the people he was paying to take care of his interests do it without giving him shit? So what if he was generous? He could afford to be. If he never threw another pass, the interest alone from his investment portfolio could keep him living the lifestyle he'd grown accustomed to. What was it Griffen had said, fresh lobster and five hundred dollar a bottle champagne? She'd pop a cork if she knew what he really paid.

"You gonna do this or not?" he snapped, dishing Steve the brunt of his irritation.

"Sure, Jed. Calm down. Give me the details." Steve's tone turned efficient and businesslike.

Jed gave him as many of the details he knew, receiving non-committal responses from the attorney. "And keep it away from the press." The last thing he wanted was to wake up in the morning to find ESPN or some other cable network running a lead story about Jed Maitland's latest love child.

"I'll do my best," Steve assured him. "Jed, as your attorney, I wouldn't be doing my job if I didn't advise you—"

"Save your breath. The kid is mine." Then he took the time to explain the situation to Steve.

When Jed finished his explanation, Steve sighed again. "I've known you a long time, Jed. What else is going on? No one has heard from you in over a week."

"Leave it alone." He wasn't prepared to answer that question. How could he when he didn't know the answer himself?

He'd wanted a break. Needed to get away, sober up and clear his head. He'd been mad as hell over the team's offer to come back next season as an assistant offensive coordinator. Because it hadn't been an offer. Not really. It'd been an ultimatum. Either come back as a coach or sit the bench as a third string loser.

He was thirty-five years old. Montana hadn't retired until he was thirty-eight. Len Dawson hadn't turned in his shoulder pads until forty-one. Okay, so maybe the past two seasons he had spent more time on the sidelines. He'd nursed bruised ribs, a busted hand, a pulled hamstring, and then finally, the shoulder injury that had ended the season for him two games away from the playoffs. Maybe it *was* time to quit.

And do what?

"We've got a problem, Jed," Steve said. "Your agent called two days ago. The owners are pissed. The BMW people are threatening to sue you for breach of contract because you missed another commercial shoot. Adidas catches wind you're blowing shit off, and your product endorsements are going to start disappearing."

Jed chucked the remote across the room, then dragged his hand down his face. He wasn't ready to make a decision. At least not one as important, or as life altering, as his career. Or lack of one. "Bob Yorke is a fucking mother hen."

"Get your head out of your ass, Jed. It's going to cost you if you don't."

"Fuck off."

Steve was quiet for a moment. "You have a lot to lose."

"Let me worry about that."

"Talk to me, buddy," Steve pleaded. "We've been friends a long time."

"It's late. I've gotta run."

"You can't keep running."

Jed swore again. He didn't need this shit. All he'd wanted was to make sure his son was provided for financially, not receive a lecture from his lawyer. "You're my attorney, not my mother. Get off my goddamn back," he shouted, then sent the phone sailing across the room where it crashed against the wall and shattered.

Jed turned off the trashy excuse for a talk show he hadn't really been watching for the past forty minutes, wondering what on earth he was going to do to keep himself occupied. He had no clue where Griffen had disappeared to for the day. She wasn't home and her antique store was closed up tight. A phone call to her father had turned up nothing because the doctor hadn't been home, either.

He was going fucking stir crazy.

School would let out soon for the day. He supposed he could pick Austin up after classes. And do what?

Maybe get to know each other.

That thought didn't spook him half as much as he'd expected. After all, wasn't that why he was sticking around? To get to know his son? He should spend some time with the kid, without Griffen's interference. Without her hovering, they might even have a decent conversation. And it was better than hiding out in a cheap motel room wondering what he was going to do with the rest of his life.

After driving to the next town to buy himself a new smart phone, he called Steve to apologize for being a prick, then drive to Hart High School to pick up Austin. He pulled into the parking lot and killed the engine, and before he could change his mind, the dismissal bell rang. A few moments later, he spied his son's lanky body and honked. Austin waved and loped toward him, then slipped inside the SUV without so much as a greeting. He chucked his backpack onto the floor board.

Jed started the Escalade, but didn't pull out of the parking lot. "Problems?" he asked, wondering at the cause of Austin's sullen expression.

The boy slid down until his head rested against the seat. "I got suspended for kicking Vic Krueger's sorry ass."

So his kid was a trouble maker. A skill he obviously came by naturally. "What's your mom gonna say about that?" he asked, seriously doubting this was a common occurrence.

Austin kicked at the backpack. "She'll probably ground me."

"I imagine she will. You want me to talk to her?"

Austin sat up and grinned. "You'd do that?"

"Sure." He didn't see a problem with telling Griffen the

boy had been suspended. "I doubt she'll go any easier on you though."

Austin sighed. "Not Mom," he admitted. "She hates fighting."

"Most women do," he said, then pulled out of the parking lot. He drove to the center of town toward Goldie's. If Austin was going to end up on restriction, the least he could do was soften the blow with junk food. Maybe he'd even tell him what had caused the fight.

Goldie looked over her shoulder at them when they walked into the local diner. Jed waved, but she didn't wave back, she just kept staring at the two of them over the rim of her bifocals.

Jed led them to a booth while Goldie continued to stare. He knew the resemblance between him and Austin was obvious, but he hadn't expected an open-mouthed stare from the gruff diner owner.

"Are you mad at me because I got suspended?" Austin asked climbing into the booth.

"No." Jed took his seat opposite Austin. "But I'd like you to tell me about it."

"No cobbler today," Goldie said to Jed when she approached their booth. "You want coffee?" She continued to look back and forth between the two of them, as if she couldn't quite believe what her eyes were telling her.

"Just a couple of banana splits," Jed said.

"With extra whipped cream," Austin added.

Goldie lowered her bifocals. "Austin Somerfield, you know your mama don't like you loading up on sweets before supper."

The grin Austin flashed at Goldie made Jed chuckle. The old saying about apples and trees sprang to mind.

"Yes, ma'am," Austin said. "No extra whipped cream."

Goldie nodded. She gave them both another curious glance before moving on behind the counter.

Jed leaned back into the booth and looked at his son. Austin tapped his spoon on the napkin and wouldn't look at him. "So what was the fight about?" he asked again.

Austin shrugged. "Nothing. Vic Krueger is a jackass."

"He probably is, but I think you're smarter than you showed everyone today."

Austin's head snapped up. "How would you know?"

Jed ignored the hostility in his son's voice. "I'm a pretty good judge of character." A skill that had kept him from getting screwed over or taken advantage of when he'd started making serious bank playing football.

Austin looked back down at the table and started tapping his spoon on the napkin again. "You don't know me."

"Isn't that what we're supposed to be doing? Getting to know each other?"

Austin shrugged and continued his tapping. Something was bugging the kid and it went beyond his fight or being suspended. A part of him wished Griffen were there so she could intervene. If anyone knew Austin and his moods, it would be his mother, but he tossed that thought aside. He and Austin needed to forge a relationship.

Austin set the spoon aside and looked at him, wariness evident in his eyes. "When are you leaving?"

Jed scrambled to find the right answer. "I don't know." How long could he stick it out before the vultures tracked him down? He hadn't done much to get his shoulder back in shape, but for what? Now that the bulk of his anger had dissipated, he could admit that his options were definitely limited.

"You gonna be here for the tournament this coming weekend?" Austin asked.

"Probably."

Austin crossed his arms over his chest and lifted his chin. "What about when training camp starts in a few months? How you gonna be around then?"

Jed let out a sigh. "I'm not sure." Since the day Dani left him, he'd answered to no one but himself. He did what he pleased, when he pleased. And he sure as hell didn't appreciate being interrogated, even if it was from his own kid.

Austin's frown deepened. "You don't know much, do

you?"

Jed's temper spiked, but he fought to keep it under control. Leaning forward, he braced his arms on the table and gave the kid a level stare. "Listen, pal," he said, keeping his voice low so Goldie couldn't hear them. "You've got a chip on your shoulder. What's this all about?"

Austin glanced around the diner, then turned back to Jed. "How come you didn't marry my mom?" he asked.

He didn't need a clarification as to which mom Austin was referring to—the answer was simple. His birth mother. "She left me. I didn't know she was pregnant, either. She never told me."

Austin's eyes narrowed and the hostility in them set Jed's teeth on edge. If this was anyone but his own kid, he wouldn't have hesitated to tell them to fuck off and mind their own business.

"Would you have married her if you had known?" There was a brave front to Austin's voice, a poor attempt at masking the pain beneath the question.

"I wanted to marry her even when I didn't know about you." But Dani had had other plans.

After a moment, Austin nodded, seemingly satisfied with the answer. There was no telling how much the kid knew about his relationship with Dani. He supposed the answers were in the journal copies he'd burned when Griffen had first come to see him. He should probably ask her about it because chances were pretty good that Austin would have more questions the more time they spent together.

Goldie returned to their table, two banana splits in hand, one overflowing with whipped cream. "You be sure you eat all your supper, or your mama's gonna be after you."

Austin grinned at Goldie. "Yes, ma'am."

The boy dug into the banana split and Jed didn't bother to question him on the fight since it was obvious Austin wasn't interested in providing answers. By the time Austin pushed the empty dessert dish aside, their conversation had shifted to sports.

"So what are we gonna to do now?" Austin asked.

Jed dug his wallet out of his hip pocket, then tossed a few bills on the table. "We shouldn't do anything that's too much fun or your mom will skin us both alive." Hopefully that didn't include the video game unit and games he'd picked up along with his new cell phone.

Austin laughed and slid from the booth.

"Speaking of which, where is your mom?"

"Dallas. She's looking for a job."

So that's where she'd gone. It didn't take a genius to know that something was going on in her life. The going out of business sale a few days ago, the "for sale" sign on her front lawn, and now the news that she was job hunting. Once the wire transfer came through, she wouldn't have to worry about money. He'd tell her tonight.

Jed nodded a good-bye to Goldie. "That doesn't sound like much fun."

"Yeah, we need to make supper or clean something. You know, soften her up." Austin pushed through the glass door. "Maybe then she won't ground me for the rest of my life."

"Trust me, pal," he said when they slipped inside the Escalade. "Leave this one to me. I happen to know a thing or two about softening up women."

Griffen gripped the steering wheel of her Jeep, willing herself not to cry, to remain calm and think about her next move. She needed a secondary game plan because Plan A had just been shot to hell.

She pulled in a deep, shuddering breath and let it out slowly. A heavy weight had settled on her shoulders that sent her confidence spiraling south. No matter how hard she tried to hold on, she couldn't get a solid grip. She'd been delusional in thinking her old boss would welcome her back to the firm with open arms. Unfortunately, the Dallas investment firm now laid claim to being a victim of the crappy economy and anti-corporate sentiment. In other words, there'd been no job for her. He had promised to call if anything developed, but she couldn't afford to wait around for the phone to ring. She needed a job now. Even the corporate head hunting firm she'd visited hadn't offered her much hope.

By the time she finally pulled into Hart, it was well after six o'clock. After her disastrous meeting with the executive employment agency, she'd sent Austin a text to let him know she'd be late. She didn't get into the city all that often and since they were low on groceries, she took advantage of the time and made a couple of stops. She'd received a text back, but from Jed instead of Austin, telling her not to worry and that he and Austin were fine and dinner would be ready by the time she made it home.

She hadn't even heard the timbre of his voice and the tempo of her heart had picked up speed. Just seeing his name on her iPhone was enough to kick start the memories of what they'd done, of what she wished they'd finished, the night before.

She pulled up in front of Antiquities. While in the city, she'd also taken the time to hire the auctioneer who would sell the remainder of her stock. She needed her tablet with her inventory list before their meeting the next morning.

There was enough sunlight left for her to make her way through the showroom to the back without turning on the lights. The red light on her cordless phone base flashed, alerting her to voice mail messages waiting. She punched in the appropriate code.

"Griffen, this is Keith Shelton at the bank. Give me a call as soon as possible. Call me on my cell if it's after hours," he said, then left the numbers.

Maybe he had a job for her, after all, she hoped for all of two seconds. She listened to the rest of her voice mail, then with more dread than excitement, dialed Keith's cell phone number. The only reason he could be calling her was to remind her that her store was about two weeks away from foreclosure.

Her insides went all jittery with nerves. She aimed for calm, and prayed she conveyed it to the banker. "Hi, Keith. Griffen

Somerfield."

"Griffen," he said, sounding relieved. "I'm so glad you called. Hey, we had a wire transfer come in today in your name. I wasn't sure what you wanted me to do with it, so I'm holding it until I could talk to you."

"How much is it?" she asked cautiously. Who would give her money?

"One hundred thousand dollars," he said.

"What? Is it from Ross?" But she knew it wasn't. Only one person she knew could afford to throw that kind of money around, and it sure as hell wasn't her ex. Then again, maybe guilt over cleaning her out had plagued Ross and he recovered a modicum of decency.

"That's the thing. I have no way of knowing who actually sent it," Keith said. "The sender is only listed as an escrow account from a Dallas law firm. I called both the originating bank and the law firm, but other than the name Steve Rafferty, who wasn't in when I called, no one would give me any information."

"Do you have the numbers?" She jotted down the information. Although it was after six, she still might be able to find out if the money was indeed from Jed. It had to be, because no one else would just give her one hundred grand. Life didn't work that way, especially hers.

"Do you want me to apply this to your loan?" Keith asked, a hint of awkwardness in his voice.

She winced. "I don't know yet, Keith. Let me get back to you on that." She wasn't doing a thing with that money until she knew for sure its origin. The money would satisfy the business loan and pull her mortgage on the building out of foreclosure. In other words, save her from bankruptcy—and humiliation.

As she slid her iPad into her purse, she promised to call Keith as soon as she made a decision. She then placed a call to the Dallas firm.

She asked for Steve Rafferty and was put on hold. A rock and roll station filtered through the line. She flipped through her mail while she waited, relieved she found nothing more important than junk mail. Steve Rafferty. Where had she heard that name before? Ross's attorney had been from a large firm in Houston, a former client of his, if she remembered correctly. Besides, she seriously doubted the money was from her ex.

The line clicked and so did her memory.

"Steve Rafferty."

"This is Griffen Somerfield. I just got off the phone with the bank manager at Hart Savings & Loan. He tells me that a wire transfer for a substantial sum has been sent to my account. Can you please tell me the origin of those funds?"

"I'm operating under my client's discretion, Mrs. Somerfield," Rafferty explained, his gravelly voice all businesslike and efficient. "There is no mistake. The money is yours."

"Who is your client?" She didn't need to ask, she already knew, but she wanted to hear it.

"Jed Maitland."

Her world started spinning, anger its vortex. "I'll be instructing Mr. Shelton to return those funds immediately."

She didn't wait for a response, but hung up and stalked out of the shop. She'd call Keith when she'd calmed down, but right now, she had an arrogant bastard to confront.

By the time she arrived home, her temper hadn't cooled. Oh no, she'd just begun, and by the time she was finished with him, Jed Maitland wouldn't so much as give her a quarter for a parking meter.

She pulled into the garage and started hauling groceries and supplies from the back of the Jeep. Her limbs wouldn't stop shaking. She couldn't remember the last time she'd been so angry. With half a dozen bags in hand, she stalked across the garage, around the boat, jet skis and dirt bikes that would be sold in a few days. That's where her money was coming from—from the man who'd ruined her. She'd be damned if she'd let Jed bail her out. It was her own fault she was in the financial mess she'd been dealing with the past six months.

Not that she'd caused it, but in her opinion, she was equally at fault because she'd been foolish enough to trust Ross. Foolish enough to take him at his word that everything was fine and they could afford to buy a huge monstrosity of a house or take out a hefty loan so she could build an substantial inventory for the shop.

She walked through the door and into the kitchen, or what had once been her kitchen and surveyed the pans cluttering the sink and counter top. She set the bags on the floor. Austin stood at the table, tossing a salad, laughing at something Jed said as he added a generous portion of salt to a stock pot full of boiling water. The father and son bonding scene only fueled her anger.

The door closed a little harder than she'd intended.

"Hey, Mom," Austin turned to face her, a bright smile on his face, his chocolate eyes filled with a happiness she hadn't seen in months. "We made supper."

"I can see that," she managed, trying to shake her anger. She looked at Jed. He wore a black, graphic t-shirt tucked into faded jeans. A black button down shirt hung open, the sleeves rolled back. He looked sexy and completely at home in her kitchen. "I need to talk to you."

"Spaghetti's almost ready," he said as he dropped the pasta.

"Now, Maitland." She set her purse on the counter and gave him a pointed look. "Austin, there are more groceries in the Jeep."

"Yes, ma'am," he said, looking from her to Jed, then back again. The happiness disappeared, replaced by confusion and wariness.

Griffen blamed Jed, which only made her simmering anger boil to the surface and spill over. "You had no right," she said once she was certain Austin was out of earshot. "One hundred thousand dollars, Jed? Was that for services rendered? Jesus, how much for a blow job?"

"Give me a break." He turned on the faucet and rinsed his hands, drying them on the dishtowel slung over his shoulder. "I told you last night I was taking responsibility for my son."

She gripped the top rung of the ladder back chair so hard her fingers ached. "I don't want your guilt money."

He leaned against the counter, his hands braced behind him. A muscle twitched in his jaw, telling her she'd pushed a few buttons.

"It's not guilt money," he said, his tone even and controlled, belying the irritation she sensed lurking just beneath the surface.

"We don't need your money."

"Oh, really?" He crossed his arms over his chest. Despite his casual stance, Griffen had learned one thing about Jed the past few days, the man was anything but casual. "Seems to me like you do."

"Stay out of my business." She stormed out of the kitchen. She'd change clothes, she'd calm down and they could talk about this reasonably. Maybe if she tried a calm, rational approach she could get through to him, instead of yelling like she really wanted to do. Loudly.

She made it up the stairs and into her bedroom without him following her. She tossed her suit jacket on the bed, then unzipped her black skirt, grateful for the reprieve to pull her anger back under control. After hanging up her clothes, she slipping on a pair of yoga pants and a loose-fitting tank, then pulled the pins from her hair and shook it loose, scrubbing her fingernails over her scalp as it fell around her shoulders. As she dropped to her knees to look under the bed for her gym shoes, the door opened.

"Don't you ever knock?" she asked when the source of her anger stepped through the door.

"No." He closed the door behind him.

She ignored him, intent on finding her gym shoes. She didn't want to talk to him until she was calm, and she'd nearly been there, until he barged into her room uninvited.

"The pasta's going to overcook."

"It's taken care of."

"Can I please have ten minutes to myself?"

"Your ten minutes were up fifteen minutes ago," he said,

his voice hard. "Look, your life affects my son. That makes it my business."

"Go away."

"You're selling your house," he said, ignoring her demand for solitude. "You're selling your business. You're selling practically everything you own, according to Austin. He also told me you were in Dallas looking for a job today. What the hell is going on?"

She found her gym shoes and pulled them out from under the bed. "It's none of your concern." If she looked at him, she'd weaken. He'd smile at her or show concern or tenderness, and she'd fall apart. Instead, she crossed the room to her dresser for a pair of socks, determined to remain strong.

"I disagree."

She walked to the chaise in the corner and sat to tug on her socks. "Tough."

"Oh, that's mature," he fired back.

Just as immaturely, she shrugged, then tied the laces of one shoe before looking at him. He stood by the door, one hand resting on the knob, the other at his side. "You're a fine one to talk about maturity."

His eyes narrowed. "You haven't answered my question."

She turned her attention back to her task, shoving her foot into the other shoe and tugging on the laces. "I'm instructing Keith to send that money back. We don't want, or need your money."

"Looks to me like you do."

"My life is my concern."

"And your life affects my son," he repeated, his rising voice indicative of his increasing frustration with her. "If you're in trouble, I can help you."

She sighed and stood. Calm and rational. No shouting matches. She repeated the mantra twice before the spoke. "I'm going to be honest with you." She shoved her hands in the back pockets of her yoga pants so she couldn't clench her fists. "I don't like the fact that you're dead set on insinuating yourself in Austin's life because I still think he's going to get hurt, whether you mean to or not. If you want to be a part of his life, fine. I can get used to that. I don't have a choice. But you don't have to buy my cooperation."

His eyes narrowed further. "Is that what you think I did?" he asked, the words spoken slowly.

She shrugged again. "I don't know. That's what it looks like."

He looked past her to the solid brown draperies, then back again. "I've got a lot of time to make up for." The pain that flashed through his eyes, matched the ache she detected in his voice. Yes, he did have a lot of time to make up for, but that wasn't his fault. Dani had made choices. Choices which had affected many lives.

For the space of an instant, she felt guilty and selfish. All this time she'd been too busy wallowing in her own self-pity to understand what he must be feeling. A few days ago, she hadn't thought him capable of anything other than his own self-serving needs. Mattie had been right when she'd said Jed could be hurting, too. He had a son he'd only just learned about, a son Dani had kept from him.

"That isn't your fault," she told him. "You didn't know about Austin."

"No, I didn't." The anger in his voice was unmistakable. He pushed away from the door and paced the confines of the bedroom. "I wasn't given options here, dammit."

"Don't you dare blame me for this."

"Dani's been dead a long time. What took you so long?" His angry words lashed at her.

"We've been over this," she argued heatedly. "I've only known you were Austin's father for a couple of weeks. Dani's journal—"

"Yeah? And where is this mysterious journal?" he demanded.

"Austin has it." She pulled in a deep breath. *What happened to calm and rational?* "I'm sure if you asked him, he'd give it to you. She tells him about her relationship with you. How much she loved you."

"Loved me?" He laughed, but the sound held no humor. "She sure had a hell of a way of showing it. If she loved me so goddamned much she might have at least given me a chance to know about my own son. Austin was four when she died. I think she had plenty of time."

"No, Jed. She didn't. Not really." She crossed the space between them and rested her hand on his arm. "Having Austin was too hard for her. Dani's body just couldn't take the stress of having a child. I know it was wrong, but she never wanted to burden you."

He looked down at her and her heart snagged at the torment in his eyes. "Dammit, Griffen," he said in a harsh, pain-filled whisper. He started pacing again. "She never would have been a burden. I loved her."

He strode to the bed and sat on the edge, propping his elbows on his knees. He didn't look at her. He was lost in the past. "We were going to elope to avoid the press. I was in Las Vegas for the draft. She was going to fly in and we were going to get married once the draft was over. I'd even talked to her that morning. We'd planned to come here afterward to tell your parents."

Griffen hadn't known. Dani had only told her that the father of her baby had offered to marry her, but she'd refused and had come home. Her sister had known the risks involved if she carried the baby to full term, but she'd wanted the child so desperately. She realized now just how self-centered Dani's actions had been.

"When I got back to my hotel after all the press bullshit, she wasn't there. When I called her, there was no answer, so I figured her flight was delayed. After I checked with the airline, I found out she'd never used her ticket."

Griffen moved to the bed and sat beside him. "Jed, I'm so sorry."

"No explanation. Nothing," he said. "I thought about searching for her, but pride got in my way."

She resisted the urge to wrap her arms around him in an attempt to ease his hurt over Dani's betrayal. "I didn't know," she whispered instead. "Dani wouldn't talk about it."

He turned to face her, a wry grin canting his mouth. "I didn't publicize the fact that I was dumped, either."

He searched her face, and an understanding passed between them. She hadn't been lying when she'd told him she'd eventually get used to the fact that he was Austin's father. Now that she knew the truth, there was no way she would deny him his son.

He took a deep breath and smacked his hands on his knees. "It was a long time ago." He stood and headed toward the door. "Come on. Austin and I didn't slave over a hot stove all afternoon to let that spaghetti go to waste. I hope you're hungry."

"I'll be right down," she said, not fooled by his sudden shift of gears. Jed felt betrayed, and she couldn't blame him. But that didn't change the fact that she was sending the money back.

ELEVEN

GRIFFEN DOUBLE CHECKED the inventory list one last time. Satisfied she had it as comprehensive as possible, she started adding a list of personal items she'd selected from the house to sell, as well. The bungalow in town didn't have half the square footage of her current home, so downsizing was a must.

From her place at the kitchen table, she looked over at the family room and Austin, who lay sprawled on the sofa watching a sit-com on television. Jed dozed in the recliner. A lock of dark hair fell across his forehead, softening the hard lines of his face. She should send him on his way, but he looked so peaceful, she didn't have the heart to wake him.

That, she decided, was her problem. Her heart. Jed infuriated her, made her edgy and confused. Made her want to be reckless and daring. When she was with him she felt anger, passion, emotions she'd never really understood were missing from her life—until him.

After supper, she'd offered to clean the kitchen since he and Austin had cooked. They'd gladly relented, but instead of disappearing at the first sign of real work, Jed offered to help Austin with his pre-algebra homework. So while she'd put a semblance of order back into her usually organized kitchen, Jed described the algebraic theory behind exponents. For someone with a short fuse, his patience had amazed her as he'd carefully explained the why's behind each equation until he was certain

Austin understood.

The entire scene had been so domesticated, so homey, and it bothered her because she knew it was temporary. Apparently she was the only one willing to admit they weren't a real family and the domesticity definitely wouldn't last.

The problem was, when Jed wasn't being pigheaded or trying to shove a crap ton of cash at her, she could easily get caught up in all that wicked charm. While he hadn't raised the money issue again, she wasn't fooled. So far, Jed Maitland hadn't taken no for an answer on anything. No reason to believe he'd start now.

"Mom?" Austin quietly called to her. "Do we have to sell *all* the dirt bikes? Can't we keep at least one?"

She sighed and looked at him over the lid of her laptop. "I'm sorry, Austin." She kept her voice down so as not to awaken Jed. "But we need the money. Maybe later I can manage to pick up a used one for you, but for now every penny counts."

Austin's dark brows creased, making him look like a much younger version of his father. "This sucks, Mom. Everybody's going to be riding this summer and I'll be stuck at home."

Just take the money.

"I know, honey, and I am sorry." Guilt slammed into her. She'd make it up to him somehow. On her own.

Other than a dramatic sigh, Austin didn't argue and turned his attention back to the television. She looked over at Jed. He looked back. Her stomach tightened at the sight of the hard line of his jaw coupled with the intensity in his eyes. She wasn't taking his money. She was in financial hell because she'd depended on another man to take care of her. She'd be damned if she'd repeat history.

She tried to ignore him and returned to her task, but she could feel him watching her. He distracted her and she couldn't concentrate. He wanted answers. She'd managed to evade them earlier, but once Austin disappeared to his room for the night, she suspected he'd start badgering her again about her finances. Perhaps she should tell him the truth, then at least he'd understand her reasons. Plus, he did have a point. Her life, her choices, did affect Austin. The only problem was, she wasn't exactly keen on the idea of him knowing she'd been so incredibly stupid.

She powered down her laptop and headed to the sink. Resisting the urge to run as far away from Jed as possible took willpower she wasn't sure she still possessed. She filled a mug with water and set it in the microwave. Nothing was working out according to her grand plan for reorganization. She'd been so confident she'd pull herself out of the hole, but realized her mistake had been counting on a job at her old firm.

She tugged her sweater tighter around her, afraid she'd fall apart again. She needed to hold it together, for herself and for Austin. But if she didn't find a job, a decent paying job, they were sunk. There were too many variables, too many outside influences left to chance. A bad economy, the fact that she'd been out of the job market for a number of years, all worked against her. A failed business didn't help, either. But she needed something solid beneath her, and until she had it, the ground would continue to shake with each tentative step she took toward recovery.

"I can help you, Griffen."

She spun around at the sound of Jed's voice. He stood in front of her, compassion and sympathy lighting his gaze.

The microwave dinged but she didn't move. "I don't want your money."

"Is it just my money, or anyone's?" he asked. He settled his hands on her shoulders, his touch warm and oddly comforting. "How much do you need? One phone call and you can have what you need right now."

She pulled in a deep breath. She wasn't about to depend on someone else to solve her problems. Problems created by her own blind trust. "I appreciate the offer, but no."

He dropped his hands. "Why the hell not?" he demanded, frustration lining his voice.

She moved away and pulled her mug from the microwave. The man was worth millions, that much was common knowledge. The money he'd had sent to the bank little more than pocket change to someone like him.

"I have to do this myself."

"No, you don't. Dammit, you're stubborn."

She dropped a tea bag into the mug, then turned to face him. "You don't understand. It's a matter of—"

"Pride?" he retorted with a laugh that held no humor. "Trust me, Sister, I know all about pride."

Her refusal had nothing to do with pride and everything to do with her own survival. "It's a matter of taking care of myself. And Austin."

He narrowed the distance between them again, standing so close she caught the spicy scent of his aftershave. He reached out and ran the back of his hand down her cheek, a touch so feather-light and gentle, her breath caught. "Let me help you."

There was only so much a person could expect to withstand at one time without falling apart just a little. For a split second, she hesitated, then came just as quickly to her senses. Allowing Jed to fight her demons would be so simple, an easy way out, but she couldn't let him.

Oh, God, she was going to cry. She pulled in a shaky breath, fighting to hold onto the strength and determination that had carried her this far before her world started crashing down around her. She blinked, trying to hold the tears at bay.

Jed slipped his arms around her before the first tear hit her cheek. He pulled her against him and held her close. He'd never known anyone as brave, or as hardheaded, as the woman drenching the front of his shirt. He let her cry, let her get it out of her system. In his experience, when a woman cried she was trying to get something from him, but not her. No, the woman pressed intimately against him, clutching his shirt in her delicate hands, wanted nothing from him. Didn't she realize he'd give her the world if she'd let him?

His heart skidded to a halt. Suddenly, he forgot how to breathe. The realization of exactly what Griffen was starting to mean to him should have made him run. Instead, he held her tighter. He should leave, ditch this town so fast no one would even remember he'd been in Hart. Only his days of disappearing when things got tough were behind him. No longer did he have only himself to think about. Now there was Austin. And Griffen.

He held her, stroking her back, running his hands over her sleek chestnut hair, murmuring nonsensical reassurances, and loving the feel of her slender curves tucked against him. Like he hadn't wanted another woman in a long time, he wanted Griffen. Previous thoughts of having her to get her out of his system evaporated. He'd never be able to forget her once they made love. And they would, too. He didn't doubt it for a second. He wanted her. After last night, there was no question that she wanted him, as well. But could they share a relationship with Austin and still enjoy each other on a deeper, more intimate level without complications?

Not a chance. Griffen was all about complications. The question was—did it matter?

She pulled in a ragged breath and looked up at him. "I'm sorry," she whispered. "I never cry, but lately—"

"Shhh." He swiped at the moisture staining her cheeks, then brushed his lips across hers in a quick kiss. "Everyone is entitled to few tears once in a while. Even you." How had she gotten into her current predicament? Divorce was never easy, or cheap, but what she was going through went beyond the norm. "Sweetheart, talk to me."

She moved out of his arms and the loss of heat made him want to pull her back. The forgotten mug of tea sat waiting on the counter, and she concentrated on removing the tea bag and dropping it into the garbage can.

"What do you want to hear?" she asked, a trace of bitterness filling her voice. "Do you want to hear that I was an idiot who lived a fairy tale that wasn't there? Or would you rather hear how I was dumb enough to trust a man. My husband, no less?"

"What did that bastard do to you?"

"Screwed me for the last time." Griffen wanted to tell him everything, but she couldn't let down the barriers she'd erected over the past six months far enough to let out the truth. All her life she'd had someone who took care of her. She'd gone from her father's care to Ross's. Oh, she'd thought she'd been independent, but not really. At least not in the truest sense of the word. She'd been free to make her own choices, but she'd always had a safety net in case she fell. Now she was truly on her own, and she realized she wasn't willing to relinquish that independence again. She had to prove to herself she was capable of running her own life. No matter how hard, no matter how many setbacks, she refused to allow anyone to hold that net for her ever again.

She looked at Jed. He stood silent, waiting for her answer. Waiting for her to give him a sign that she'd accept his offer. All she needed to do was say the word, and he would make her problems disappear.

Just take the money.

She swallowed, trying to form a response that would make him understand she just couldn't accept his help. He'd called her stubborn. True, but she was determined to prove her own self-worth. "I really do appreciate your offer, but I can't accept it. I have to do this myself."

"There's nothing I can say to change your mind?" he asked. He didn't look angry, just resigned. For that, she was grateful.

"No," she said with a shake of her head. She reached for her cooled tea and took a sip. "Thank you for understanding."

He rubbed at the back of his neck. "You're a pain in the ass, you know that?"

She managed a smile. "I'm really not trying to be difficult. Just...smarter."

He took a step toward her. The intensity in his eyes held her spellbound.

Taking the mug from her, he set it on the counter, then cupped her face between his palms. His hands were rough, warm, and she wanted them all over her body. A shiver of apprehension shimmied down her spine.

"I think you're a fool for not letting me help you."

She opened her mouth, but he placed his thumb over her

lips, stilling her words.

"And I think you're one of the most courageous people I've ever known."

Courageous? Her? She didn't think so. Not when her insides were jumping all over the place because he was touching her. "Is that a compliment, Maitland?" she whispered.

He leaned in close, his breath fanning her lips. His eyes darkened and her pulse quickened. He was going to kiss her, and she couldn't, or wouldn't, stop him even though Austin was a mere twenty-five feet away in the family room. Besides, after what she and Jed had done the night before, playing coy now would be more than a little hypocritical.

"Austin—"

"Is half asleep," he said, dispelling her argument, seconds before his mouth pressed against hers. His tongue teased her lips, and she opened to him, mating her tongue with his.

She wrapped her arms around his neck and sighed. Kissing him back wasn't smart, but a defensive line crashing through her kitchen would have been hard pressed to stop her from rubbing up against him like a cat in heat. There was no denying she wanted him in the most primal way possible. She wanted him hot and hard and inside her.

His hands moved from her face, down her sides, lightly teasing the swell of her breasts, to land on her ass. He urged her closer and she nearly purred when his arousal pressed against her belly.

Making love to Jed would be a mistake, but she didn't care. Sex would only complicate their already complicated relationship. Their connection wasn't elemental, their bond wasn't born of mutual affection and attraction, but one which had evolved because of their relationship to a thirteen-year-old boy.

"Hey, Mom, do we have any...uh...excuse me."

Griffen scooted away from Jed. Heat scorched her cheeks. "Do we have any what?" She managed to sound relatively calm, despite the wild beating of her heart and her embarrassment at being caught making out with Jed.

Austin's glare was nothing short of hostile as he stormed into the kitchen. "Never mind," he said, his tone insolent. "You're *busy*."

He didn't wait for her to answer. He stalked to the fridge and yanked open the door.

"It's late," she told him. She didn't want to make an issue out of it and decided the best course would be to discuss her and Jed going at it like a couple of hormonal teenagers when they were alone. "You should be getting ready for bed."

The phone rang just as Austin slammed the refrigerator door closed. "Yeah, well, I'm not tired."

She glanced at the Caller ID screen, but didn't recognize the number, so she let it roll into voice mail. Jed grabbed hold of Austin's arm and steered him over to the table and into a chair.

This was her fault. She should've talked to Austin sooner, but what would she have told him? That his mom needed to get laid? Hardly.

Jed stood with his arms crossed, his feet braced apart. "I don't want to hear you talk to your mother that way again."

Austin looked up at him, his expression the epitome of defiance. "You can't tell me what to do."

Jed let out an impatient breath. She could see his struggle to hold onto his temper and almost felt sorry him. Teenagers weren't easy.

"That's enough, Austin," she warned. Under any other circumstances, she would've been shocked by her son's rude behavior. Generally, he was a good kid, easy going for the most part. Since he'd busted them going at it, she decided to cut him a little slack.

"I'll handle this," Jed told her, his voice biting and cold.

Her back stiffened at his harsh tone. Her first instinct was to step in and protect her son, and she would, without question. But she also understood that maybe Jed needed to be the one to deal with the situation. They were all in the middle of unfamiliar territory. The lines were blurred and a new order needed to be established. While she wasn't fond of giving up an ounce of control, she had a feeling Austin was in for a rude awakening. Having Jed around wasn't going to be filled with the hero worship he had once envisioned.

"You," Jed said, looking back at Austin, "need to apologize to your mom."

"Screw you," Austin shouted. "And her. She's gonna ruin everything."

Jed's frown deepened, his exasperation clear. "How is she going to ruin anything?"

"She'll get rid of you like she did my other dad. And then I'll never see you again." He threw another antagonistic glare her way that reached clear to the bottom of her soul and scraped it raw.

Austin had never blamed her for Ross's leaving, and the fact he did so now, hurt. She tried to understand his confusion. What else could he possibly think when the only father he'd ever known had walked away without so much as a backward glance?

"Austin, that isn't true," she told him.

His face flushed with anger and his eyes were bright with unshed tears. "You're a liar. You made him leave. And when he disappoints you, you'll make Jed go away, too."

Jed pulled out a chair, and sat, facing Austin. "Whatever happens between your mother and me is our business. But I promise you, nothing will ever affect our relationship."

"You don't know that." Austin's voice caught, and he sucked in a deep, wavering breath. "You could end up hating her as much as my other dad does."

The raw torment in her son's eyes broke her heart. She despised Ross for the hurt he'd caused Austin. Easing his pain over Ross's rejection she could manage. His fears of rejection by his biological father were up to Jed to erase.

"Ross and I never hated each other," she told Austin. Maybe because they had never really loved each other, not in that all consuming, passionate sense. Oh sure, they cared for each other, and in their own way, they did love. They were a partnership, or so she'd once believed. But looking back now, she saw their relationship for what it really was...empty.

"I heard him, Mom. I heard what he said to you."

She frowned. What could he possibly have heard? She and Ross hadn't even argued. Not like her and Jed disagreed. In fact, Ross had never fought with her, he shut down then made her feel foolish and emotional.

"I heard him." The tears shining in her son's eyes spilled over. "The night you told him to leave, I heard him say he hated being with us." His voice caught on a sob, and her heart broke all over again.

"Oh, Austin." She went to him and pulled him out of the chair and into her arms. "He didn't mean it." She looked over his shoulder to Jed. His jaw clenched and a muscle ticked in his cheek. Anger, no doubt directed at Ross for hurting Austin.

Get in line.

Austin's outburst wasn't about busting her and Jed making out in the kitchen, or even the possibility of Jed abandoning Austin. No, this had Ross's rejection written all over it. How on earth did she explain mid-life crisis to a child?

"He didn't hate us," she said, smoothing his hair.

Austin let go of her. He scrubbed his hand down his face, same as she'd seen Jed do several times. "That's what he said, Mom. I heard him."

"He didn't leave because of you or even me. Not like you think. He despised what his life had become. He wanted to be free, Austin. He didn't want to face his responsibilities. That's on him. It had nothing to do with you."

"Yeah, it kinda does," Austin said, but shrugged his shoulders. "But, whatever."

"Regardless of what happens with your mom and me, that has nothing to do with us," Jed reiterated. "You got that?"

She half expected Austin to shrug again, but after a moment, he simply nodded in agreement.

Austin looked at Jed, caution and hope warring in his dark brown eyes. "Promise?" he finally asked.

"Yeah," Jed said. "I promise."

Griffen prayed Jed would keep his word. Because if he

reneged when whatever was going on between them ended, her own relationship with her son could be damaged forever.

TWELVE

THREE DAYS LATER Griffen had finished packing up the last of her private collection of collectibles she'd planned to auction off on Saturday. She had hoped keeping busy would have given her something to think about other than Jed, but she'd been wrong. Instead she'd been obsessing over him, fantasizing about him. Hell, she'd even dreamed about the man last night.

She had it for him...bad.

Tuesday afternoon he'd sent her a text message, telling her he'd be in Dallas for a few days but would be back before Friday to help her move the boat, jet skis and dirt bikes to the parking lot behind the store for the auction. Logic told her that when a car drove by her house that it wouldn't be Jed, but that didn't stop her from feeling a stab of disappointment every time it wasn't him.

She sidestepped a box of collectible books she refused to sell. At least her job situation had improved. Carol Reynolds from the Hart branch of the Texas Federal Credit Union had called her that morning, letting her know they were looking for a loan manager. Apparently, Keith Shelton had mentioned she was in the market for a job and Carol had thought of her when their current loan manager had announced his retirement.

Not everything was sunshine and roses. She still had to pass all the background checks and make it through the interviews with the board of directors. Plus, the current loan manager wouldn't be retiring for another two months. If the auction pulled in enough money, she wouldn't have to worry too much. Things would be tight financially for a while, but they'd grown used to cutting corners the past few months.

She hefted a box filled with crystal stemware into her arms and made her way back into the warm sunshine to the rear of the Jeep. Having the extra time between jobs just might be a blessing in disguise since she'd have an opportunity to settle them into their new home.

Life, she'd learned, wasn't about what happened to a person, but how they handled the obstacles thrown in the way. In the past few months, she'd become adept at looking for silver linings.

She set the last box on the back seat of the Jeep, turning when she heard the sound of Jed's Escalade pulling into the driveway. Since she was eons past the point of playing it cool, she smiled like a fool when he slid from the SUV. Her pulse picked up speed as he walked toward her. The man was gorgeous. Just looking at him made her girl parts twitch. He wore a pair of jeans that fit his long, muscular legs perfectly. She hadn't wanted to like him, but he'd proven time and again he wasn't the shameless scoundrel the press had painted him.

Even the gentle breeze couldn't cool the flush of heat that rushed through her at the sight of him. Their relationship had changed. She wasn't exactly certain how it happened, but it had. Maybe because she'd stopped thinking of him as the enemy.

God help her, she cared about Jed Maitland. She desired him, too. And that brought an urge difficult to resist, because she really wanted to run up to him and launch herself into his arms. Kiss him stupid and insist he make love to her. A little extreme, especially for her, but the man made her want things she'd forgotten existed. She'd racked up half a week of sleepless, restless nights as proof.

Grateful he couldn't hear the wild beating of her heart, she smiled at him. "Just like a man to show up when the work's half done," she teased.

He slipped off his sunglasses and stuffed them into the

pocket of his shirt. "You should have called me. I'd have been here sooner."

Alone. With Jed. She knew exactly how that would've ended.

Yeah, she should've called him.

"I had more things I wanted to pack." She closed the back end of the Jeep, then walked into the garage. "You'd have only been in the way."

He laughed, a low, comforting rumble of sound. "I don't think a woman's ever accused me of being in the way before."

"Don't let it wound that oversized ego, Maitland." She waited until he stepped into the garage before she hit the switch on the garage door opener.

He moved closer, a predatory light shining in his gaze. "My ego is never wounded." His voice was low and flirtatious. She'd told him once not to flirt with her. What had she been thinking?

He stopped a few inches from her. "Bruised?" she asked.

"I don't bruise easily." He braced both hands on the wall behind her, trapping her within the strength of his powerful arms.

"Neither do I," she whispered.

His eyes darkened.

She forgot how to breathe.

"That's good to know," he said, then dipped his head and kissed her hard and deep.

Heaven help her, he made her want, made her need, made her hotter than she ever thought herself capable of being with nothing more than a simple kiss. Although, Jed's kisses were hardly simple. More like demanding. Hot. Wet. Erotic.

She moaned and wreathed her arms around his neck, pressing closer until the tips of her breasts rubbed against his chest. Tension coiled tightly inside her. Crazy or not, fate had brought them together and there was no denying where they were headed. And if he didn't make a move in that direction soon, she'd drag him there herself. She had no qualms about being the aggressor.

He gripped her hips and rocked her against him. A bolt of electricity shot through her at the intimate contact, pooling in her belly and heading south. He made her wet, hot with a need so powerful she'd burn alive if he didn't put out the fire.

He ran his hands up her sides, to her arms, and she wiggled closer. He broke the kiss and pulled her arms from around his neck. Warm, stale air from the garage washed over her, but instead of breaking the spell, spurred her erotic thoughts into overdrive.

"Sweetheart, you're killing me." His voice was tight with frustration, his expression tighter.

Feminine satisfaction made her smile. She gave him a throaty laugh she hardly recognized as her own. "The feeling is mutual, Maitland. Crazy, but mutual."

"What's so crazy about two people wanting each other?" He didn't sound irritated, but he looked mildly peeved.

"Nothing, but our..." She didn't want to use the word relationship. They didn't have a relationship. All they really had was burning case of lust. Mutual desire bordering on insanity. "It's just not smart."

He frowned. "Smart?"

She opened the door to the kitchen and held it open. "Are you coming?"

"Really?"

She laughed. "Don't be dirty."

His grin turned wolfish. "If you only knew," he said, following her inside. He walked to the table and sat. "Is that how you would describe our relationship? Not smart?"

She pulled two bottled waters from the fridge and handed one to him. "That's the whole problem." She twisted off the cap. "We don't have a relationship."

He set the water on the table with a snap. "We have a son."

She shook her head. "No," she said, joining him at the table. "You and Dani had a son. I adopted him."

"You're splitting hairs."

Was she? Probably, but it was the truth. If it weren't for Austin, they never would have met. More importantly, they weren't the only two parties involved. They had Austin's welfare to think of, too. Hadn't his outburst Monday night shown them the fragility of their son's emotional state?

"Does it matter?" she asked. "We have a connection through Austin. Nothing more."

"That's bullshit and you know it." He came out of the chair and pulled her to him. He banded his arms around her, holding her close.

Her nerve endings started tingling all over again.

He leaned in close. Determination burned in his gaze, tension coiled his body. "Every time we get within two feet of each other something happens."

Yeah. Spontaneous combustion.

"And you think that translates to a relationship?"

"I don't know what it means other than the fact that I want you, dammit. And you want me. What the hell is wrong with that?"

"Nothing, but we're not the only two people involved."

His gaze slid from her eyes, to her lips, and back again. "Sweetheart, when I get you into bed, you and I are the only ones who will be involved."

Good Lord, just the thought of going to bed with him had her melting on the spot. He was lethal.

She pushed away from him only because couldn't think when he was standing so close, or being so blatantly sexual. "I was talking about Austin. You said yourself, whatever affects me, affects him. You think making love to you is not going to affect me? I don't go in for casual sex. I'm not one of your little gridiron groupies waiting on the sidelines."

"I never said you were."

"Let's just drop it, okay? I've got a ton of things to do today and—" Whatever happened to her being the aggressor? She was acting like a timid virgin.

"And you'd rather avoid this conversation." Irritation lined his words. "Fine. Go ahead and avoid it all you want, Griffen. But the fact remains, we want each other. And you're going to have to deal with it sooner rather than later, sweetheart."

She sighed and opened the fridge again, setting the bottled water inside. Yes, they would make love, and she was sure it would be a mistake. A mistake she didn't have a prayer of preventing.

As she followed him into the family room, her cell phone rang. She dodged a packing carton to snag it off the entertainment center. "It's my realtor," she said, then answered halfway through the second round of the ringtone.

"Griffen? Joe Gibson, here. I've got news."

She dropped into the chair. "Good news, I hope."

"Very good news," Joe said, "There's an offer. And they're willing to pay your asking price."

A surge of relief welled inside her. "That's fantastic."

"Will a twenty day escrow work for you?"

"It will if you can get me into the bungalow by then," she told him. If her luck held through the auction, she might just be able to climb out of financial hell. The proceeds from the sale of the house would satisfy the mortgages, bring the past due balances on her other debts current and allow her to put even more money down on the bungalow, lowering her mortgage payment on the new place even more.

"It won't be a problem. I'll send over the papers later this afternoon."

"Thank you, Joe. I appreciate all you've done." She disconnected the call.

"He sold the house," she told Jed, setting her cell phone on the table. "Do you have any idea what a relief this is for me?"

He sat on the sofa and leaned back, looking hot and sexy and so doable. "Yeah, I do." When he smiled back at her, she melted a little more.

She let it out a long, slow breath. "I think I did it."

Jed fought to keep the smile on his face and not let her see the truth. He'd have to tell her eventually, that it was his dummy corporation buying her house, but for the moment, he couldn't help be a tad selfish and let her enjoy the moment.

He'd spent the past three days in Dallas taking meetings. He'd met with his attorney, accountant and his broker, taking a long hard look at where he stood financially. His finances were beyond healthy, but he had no idea what to do about his career. The meetings with his agent hadn't gone as well. While the advertisers threatening to sue had been placated, he was still on the verge being cut from the roster. The last thing he wanted to admit was that his career was over. Hanging out on the sidelines like a washed-up jock left a bad taste in his mouth. Anything else just felt too much like a mercy fuck.

She sprung up from the chair and looked around the room. "Have you seen my iPad? I need to make a list. The buyers asked for a twenty day escrow." She snagged her tablet off the sofa and powered it up. "I need to make sure the carpets are cleaned, the appliances, and the lawns done. I suppose I could afford to hire a cleaning service." She bit her lip and stepped over an empty packing carton to inspect the cream colored drapes. "These should probably be cleaned, too. Or do you think the new owners will want to redecorate?"

"I wouldn't worry about it," he told her. "They're fine."

He wasn't fine. Griffen was a dilemma, a distraction, but one he couldn't get out of his mind no matter how hard he tried. While his accountant had gone over figures and investments, his mind had been on Griffen and Austin. When Steve had discussed the possible consequences of proposed career options and the BMW people with their threats to sue, he'd been obsessed with thoughts about making love to Griffen.

He tried to tell himself she was a mistake, but that didn't stop the constant ache wanting her caused. He tried to tell himself he could make love to her and get her out of his system, that they could have a few laughs for as long as it lasted, but his conscience wouldn't let him. Griffen wasn't a fling. She played for keeps.

Despite that particular complication, he still wanted her.

She smiled up him, her eyes sparkling with happiness. Guilt crashed in on him. He should tell her he was the one who bought her house. Tell her that on Saturday he planned to raise the bids himself or outbid everyone else so she'd have the money she needed from her auction. And he should tell her about the trust fund he'd set up for Austin.

Later. He couldn't stand the thought of seeing that cheerful sparkle leave her eyes.

"I feel like celebrating." She set her tablet aside, walked toward him. He snagged her hand and gave a gentle tug, urging her into his lap. She slipped her arms around his neck and moved in for a kiss.

To hell with guilt, he thought, as he obliged. She tasted sweet. She tasted like home. Regardless of the stark fear that thought evoked, his body responded to her.

She ended the kiss quickly and scrambled off his lap. "To hell with my diet. When Austin gets home from school, what do you say we drive over to Goldie's for some fried chicken and gravy?"

He couldn't have heard her right. "What do you mean Austin's at school?"

She nodded, picked up her iPad again, and started tapping the screen. "He won't be home for another...," she checked the gold watch on her wrist, "...ten minutes."

"They let him back early?"

She looked over at him, her brows puckered in confusion. "Back? What are you talking about?"

Dread crept up his spine, tightening the back of his neck with tension. "He didn't tell you, did he?"

"Tell me what?"

He rubbed at the tension but it didn't ease. "This is partially my fault. I told him I'd talk to you about it the other night, and with everything that went on, it completely slipped my mind."

"Jed, you're scaring me. What's going on?"

"Austin got into a fight at school on Monday. He was suspended for the week."

She shook her head. "No, that can't be right. He went to school this morning. He's gone to school all week."

"Not to school he didn't," he said, his tone dry.

"Are you sure?" She dropped onto the chair. When she looked at him, the concern in her eyes tripled his guilt. "At the very least, someone should've called me to set up a meeting. It's school policy. He can't go back until I meet with the principal."

"I'm sorry, Griff. I screwed up, but Austin still should've told you."

"This isn't like him," she said. "He's never lied to me about something so important."

"When you didn't ground him right away, maybe he figured you'd never find out."

"Mattie is a teacher at the high school. Of course I'd find out."

"And no one from the school called you?"

"No." She picked up her cell phone and scrolled through the list of incoming calls. "Nothing."

Jed sat forward and braced his elbows on his knees. "He'll be home soon. We'll find out where he's been hiding out all week."

"I can't imagine—" She quieted when the kitchen door suddenly slammed closed.

Austin walked across the kitchen and dropped his backpack on the table. "Hey, Mom. How long until dinner?"

"Where have you been?" Jed demanded.

Austin stopped and glared at his father. "Out," he said, his tone filled with uncharacteristic insolence.

Griffen didn't know what had happened to her sweet baby boy, but he was turning into a stranger. "Austin, sit down. We'd like to talk to you."

Austin walked into the room, keeping a wide berth from both of them, to slump onto the other end of sofa. He leaned back and propped one foot over his knee.

"Why did you lie to me?" she asked.

He wouldn't look at either of them, keeping his gaze transfixed on the half-filled box of DVD's. "I never said I was going to school."

"You said you'd see me *after* school. You led me to believe that's where you'd gone. How is that different from lying?"

Austin shrugged. "So am I grounded or what?"

"You bet your ass you're grounded," Jed bit out.

Austin looked from Jed to her. His dark eyebrows pulled into an angry frown. Anything was better than the I-don't-give-a-damn attitude he'd given them since walking in the door. "Fine. For how long?"

She looked to Jed, but he kept silent. "Two weeks," she told Austin. "No privileges."

"And you can forget the tournament this weekend," Jed added.

Austin shot off the sofa. "You can't do that."

"Can't I?" Jed countered. "Watch me, pal."

"Mom. Do something."

Identical pairs of chocolate eyes turned to her. She had the distinct impression she was being asked to choose between them. She knew what she had to do. No matter how much it hurt Austin now, she had to side with Jed. Austin had to learn he wouldn't be allowed to pit the two of them against each other.

"Yes, Austin. He can," she said quietly.

"You're going to let him do that to me? He doesn't have the right."

The torment in her son's voice nearly broke her resolve, but she had to stand firm. "Yes, he does. You wanted your father in your life. This is part of the deal."

Tears and accusation welled in Austin's eyes. She nearly caved.

"I hate you. I hate you both," he said before running from the room. His feet pounded on the stairs, then moments later, his bedroom door slammed closed.

"That went well." She blew out a stream of breath. She needed to talk to him, needed to let him know what he'd done was unacceptable. They were only punishing him so he'd learn that deceit came with consequences. She stood but Jed reached out and clasped her arm in a firm grip.

"Don't, Griffen."

"I have to go to him." She tugged but his iron-hard grasp held her tight.

He shook his head and stood. "Give him time to cool off first."

That sense of choice warred inside her again. In doing the right thing for her son, she'd hurt him. But if she hadn't backed Jed up on the tournament issue, in the end, Austin would walk all over both of them, playing both ends against the middle time and again. Austin needed to understand she and Jed were a united front.

"Let him think about it awhile." He took her hand again and pulled her to him. "He'll get used to the idea."

She sighed when he slid his arms around her and held her close. She needed to be held, needed the comfort.

"We have to put a stop to this before it becomes a habit," he said, running his hands over her back.

She leaned back to look up at him. "We?"

"He's my kid, too."

Yes, Austin was his son, she'd never denied that. She'd even gotten used to the idea. Austin might not like Jed disciplining him, but she knew he'd be hurt if Jed suddenly decided not to hang around. Hadn't they already established that fact when Austin had caught them kissing? "What are you saying?" she asked.

He frowned. "I can't just walk away from him. He's my son."

She stepped out of his embrace. "What about your career?"

Jed shoved his hand through his hair, fighting the frustration her questions caused. "What about it? One has nothing to do with the other."

When she frowned at him, he moved to the window. "I don't know yet," he finally admitted.

"Do you plan on being a part-time father? A weekend dad? For Austin's sake, we should discuss this."

Why couldn't she just stop the interrogation? He was here now, wasn't that enough? "I don't know," he said again.

"Jed, children need rules, they need boundaries. How can we set those if you don't even know what you're doing with your life?"

God, she was so right. If it hadn't been for the rules and boundaries his grandparents had set and made sure he followed whether or not he liked it, he never would have gotten through high school. He was the man he was today because of his grandparents. He knew that. And he was grateful.

She wanted promises, not for herself, but for Austin. Only he wasn't capable of providing them. How could he, when he had no clue what he was doing next? His grandfather had taken his responsibilities seriously. Shouldn't he do the same for his own kid? What would he be saying about the old man's memory if he walked away from the one person who really mattered—his son?

He turned face to Griffen. She stood in the center of the room, her expression solemn. And what about her?

"I'll be there for Austin."

It was as far as he was willing to go.

THIRTEEN

JED HIT THE mute button on the remote control, silencing the late night talk show host. He pushed off the bed and paced the confines of the motel room, coming to a stop at the window in time to see a flash of lightning in the distance highlight the patchy clouds in the night sky. Springtime in Texas was in full swing.

He needed to make a decision, and he was leaning more and more toward retirement. Just cut out now while he was still considered one of the best, not make a fool of himself like Favre had done by refusing to give up on a career that had been over for some time. No, it was much better to go out with a bang, not a whimper.

And do what?

He didn't know anything except the game.

Football had been his life since he was ten years old. His grandfather had signed him up in hopes it'd help him settle into his new life without his parents. The old man might have been a hard-ass, but Austin Maitland had been one smart son-of-a-bitch.

So what are you going to do?

Dammit, he didn't know anything except the game.

And it had made him rich. If he wanted to go fishing every day for the rest of his life he could. But he knew himself. He'd grow bored, he'd want something more, something to challenge his intellect.

So what were *you going to do?*

He'd planned on a degree in history and going on to earn his master's degree before the scouts started showing up in his grandparents' kitchen with their college scholarships and promises of fame. And they'd delivered. But he was thirty-five-years-old. Starting a new career at his age seemed ridiculous.

Or maybe not.

He turned and his cell phone on the bedside table caught his attention. He should call Griffen, check-in to see how Austin was doing.

And talk to Griffen.

He'd disappointed her. He'd known it the minute he'd said he'd be there for Austin. He was too much of a coward to tell her how he felt about her.

Before he could question his motives, he called her. She answered on the second ring.

"Hello?" Her sweet husky voice drifted over him, increasing his regret.

"Hi."

"Jed?"

He frowned. "You have other men calling you at this time of night?" he asked, feeling territorial.

She laughed. "Not lately."

"How's Austin?" Their son *was* the purpose of his call. He absolutely had *not* called to hear the sexy voice of the woman responsible for his sleepless nights.

Yeah. Right.

She sighed and he heard a rustling noise. She was in bed. The realization kicked his fantasies into high gear.

"He came out of his room for supper. We had a talk."

"And?"

"And he's feeling better. He's confused, though."

He didn't doubt that for a second. How else would the kid feel? Jed didn't have to be a trained psychologist to know Austin's confusion stemmed from abandonment issues. He was acting out now, pushing the limits to find his footing in this new relationship. And it was up to him and Griffen to help him navigate. "Does he understand why we grounded him?"

"He gets it," she said. "But he's still not happy about you keeping him from the tournament this weekend."

He shifted, propped the pillows against the headboard and leaned back. "We had to. You know that, don't you?"

"I do. And Austin will, too. Eventually. You were right. He needs time."

"Good." He glanced at the muted television as Kimmel interviewed a bleached blonde pop tart headed for trouble. He'd met the kid briefly at a party last year. She wasn't a bad person, just barreling out of control. Another casualty of fame.

"What are you doing?" he asked, not wanting their conversation to end.

"Reading."

"What are you reading?"

"A book," she said after a moment.

Her shy, noncommittal answer piqued his curiosity. "What kind of book?"

"A fiction novel." Her voice sounded all prim suddenly.

"Horror?"

"No."

"Fantasy?"

She paused. "Kinda of."

"A fairies and gnomes kind of fantasy?"

Her throaty chuckle heated his blood. "Not quite."

"A romance?" The thought of Griffen reading a romance novel intrigued him. A lot about her intrigued him. Her fiery spirit. Her fierce need for independence. Then there was the fact he was hard just thinking about her.

She gave a little laugh. "Don't sound so appalled."

He chuckled. "I thought only bored housewives with lousy sex lives read those."

"Now you're being a jerk. You should try one before you ridicule an entire genre." That prim note was back in her voice.

"No, thanks." He enjoyed fiction on occasion, his reading tastes leaning more toward legal thrillers or a good horror novel. "So is it a sexy book?" His mind filled with Griffen and all sorts of interesting, erotic images.

"Hmm, very." Her voice was a throaty purr.

He felt the first, subtle swell of his cock. "Does it make you hot?" Oh, he was going to be in pain if he didn't head this conversation into a different direction.

Her breath caught in response, and he grinned. "Tell me, Griffen? What turns you on?"

"A lot of things," she whispered.

His erection intensified. "A woman of variety. Tell me. What do you like?"

"Jed..."

He could almost feel her blush through the phone. Worse, he could imagine the pink tinges on her cheeks, and once again wondered where else she blushed. "I'll make you hot, babe."

He heard a rustling noise again. The thought of her wearing nothing but a sheet had his erection straining. He was a fool for torturing himself like this.

"You already do."

Jed curled his fingers into his palm at her admission. "I can make you come."

"Now?"

He chuckled. He'd meant to shock her, but the hint of anticipation in her voice was a challenge he had no intention of ignoring. "Close your eyes."

"Wait a minute," she said. "I want to turn off the light."

"Take off your clothes while you're at it." Man, was he ever on a collision course now.

"Jed..."

"Trust me."

She let out a sigh. "Hold on."

He didn't know if he could hold on for much longer. His dick throbbed and just the thought of her naked had his temperature spiking.

"Okay," she said. "This is crazy."

She didn't know the half of it. But he'd started them down this path, he wasn't about to stop now. "Close your eyes," he told her again. "And imagine my hands sliding over your body."

"Hmm..." she murmured.

He imagined her touching herself, of her own hands gliding purposefully over her curves as she envisioned them together. "Cup your breasts. Are they heavy?"

"Yes."

"Now drag your thumb over your nipples. Imagine my mouth closing over them, licking, sucking. I bet you taste so sweet."

"Oh, Jed..."

"Are you hot?"

"Yes," she said in a throaty whisper. "Hot and wet. I can feel my clit throbbing for you."

He dragged his hand down his face. At least the woman was honest.

This was dangerous. He was playing with fire, but not even that thought could stop him from continuing with the reckless, shameless game he'd started. "I want to taste you. Would you like that?"

"Oh, yes," she said, her voice coalesced into a soft moan of pleasure that caused him bodily harm. "Yes."

His erection pressed insistently against his shorts. He should hang up the phone and stop this insanity. Hadn't he spent enough sleepless nights remembering the way her eyes darkened when she came, the way she'd sounded, the way her body came alive under his touch?

"I—" She moaned again, sweet and heaven-filled. He nearly came out of his skin at the coil-tight sound of her voice. "I need..."

"I know you do, baby," he said. "Go ahead. Tell me how wet you are for me."

Her startled cry as she followed his instructions was too much. He took matters into his own hands and urged her to do the same. "Come for me, babe." his voice strained as he neared his own satisfaction. "Let me hear you come."

It didn't take long before the tempo of her breathing increased, followed by her keening moan as she came, sending him over the edge. His own ragged breathing rang in his ears, along with the thudding of his heart.

"Griff? You still there?" he said once his wits returned.

She let out a long, slow breath. "I can't believe you."

He chuckled at the hint of embarrassment evident in her breathy whisper. "That was nothing," he said. "Because when we do make love—baby, I'm gonna set you on fire."

Mattie stood on the round dais before a half circle of strategically placed mirrors and made a face, causing Griffen to chuckle. "Would you look at this mess?" Mattie swatted at the feathers on the bodice of the wedding gown. "This isn't me. I look ridiculous."

"No, it's not you," Griffen agreed, although she didn't believe for a second her sister looked ridiculous. "It's just too much dress for you." They were in their third and last bridal boutique of the day. So far, Mattie hadn't come close to finding a dress she deemed suitable enough for her wedding to Trenton Avery. Her sister was petite and curvy, she needed something to accentuate her curves, not bury them in a stark white, frilly confection of satin, lace and tulle.

"Help me out of this thing..." Mattie swatted at more feathers as she stepped down from the dais, "...before I start clucking."

The sales associate, Ellen, hurried back into the dressing room with more traditional white gowns. She hung them on individual stands designed to allow an unobstructed, three-sixty view of the bridal wear. "We have a fairly large selection," she said. "Perhaps one of these will be *the* dress."

Griffen gave the gowns a quick once-over and shook her head. "I don't think they'll work for her," she said to Ellen. "They're just as overpowering as the last four she's tried on." She looked to Mattie. "Have you considered something tea length?"

Mattie's eyebrows shot up. "Simple."

"Elegant," Griffen said.

"Classic," the sales woman added.

Mattie swatted at the feathers. "And not so...this. Or white."

Ellen nodded in agreement. "Ivory, perhaps."

"I'm thinking a little darker. But not beige," Griffen said.

"I might have just the thing," Ellen said with a smile. "Excuse me a moment, please."

"Help me, Griff," Mattie said, when the woman left. She turned, exposing the back of the dress. "I don't know why they make these things so impossible to get out of."

Griffen started working on the long line of pearl buttons. "They're designed this way so your husband can undress you on your wedding night. It's supposed build the anticipation."

The thought of anticipation had Griffen immediately zeroing in on thoughts of Jed and wondering how much longer before they finally made love. Not much, if Thursday night's conversation was any indication of just how far and how fast their relationship had changed.

Initially, she and Jed had planned to spend the day together at the auction, but when Mattie suggested she go with her to Dallas to shop for a wedding dress, Jed had encouraged her to go. Shopping with Mattie had turned out to be the perfect excuse to avoid having to suffer the indignity of watching strangers bid on her things, and for that she was grateful. For the first time in a very long time she'd given up control and had to admit, she kind of liked it.

Since Austin was grounded from participating in the basketball tournament, he was with Jed, who was hanging out with Trenton, her dad and Phoebe, who was no doubt running the men ragged. Which gave Griffen and Mattie all day to scour Dallas for the perfect dress.

As she slipped another pearl button out of the satin loop closure, Griffen let out a sigh. She still couldn't believe that she'd actually had phone sex with Jed. Never in her life had she ever done anything so brazen.

"What's that about?" Mattie asked.

Griffen blinked and looked at her sister. "I'm sorry. What

did you say?"

"That dreamy sigh." Mattie looked over her shoulder at her. "Oh my God. You're blushing."

"Leave it alone, Matt."

"Oh, yeah, like that's gonna happen." Mattie gasped suddenly. "You slept with him, didn't you?"

Griffen winced. "Not exactly."

"Either you did or you didn't, Griff." Mattie frowned. "There shouldn't be any confusion about it."

Griffen grasped Mattie's shoulders and turned her sister back around so she could finish unfastening the dress. "I really don't want to talk about this."

"Too bad," Mattie said, turning back around again so she faced Griffen. "And we are *so* talking about this."

Griffen let out a short, impatient breath. "Fine. If you must know, we had phone sex the other night."

"Oh." Mattie's eye rounded momentarily before a slow, sly grin spread across her face. "Way to go, Griff."

"And, no, I won't give you the details, so don't ask."

Mattie laughed, then turned back around. After a few moments, she said, "Ford and I used to have phone sex."

The wistful quality, combined with the tinge of sadness in Mattie's voice tugged at Griffen's heart. Mattie and Ford had been a couple since high school, but Mattie had been crazy about Ford from the second she'd met him. When they'd finally started dating, there'd never been anyone else for either of them. They were supposed to have been the ones to beat the odds, to make a mockery of the so-called experts and their statistics claiming young love never lasted. Griffen didn't doubt for a second that Mattie and Ford would've been together forever. In a way, she supposed they had. Only forever had showed up way too soon.

"He was away so much of the time." Mattie stepped out of the dress. "First boot camp, then OSC, flight school, then SEAL training. It wasn't the same, obviously, but it was fun. Goodness, he could be so wicked."

"Do you and Trenton?" Griffen asked, curious. Trenton

worked in Dallas and had a condo downtown. Since he was in line for a partnership, that meant putting in long hours, and she knew he rarely made it out to Hart on weeknights. "Have phone sex, I mean?"

"Heavens, no," Mattie said and laughed. "I tried once, but it was a disaster. He just wasn't comfortable with it."

That surprised Griffen. "Is he a prude?" He didn't seem like the buttoned-up-tight kind of guy, but who knew what went on behind closed doors.

"Oh, God, no." Mattie slipped on the plain, white satin robe the boutique provided so she wouldn't have to stand around in her bra and panties while waiting for the sales associate to return with more dresses. "Not at all. He's just...proper."

"Geeze, Matt. That sounds super sexy." She gave her sister a look. "Not." There wasn't a proper bone in Jed's body. The man was beyond sexy. In fact, she'd classify him as dangerous, shameless even. Without a doubt he would turn her world upside down when they finally made love. Just the thought had her nipples hardening and her inner thighs tingling.

"Trenton has plenty of sex appeal." Mattie shrugged, but didn't elaborate. "It is what it is."

Griffen sat on one of the blue velvet benches and looked over at Mattie. "Okay, but is it enough?" she asked, concerned for her sister's happiness. "I mean, I know how it feels to want something that just isn't there." Hindsight being so clear, she knew now her marriage to Ross had lacked passion. Her marriage had lacked a lot of things, but she'd settled. Ross had offered her stability and companionship. As far as she knew, he'd been faithful until he'd started banging his secretary. Shame on her for accepting the trade-off and never questioning if she'd been truly happy. The last thing she wanted was for Mattie to make that same mistake.

"I had crazy passionate once," Mattie said, "and it nearly killed me. When I lost Ford, I honestly didn't care if I lived or died. If it hadn't been for Phoebe..."

The sadness banked in her sister's eyes increased her

concern. Could Mattie still be in love with Ford? He'd been dead for five years. Did a love that ran as deep as theirs ever truly die?

"Do you love Trenton?" Griffen asked. "Don't settle, Matt. If you're not in love with him, don't marry him."

The smile that canted Mattie's mouth didn't come close to reaching her eyes. "Of course, I love Trenton. And he loves me, and Phoebe. She's even starting to get used to the idea of a man in my life. He's patient with her, and that's not so easy. You know what a little tyrant she can be."

"I just want you to be happy," Griffen said. "You deserve to be happy."

Mattie smiled again, but that hint of sadness still lurked in her sister's eyes. "I am happy," she said as Ellen returned to the dressing room. "Oooh, and that dress looks like a good start."

Ellen hung up a lovely tea length A-line wedding dress with an illusion neckline and beaded lace appliqués for their inspection. "The color is champagne," Ellen explained as she fanned out the skirt. "Now, this is only a sample and it will be a little long on you, but we'll order it in petite. If it's still a little long, don't worry. The seamstress I use works miracles."

"The color is perfect," Griffen said, tracing a lace appliqué with her finger. "What do you think, Matt?"

She plucked the dress from the stand. "Let's find out."

Ellen discretely disappeared as Mattie shrugged out of the robe and stepped into the tulle underskirt and then into the dress. Griffen fastened the back, then stood back as Mattie stepped up on the dais to study her reflection in the half circle of mirrors. When she caught Griffen's gaze in the reflection, the smile on Mattie's face was genuine.

Mattie laughed and twirled around. "It's perfect."

Ellen returned, her hands filled with head pieces. "I can get each of these in the same champagne color." She placed four different pieces on the glass table, ranging in style from a short, traditional veil with a blusher, to a simple headband encrusted with rhinestones. "But this," she said, holding up a bird-cage style veil, "is what I would suggest."

Mattie tried on the veil Ellen handed to her. "What do you think?"

"Beautiful," Griffen said around the lump that suddenly lodged itself in her throat.

"Don't you dare cry," Mattie said, her own eyes suspiciously moist. "Now we have to figure out what the bridal party is going to wear. Meaning you."

Once Mattie changed back into her street clothes, they joined Ellen in the main salon. "We have a nice selection of dresses. If you don't see anything you like, let me know. We have style books available and can order anything you need."

Griffen cleared her throat. "I guess jeans are out of the question."

Mattie shot her a tolerant look. "What do you think of teal?"

"Gangrene?" Griffen flipped through the row of dresses hanging on the rack along the back wall. "That sounds so appealing."

Mattie ignored her and turned to Ellen. "I'd like something bold. Teal, plum, burgundy maybe."

"Those are more fall or winter colors," Ellen said. "For a summer wedding, bright jewel tones are in this season. And pastels are always a lovely choice."

"What about this?" Griffen held up a tea-length, satin A-line dress in a luxurious marine blue. It had a boat neck cut, similar to the illusion neckline of Mattie's dress. A simple mock belt of matching beads and sequins were the only embellishments. "Simple. Classic. Not quite the color of gangrene, but still bold. It even has the same vintage vibe. And the color will really complement the champagne of your dress."

An hour later, they left the bridal boutique, orders placed and a date set for their first fitting in two weeks. After a quick Starbucks stop for lattés, they headed back to Hart. Since Mattie was driving, Griffen pulled out her cell phone to check for missed calls. There were two, one from the auctioneer and one from Jed, as well as a text from her dad telling her Austin would be staying with him for the rest of the weekend.

"Dad's keeping Austin overnight," she said as she sent a text back to her dad confirming.

"Oooh, sounds like Jed has plans for you tonight.

Griffen bit her bottom lip. Did he? "He called."

"Then call him back and find out. And if not, then you tell him you're taking advantage of the situation."

"I don't know."

"Dammit, Griff," Mattie said, her tone filled irritation. "You're attracted to the guy. He obviously wants you. For once in your life, just freaking go for it. What's the worst that can happen?"

She wasn't the only one involved. She had a child to think about, too. "Austin could get hurt."

"That's such a load," Mattie said. "You're afraid *you* could get hurt."

Yes, she was afraid, because she'd come to care for Jed. He wasn't the public image, not really. Sure, he could be stubborn and impossible. He pushed her buttons and made her want to throw things. But he was also caring and kind. And he made her hot. "We come from two different worlds."

"So? Who cares?"

"You say that like it doesn't matter."

"It doesn't. And you know, you don't come from two different worlds. Not really. Jed comes from the same place you do. He might have made it big, but he grew up just like we did, traditional values, small town and a strong work ethic." Mattie let out an impatient breath. "Call him back, Griff. Tell the man what you want."

"It can't last." Okay, so she cared for him. She desired him. But that was as far as she was willing to swim in that river. He'd be leaving. Soon.

"You don't know that," Mattie argued. "You won't know until you two have that discussion."

"He isn't a forever kind of guy, Matt. Even if something more did evolve, I would never ask him to stay." Her pride wouldn't allow it.

"Then don't." Mattie glanced her way, a wide grin suddenly on her face. "But that doesn't mean you can't use him for sex."

Griffen laughed, grateful Mattie had lightened the mood. The conversation had turned way too serious.

Her cell phone rang and she checked the Caller ID. "It's him." Her cheeks instantly heated.

"You've got it bad," Mattie said. "Do it, Griff. Go for it."

She took a deep breath, then hit the answer button. "Hello?"

"I missed you today."

His voice was loaded with sex and sin, and her heart skidded to a halt. "That makes two of us," she said once her heart started beating again. "Austin's staying with my dad for the rest of the weekend. I'm thinking this reeks of your handiwork."

"Thomas offered," he said. "It means we can be alone."

"All night long," she said, ignoring Mattie's quiet chuckle.

"I've been thinking about dinner, sex and you all freaking day."

Her pulse quickened at the sexy rumble of his voice. "Jed." She used her best warning tone.

"Or we could talk on the phone instead."

"I'm not alone." No way was she going there. "What were you thinking for dinner? Goldie's closes early on Saturday."

"Wine and candlelight, sweetheart. Not local diner."

"Oh. Okay." More erotic images filtered through her mind. A planned seduction. She'd never survive. "I should be home in about an hour."

"I'll meet you at your place."

She told him where to find the spare key in case they hit traffic and he showed up before she arrived. "How did the auction go?"

"You haven't talked the auctioneer?"

"No yet. Why? Were there problems?"

"No, everything went pretty smooth," he said. "You should give him a call back."

She asked about Austin, then promised to meet him soon.

"Griffen?" he said before she disconnected the call. "Do you remember what I told you the other night?"

He'd said a lot of things. A lot of erotic things that made her come apart with just her imagination and the sound of his voice. "Which one?" she asked cautiously.

"Baby, I am gonna set you on fire."

Unable to speak, she hit the disconnect button and ended the call.

"What's wrong?" Mattie asked. "Griff, are you okay?"

Griffen stared at the now dark screen of her phone. "No."

"What did he say?" Mattie asked, her voice filled with concern.

Griffen cleared her throat as she looked over at her sister, whose attention kept shifting between her and the road. "He's gonna set me on fire."

Mattie's eyes widened and she laughed suddenly. "Well." She laughed again. "I have only one thing to say about that."

Griffen wasn't sure she wanted to know, but asked anyway. "Which is?"

"It's about fucking time."

FOURTEEN

BY THE TIME Mattie dropped Griffen off at her place, Jed hadn't yet arrived, for which she was grateful. She'd wanted time to shower and change before she saw him. Regardless of the enthusiastic pep talk from her sister, she couldn't stop the case of nerves if her life depended on it. The thought of making love to Jed might had been forefront in her mind for days, but that didn't mean she'd gotten used to the idea.

After her conversation with Jed, she'd called the auctioneer. The auction hadn't only gone smoothly, as Jed had indicated, it had gone extremely well. The figure the auctioneer gave her pretty much solved the last of her financial concerns. Now she could pull the building out of foreclosure and put it up for sale, plus pay off the business loan.

She waved to Mattie one last time, then went around to the side of the house. She unlocked the kitchen door and slipped inside, tossing her purse on the kitchen table on her way into the family room. That's when she saw them. A scattering of white, pale pink and deep mauve-colored rose petals littered the floor, leading a path out of the family room toward the staircase.

"Jed?" she called, but received no answering reply. She checked the side door that led to the garage, wondering if maybe he'd parked inside. Which made sense if he were trying to avoid gossip, but when she looked, she only found her Jeep. Curious, she headed for the stairs and picked up a velvety rose petal. Cool to the touch, as if it'd recently been refrigerated.

She walked up the stairs, careful to avoid crushing rose petals into the carpet. The door to her bedroom stood open and the lights were dimmed. When she walked inside, she half expected to find him in her bed—waiting.

The room was empty.

She went to the bed. More rose petals and something else littered the surface. She gasped when she realized exactly what she was seeing.

Condoms.

Lots and lots of condoms.

Gold packets, silver packets, black packets and more rose petals covered the surface. There had to be at least one hundred of them, if not more.

"Good grief." Talk about making a statement. She couldn't help wondering exactly what he was expecting to happen.

Sex.

No kidding.

And lots of it.

She let out a nervous laugh, trying not to feel too intimidated. The sound of a car door slamming had her throat tightening, along with her girl parts, but a quick look out the window revealed the neighbors across the road, not Jed. She tried to breathe a sigh of relief, but it came out in a rush instead. Her insides were jittery and her palms were sweaty. She was a wreck.

Get over yourself.

If only she could. Jed was no boy scout. She had nowhere near the kind of experience he was probably used to from his sexual partners. Did she really think she could take him to the brink of insanity as he did her? He drove her to the edge just *thinking* about making love to him.

Maybe she should text him, tell him she'd changed her mind. So what if he knew she was hiding from him? That wasn't quite true. She was hiding...from herself. Making love to Jed wasn't a decision she'd made lightly, and she couldn't deny she was terrified on a variety of levels. Her sex life with Ross had been satisfying, sometimes passionate but rarely adventurous. To say they shared anything remotely close to the level of sexuality she had with Jed was a major credibility stretch. Ross had never set her on fire the way Jed did with one single touch, or a look, or even the sound of his voice. He was unlike anyone she'd ever known, and she knew she'd never know another man like him in her lifetime.

Soft music suddenly caught her attention. Grateful for the diversion, she gladly followed the sound into the master bath, not sure what to expect. Her iPod dock sat on the double sink, her iPod tuned to her classical music playlist.

Candles, dozens of them, surrounded the sunken, garden tub filled with water, casting the room in a soft, warm glow. More rose petals floated on the surface, their subtle scent wafting on the steam, teasing her senses. She dipped her fingers into the water, which was hot and just the way she liked it. A silver serving tray sat perched on the bench to her vanity, which he'd apparently dragged into the bathroom to set by the side of the tub. An opened bottle of Dom Perignon sat in an ice bucket, and a champagne flute filled with the bubbly sat on top of the tray, along with a glass bowl filled with plump, red strawberries.

Other than the romantic display, there was no sign of Jed. Where he'd gone, she couldn't begin to hazard a guess because he'd left no note. But she sure as hell didn't need a written invitation to know this had all been done for her benefit. As she stripped out of her clothes she couldn't help be impressed. The guy certainly knew how to turn on the romance, and she appreciated the effort.

Funny, because she'd never in a million years have pegged him for the romantic type.

Who needs romance when you have dozens of women dropping at your feet?

She stripped and pinned up her hair, then looked at her reflection in the long mirror over the double sink. Not bad, not really.

She was only thirty-two years old, hardly over the hill.

He's had a lot of women. Younger women, with perkier boobs and tinier waists.

She wanted perkier boobs. She'd like to erase the threat of crow's feet, too, while she was at it, but that wasn't going to happen. If only she had a smaller waist and slimmer hips, but she was her mother's daughter. Like her sisters, curves came with the territory.

She turned away from the mirror before she talked herself into a fit of sheer, unrealistic paranoia. Instead, she stepped into the tub and eased down into the scented, steaming water. After adjusting a towel to rest her head against, she leaned back and closed her eyes. She let out a sigh and could practically feel the tension leaving her body. A few sips of the expensive champagne, and she was pretty sure she'd gone to heaven. If Jed's intention was to relax her so she'd be putty in his hands, all she had to say was *touchdown.*

She must've dozed, because two of the votive candles had burned out and the water had turned tepid. After downing the last of the champagne in her glass, she exited the tub and dried off. Wrapped in a towel, she went into her bedroom for something to wear. She considered dressing up, slipping into a little black dress and heels, but all she had to do was look at the bed to know she'd be severely overdressed. Instead, she went into her lingerie drawer and pulled out a tissue wrapped package. Carefully, she unwrapped the shell-pink colored chemise and matching silk robe she'd bought over a year ago and had never worn.

The whisper thin fabric slid over her curves and fell to mid-thigh. After adjusting the straps, she removed the matching robe from the protective wrapping and shrugged into it.

She opened her jewelry box and sifted through it until she found a pair of emerald studs, but then thought better of it. They were expensive, a gift from her mother on her twenty-first birthday, and she'd hate to lose one. Her fingers brushed over her wedding ring and she hesitated. She'd taken off the simple gold band the night Ross had left her and she'd almost forgotten it existed. Lifting the band out of the box, she studied it in the buttery glow from the lit Victorian lamps on the night tables. The inscription was nearly worn away; *RES/GHS* and their wedding date. No words of undying love, no promises of forever, just a simple statement of fact; who and when. Even though she had every right considering what he'd done to her, she didn't despise her ex-husband. She no longer loved him, either. No, that emotion had dwindled long before Ross and his mid-life crisis ran off to Jamaica.

She dropped the ring back in the jewelry box and snapped the lid closed. Ross was the past. Jed might not be her future in the long term, but she was okay with that, too. Having sex with him would complicate things when it all ended, but she'd find a way to cope. What other choice did she have?

"I was hoping you'd still be soaking in the tub."

She turned at the sound of that voice, all whiskey rough and velvety rich at the same time. Her nipples hardened. "It was a lovely. Thank you," she said as he slowly walked toward her. All of a sudden, she didn't know what to do with her hands, so she fiddled with the tie to the robe.

"I brought dinner." He wore a pair of jeans and a black t-shirt with a red, denim company logo emblazoned across the front of his massive chest. The sleeves were snug, showing off his rock hard arms, arms that slipped around her and drew her close. She sighed and wrapped hers around his waist, resting her head against his chest. Breathing in his masculine scent made her dizzy. He was hard, all male, and she wanted him so badly she ached just thinking about him. She didn't need roses and expensive champagne. She needed him.

"I don't want food," she told him.

"It'll keep."

Thank goodness, because neither one of them moved. They stood there just holding each other while a haunting Brahms melody drifted into the bedroom. Finally, she pulled back and looked up at him. Tenderness and promise were banked in his eyes, and her insides did a funny flip. Oh, but this man was dangerous. To her mind, and her heart.

"I've thought about this all day long," he said, then dipped his head to skim his lips along her throat, gently nipping with his teeth, then soothing with his tongue until he reached her mouth. A shiver passed through her and she moaned as his tongue slipped between her parted lips. She lifted her arms to wrap around his neck, then slid her fingers into his thick hair and returned his kiss with a passion that no longer surprised her.

Need twisted and knotted inside her, and when his hands slid down her back to cup her bottom, she moaned and arched against him. She wanted so much more. She wanted his skin pressed against hers, his body poised over hers, him deep inside her.

His mouth left hers and she whimpered in protest. Her breath came in short gasps, her body burning for him.

He pushed the robe from her shoulders and the silk puddled at her feet. She tugged his t-shirt free from his jeans. "Take off your shirt." When he complied, she stared in awe. Just as she'd imagined, he was pure masculine perfection. She knew he had a great body. The man was a professional athlete, after all, but she'd been unprepared the sight of all those hills and valleys of his chest and ripped abs.

"Wow." She was never getting naked in front of him. "Work out much?"

He chuckled. "It's part of the job."

She didn't care. She still wasn't getting naked in front of him. But that didn't mean she couldn't enjoy the hell out of him. She smoothed her hands over his torso, using her fingers and lips and tongue to explore all that gloriously hard male flesh.

He sucked in a sharp breath. She looked up to see his eyes darken. Desire ignited in his gaze and his body tensed. He pushed her hands away, then pulled her up against him. He kissed her, and there was nothing gentle or romantic about it. He kissed her hard, demanding, letting her know in no uncertain terms exactly what he expected from her.

She groaned. Need licked through her. Warmth pooled in her belly and there was a heaviness inside her that responded to his sensual demand. She reached for the fly of his jeans and dragged the zipper down, then pushed the denim over his hips. Pressing her lips to his torso, she licked and tasted and teased. When she settled to her knees in front of him, a wave of satisfaction pulsed through her when she freed his erection and heard his sharp intake of breath.

"Griffen."

"Hush," she said, then took him inside her mouth.

Making love to Jed had to be most idiotic stunt of her life, but nothing short of a natural disaster could prevent her from charging down that path with him tonight. By his actions, her hardened heart had softened, enough to let him inside where she would hold the memory of this night, and him, for the remainder of her days.

Jed clenched his jaw as Griffen loved him with her mouth. He balled his hands into fists, fighting to hold onto the thin thread of his control. He was afraid to move, afraid to breathe, but if he didn't touch her, he'd go crazy.

She pulled him deeper into her mouth and he nearly lost it. He grit his teeth and growled, the sound low and savage. Good God, she was trying to kill him.

He reached for her, hauling her back to her feet and crushing her against him. He claimed her mouth, his tongue sliding over hers. But kissing her wasn't anywhere near enough. He wanted more. He wanted, needed to taste her—every enticing inch.

He ended the kiss long enough to toe off his shoes and shuck his jeans. He lifted her into his arms and carried her to the bed where he gently lay her upon the mattress. She gasped, and then he remembered all the foil packets, the dozens of boxes of condoms he'd arrogantly purchased just to shock her. He supported her back with his good arm and shoved the packets aside.

A sweet sigh escaped her lips when he settled her back on the bed. She pulled him with her. "I want you," she murmured against his mouth.

His blood pressure spiked. God knew he wanted her, too. So much.

"Shhh, sweetheart. We have all night," he said as he smoothed his hands up her impossibly long legs. He pushed beneath her silky slip of fabric shielding her curves and groaned when he discovered she wore no panties.

He wanted to take things slow. He intended to savor every inch of her long and luscious body, but need pulsed through him in hot waves, making a mockery of his control. He stretched out alongside her and dragged his hands over the dip in her waist and upward to cup her breast in his hand, then lowered his head and suckled her through the silky material.

Griffen moaned and arched against him in silent demand for more. His mouth left her breast and he slowly moved down her body. Pleasure speared through her when his hands slid over her hips to the inside of her thighs, his fingers lightly brushing against her curls. He shifted and moved between her legs. She rolled her hips, seeking his touch, crying out when he lightly teased her clit. He slipped his fingers inside her and his groan of satisfaction heated her blood, pushing her closer to heaven.

His breath fanned against her sensitive flesh as he coaxed her closer to completion with his hands. She felt so reckless, as if she were charging toward a place she couldn't remember ever being before. And there was nothing she could do, or wanted to do, to stop. Whatever she needed, he sensed and gave selflessly.

She widened her legs and he kissed her inner thigh, moving closer and closer to where she craved his kisses the most. When he finally brought his mouth down on her sensitized flesh, every inch of her body responded as spirals of pleasure drew her closer to sweet oblivion. He dragged sensation after sensation out of her, using his mouth, his hands, pushing her ruthlessly toward an earthshattering orgasm.

He turned his hand and pressed his fingers upward, finding that spot that had her entire body trembling. Her breathing deepened and she couldn't help the cries that escaped her lips as a powerful orgasm rocked her body.

"You sound so sexy when you come," he said. "Come for

me again, baby."

Without giving her time to recover, he suckled her clit. Hard. As if she had no control over her own body, she tensed, her body bowing as she flew apart again almost immediately, the orgasm rocking her so hard she lost her breath and her ability to think. The intensity of her release spooked her. Never in her life had she ever experienced anything so powerful, so all consuming.

As if he sensed her sudden unease, he slid up alongside her and cradled her against him as aftershocks of pleasure pulsated through her. She clung to him, seeking balance, needing grounding, as she waited for her world to turn right side up again.

But he wouldn't have it. He dragged his hands down her back and held her close as he brought his mouth to hers, urging a renewed response from her with his deep, drugging kisses. His mouth left hers long enough to remove her chemise, and she didn't care. Nothing mattered now except their two bodies coming together in an explosion of heat and need.

He trailed hot kisses down her throat, his tongue teasing that sensitive spot just below her ear. She held him to her, her breasts crushed against his chest as he slid over her. She parted her legs and he settled between her thighs.

Her world narrowed when he slid his long, hard length inside her. She was slick, drenched with need. His mouth came down on hers, the erotic dance of his tongue, combined with the slide of his body into hers, had her arching her back and holding him to her. He reached down and lifted her bottom, holding her up as he drove into her, increasing the tempo.

"Jed," she cried, but he didn't stop. Instead, he pushed her harder, higher. He made her insane, burning her from the inside out, consuming her as he continued to make love to her.

She neared the edge again, straining for the pleasure until her entire body trembled. He pushed her, taking her in a maelstrom of emotion and need. Each stroke of his body was like a match to kindling and before long, she ignited into a flame that burned so hot she feared she'd never survive.

Driven to the brink of mindlessness, he pushed her over that edge one last time. Inch by sweet inch, he plunged deep inside her, sinking to the hilt. Elemental desire, a deep primal need to make him hers, completely hers, overwhelmed her.

He demanded and she gave without restriction. He stripped her emotions bare and without a doubt, she knew there would never be any turning back where Jed was concerned. So she responded with demands of her own, demands he mindlessly met until she cried out and the waves carried her into sweet oblivion, taking him with her until his control finally shattered. He buried himself inside her and together they went to that place where rational thought ceased to exist and only pleasure and heartbeats remained.

Jed didn't think his pulse would ever return to normal. His doctors would hospitalize him for fear he'd stroke out if they heard the pounding going on at the opposite end of a stethoscope. Sweet heaven, he couldn't recall another woman who'd ever given herself to him so completely. The thought didn't sting half as much as he imagined, but he'd been right. There would be no forgetting Griffen.

He rolled, wincing when the edge of a foil packet dug into his back. He took her with him until she lay sprawled across his chest and she shivered from the sudden chill against her creamy skin. Maneuvering them beneath the covers wasn't easy, and his shoulder caught. He tensed, but she hardly seemed to notice by the time he settled the comforter over them then waited for her to get comfortable again. She snuggled against him, and he held her close, feeling the beat of her heart against his.

Lust didn't equal love, and the rationalization gave him some comfort. He didn't know what he felt for Griffen, but he didn't think his feelings could ever be categorized as something as simple as lust. Sure, his body craved her touch, and now he'd made love to her, he didn't think he could ever get enough of her. But that was as far as he was willing to examine. Instead, he held her close, liking the way she curled next to him.

"I think I've died," she said against his chest, "and gone to heaven."

He chuckled and ran his hand down her back to rest on her hip. "Yeah, but what a way to go."

Her long, slim legs tangled with his. She rested her head against his good shoulder and sighed, her warm breath fanning his chest. "If I had the strength, I'd pinch you for that remark."

He wondered what she'd do when she found out he'd bought the house, not to mention the stunt he'd pulled at the auction. He'd arrived early and he'd made an offer on the entire lot, more than enough to cover whatever she owed. The guy Griffen had hired was a sly old fox who loved the thrill of negotiations. The old man had haggled until Jed agreed to pay way more than he should have, plus put a thousand dollar bonus in the guy's pocket just to keep his mouth shut about the whole thing.

He had to tell her. From their conversations, he knew she'd be ticked at him for interfering. Griffen could become pretty damned prickly when it came to her independence. Her reaction to the monthly support allowance he'd arranged should have told him to mind his own business.

He hated the idea of destroying their momentary bliss, wanting instead to keep the real world at bay. For the first time in a long time, he felt a sense of peace. Oh, sure, he had to confess the truth to Griffen, and she'd be angry as hell at him, but he wasn't too worried about getting her to see things his way. Like he'd told his son, he knew a thing or two about softening up women, and Griffen was, after all, a woman. One hell of a woman, who was bent on taking nothing from no one, himself included.

He ran his hand from her hip, up the length of her spine, to cradle the back of her head in his palm. She sighed when he kissed her, long and slow, hard and deep. For now, it was just the two of them, and he'd be damned if he'd let the outside world intrude.

FIFTEEN

GRIFFEN SLOWLY OPENED her eyes, smiling when the morning sun peeked through the draperies of her bedroom. She stretched, then let out a groan when nearly every muscle she could name, and some she couldn't, screamed in protest. Her body ached, but she'd never felt more fulfilled in her life after a night of making love to Jed.

Turning her head on the floral pillow, she looked over at the cause of all her muscle aches. His hair was mussed and hung low over his forehead, shielding his eyes. The heavy shadow covering his strong jaw did little to abate the illusion of strength. In sleep, his chiseled features were somewhat softened, but she didn't think anything could completely alleviate that dangerous, bad boy appeal. One arm was thrown back over his head, the other cradled against his chest. The sheet slung over his hips exposed his torso for her viewing pleasure.

The night she'd spent with Jed had been glorious. After a brief rest, they'd ventured downstairs for sustenance but ended up continuing their sensual exploration on the kitchen counter. She fully expected a blush to cover her from head to toe as she thought about some of the things she and Jed had done during the night and into the early morning hours, but all she felt was a rush of exhilaration.

With a dreamy sigh, she slipped from the bed, drawing the silk robe around her. She headed into the bathroom for a shower, glad that Jed still slept because she didn't think she had the ability to keep her feelings to herself after the night they'd shared. And she simply wasn't ready to face him, or the truth, quite yet.

Impossible, she chastised herself, picking up the brush and running it through her tangled hair. There was no way he'd know what she felt for him, especially since she wasn't even ready to put a name to those feelings. Her heart ached for him. Her body ached as well, humming like a well-tuned engine under his expert and gentle touch. He made her feel things she'd never believed possible between a man and woman, and she was a far cry from a blushing virgin.

She turned on the tap and waited for the water to heat. Could she love him? If he walked out her door and never looked back, would her heart shatter into a million tiny pieces? She didn't want to search for the answer, uncertain she'd like what her heart was trying to tell her.

No, she couldn't love Jed. No matter how much she wanted him, she would *not* love him. She would never put herself in a position to trust and depend upon a man to be there for her. Never again. Especially not since she'd proven she could take care of herself.

After she finished working out the last of the tangles, she dropped her robe and stepped into the shower. Determination to pretend nothing earthshattering *had* happened between them spurred her, but the truth had her wincing. She'd crossed a line last night. Hell, who was she kidding? She'd given a part of herself, and that frightened her. Wherever she dared to venture from this moment on could determine the outcome for the rest of her life. The stakes had shifted and Austin was no longer their only common ground. Oh, no, what she felt for Jed was more elemental, more basic, and more frightening than anything she'd faced in the past six months.

For their son's sake, as well as that of her own heart, she prayed she hadn't made a monumental error. Because deep in her heart, she knew the truth. If Jed walked out her door right now and never looked back, her heart would most definitely shatter into a million tiny pieces.

*

Jed looked up from the Sunday newspaper he'd been reading when Griffen walked into the family room carrying two mugs of coffee. He set the financial section aside and made room for her on the sofa next to him.

He took the mug from her, setting it on the table beside him, then slung his arm over the back of the sofa. His shoulder caught and he flinched, then swore.

"I heard your shoulder catch in your sleep this morning. Does that happen often?" she asked, settling in beside him.

"More than it should." He rested his hand on her shoulder and rubbed, moving his hand to her neck, letting his fingers sift through her silky hair. God, he'd never get tired of touching her.

She leaned forward and set her mug on the table, then scooted back and curled against him, laying her head on his shoulder. She peered up at him, concern filling her eyes. "Can you still play?" she asked quietly.

Could he? He honestly didn't know any longer. The doctors had never promised him a one hundred percent recovery, but he'd been optimistic. Or was it denial? Denial, he decided. The orthopedic surgeons had been anything but promising when it came to the use of his shoulder as far as his career had been concerned. His rotator cuff was shot, and the clavicle resection hadn't completely alleviated the pain. He had plenty of strength, but as far as throwing a decent pass, he wouldn't know until he went out there and tried. He was sure he could play football again, but he began to have serious doubts about his ability to remain on top. And for him, it was an all or nothing proposition.

"I don't know." A surge of anger rushed forward at the reluctant admission and he tensed. He couldn't be over the hill. Not him.

He set Griffen away from him and stood. Damn her for making him look in places he didn't care to have uncovered. He started pacing the length of the family room, agitation and anger filling every step he took. The sensation of feeling trapped gripped him hard.

"Jed?"

The concern in her voice irritated him. "Don't." He didn't want her concern, and he'd be damned if he'd allow her to pity him like he was some washed up legend.

A spark of fire lit her eyes. "Would it be so terrible if you couldn't play again?"

He gave her a withering look. "And what do you suggest I do for a living?"

"You could work as a commentator," she said. "Austin always watches the pre-game shows every week with those old football players, Terry Bradshaw and Howie Long. They don't look as if they're starving."

"*Old* football players?" He cocked a brow. "Thanks a lot, Sister."

She curled her feet beneath her and clutched the coffee mug in her hands. "You know what I mean. *Retired* pros."

He turned away, unable to face her, the truth, or his own fear. He didn't know which, or maybe he just wanted to continue to avoid the inevitable. He paced to the fireplace and propped his foot on the hearth, resting his injured arm on his upraised knee. "What if I don't want to retire?"

But he had been thinking about it. A lot. Hadn't that been part of the reason he'd spent three days in Dallas in meeting after meeting? He didn't have to continue with the game. He didn't need the money. But he didn't want to give it all up, either. Or was it the fame he wasn't willing to let go?

"Can you honestly compete to the best of your ability?"

"I don't know any more," he said.

She stood and came to stand beside him. "I've seen you play, Jed. It's impossible not to since Austin never misses a game. Can you still create that same magic, or whatever it is you do out there on the football field?"

He couldn't look at her. He couldn't bear to see the truth in her eyes. Hearing it in her words was hard enough for him to face. "What if someone told you that you could no longer do what you wanted?"

She laughed, a caustic little sound that had him looking at her. The expression in her eyes was chilling in its intensity. "I just lost my business, remember? I know what you're feeling. You don't know what you're going to do with your life. I have skills to fall back on. Surely you majored in something useful in college."

He ignored her sarcasm and straightened. "I made sure I earned my degree. I have a bachelors in history with a teaching credential."

She propped her slender backside against the Queen Anne desk and wrapped her long slim fingers around the edge. "What had you planned on doing before you went pro?"

"Get my master's, maybe my Ph.D., and teach."

Her eyes widened in surprise and he tried not to take offense.

"Then do it," she said.

She made it sound so easy. Only it wasn't. "It's a little late to be starting a new career."

"No, it's not."

"Griff, I'm thirty-five years old."

"Wait, I'll alert the nursing home."

He really didn't appreciate her sass, but he got the point. There were older than average college students embarking on new career fields, especially in the current economic climate. And it wasn't as if he hadn't been considering retirement. "I don't know."

She pushed off the desk and crossed the room to pick up her mug. "What can you do now? Can you stay involved somehow?" she asked before taking a sip of coffee.

"I can coach and work the sidelines, or ride the bench until my existing contract ends in two years," he said, wondering where she was headed. She should have been a lawyer. She had interrogation down to an art. "They want me to train the new draft pick."

"Training is teaching," she said, moving back to the desk to sit in the chair. "Even working the sidelines would put you—"

196

"No," he said more sharply than he intended. "If I go anywhere near a stadium, it's going to be leading my team."

She set her mug on the desk. "And if you can't?"

"Then to *hell* with all of them," he said. "Let the advertisers sue me, I no longer give a damn. The owners can go to hell, too." He felt like a jerk for raising his voice and yelling at her. This was not her fault, but dammit, she was probing an open wound. And using a damned sharp stick.

"Jed, that's not true." Her voice was calm, reasonable and understanding, and set his teeth on edge. "You do care," she said. "You care too much. This has been your life. I know how hard it is to give up something you love so much."

"Love?" He gave a bitter laugh. "It's all I know. Believe me, it's not all fame and glory, either. They'll suck every bit of life out of you, then toss you aside when you're so broken you can't even hold the ball in your hands."

She shook her head. "You don't know that."

"The hell I don't," he countered. "Remember Linc Monroe? We were drafted together."

At her nod, he continued. "The sport bled him dry. Sucked the life right out of him. Used him until there was nothing left for him to give."

Memories rushed in, and there was nothing Jed could do to stop them, or from telling Griffen his most painful secret. He dropped onto the stone hearth, propped his elbows on his knees and looked at her.

"He had a pretty bad knee injury early in his career that flared up from time to time. In taking the edge off the constant pain, he'd gotten addicted to painkillers. It got to the point where he thought he couldn't function without them. When his knee finally did blow, you know what the owners did for him? They cut him loose. They dumped Linc Monroe like he was some nobody walk-on. He was the best fucking wide receiver who ever played the game, and they treated him like he was nothing."

He shifted his gaze away from her. He remembered the doctors shaking their heads, the solemnity that had surrounded the locker room that horrible day. The whispers, the rumors, and finally the truth. Linc's career was over.

"Where is he now?" she asked.

"New Orleans, Louisiana—in the Monroe family crypt."

More memories. Linc's fiancée crying softly, each tear a twist to his gut. The pain on Linc's father's face and his mother's quiet tears. Most of the team had gathered beneath the sweltering heat of the bayou sun. Even the head coach had been there, but no sign of the owners.

"What happened?" she asked.

He turned his attention back to Griffen. "I killed him."

She stood and came to sit beside him on the hearth. "You're not serious," she said, resting her hand on his arm.

Oh, yeah, he was serious. Dead serious. "Linc was broke. I wanted to help him, but he wouldn't take my money. His damned pride wouldn't let him. He knew he needed to retire, but he was getting married. His future bride was two months pregnant. One last season, that's all he wanted. Marilee was good for him and she'd helped him get clean. But his knee was hurting and he begged me to get him something for the pain, so I did."

He looked down at Griffen, at the patience and understanding in her gaze. In another minute, she'd have nothing but contempt for him. "Don't go getting any noble ideas about me. I didn't do it because he was my friend. I did it because he made me look good. No matter where I threw the ball, Linc could pull it out of the sky and put it in the end zone. Maitland to Monroe. We were one hell of a combination."

"But the pills didn't kill him."

"No, they didn't," he said. "But he'd had taken a bad hit in the third quarter and never said a word to anyone about being hurt. Halfway through the fourth quarter, he could barely walk. The damage to his knee could be repaired, but he'd never play again. They could've placed him on injured reserve, but instead, the bastards cut him."

"How is that your fault?"

"Linc was desperate. If I hadn't give him those goddamn

pills, he would have recognized his limits and stopped before so much damage had been done."

Griffen shook her head, trying to make sense out of what Jed was telling her. "His injury wasn't life threatening," she said. "I don't understand."

Pain filled his gaze. "He swallowed the barrel of a .45," he said quietly.

Jed was not responsible, no matter how much he tried to convince himself otherwise. Somehow she had to make him realize the truth.

"Ever hear about a paternity suit I settled out of court?" he asked.

Of course she'd heard about the suit. Anyone who was even in the same room as a television during the playoffs that year had heard about the paternity action he'd settled. The night she'd questioned him on his other exploits in the press, she'd purposely avoided the paternity issue because she didn't want him to misconstrue her curiosity with the belief she'd contacted him because of money.

"She's not my daughter. She's Linc's," he said. "Steve Rafferty and I convinced Marilee to leave Linc's name off the birth certificate, then to file the paternity suit against me. A lot of people thought that was why Linc had shot himself. It didn't help the feeding frenzy, either."

"So you let everyone believe you were the father of Marilee's baby because you felt responsible for Linc's suicide?"

"I did what I had to do to make sure that Linc's kid and Marilee were taken care of. They weren't married, so she got nothing." There was a note of defiance in his voice, as well as a subtle challenge.

She stood and crossed the room to stand in front of him. The look in his eyes dared her to question his motives. "You took responsibility for something that was not your fault."

He shoved his hand through his hair. "I gave him the goddamn pills."

His glare burned through her, but she wasn't going to give up. She had to make him realize that Linc made the choice to end his life, and Jed had nothing to do with that. "If you hadn't, someone else would have."

"You don't know that."

She took hold of his hands and held them tight. "Neither do you," she said gently. "No one does."

Moving closer, she slipped her arms around his middle and rested her head against his chest, hoping to offer him the comfort she knew he'd never ask for. She didn't question why she cared, she only knew that she did. He tensed, but he didn't push her away. "I think what you did for Marilee is wonderful, even if you did it for the wrong reasons."

He grabbed her shoulders and set her away, but didn't remove his hands. "Wrong reasons?" he asked incredulously, his strong grip biting into her flesh. "I took away his last chance to find happiness."

She shook her head. "No, Jed. Linc did that himself when he took his own life." Lifting her hand, she cupped his cheek in her palm. "I know you admired him, but what he did was selfish. You can't take responsibility for that."

She wanted to ease his pain, to help him put the hurtful memories to rest. He was kinder than he wanted anyone to know. When he could have sued the press numerous times for their false reports, especially surrounding the paternity suit, he hadn't, setting more value on Linc's child and the woman his friend had been engaged to marry. No. What Jed had done was selfless and admirable.

"It wasn't your fault," she said again.

He pulled her against him and held her tight. She slipped her arms around him, hoping the love she felt for him could heal his old wounds.

Love?

The thought was staggering, but yes, she did love him. She hadn't wanted to fall in love with him, but somewhere along the way, she had. Without even trying, he'd gotten under her skin and into her heart. Something happened between them, and she could no longer deny her feelings for him.

He was a complicated man, with many layers to his

personality. There was the public figure, the legend, who drew attention where ever he went. And then there was the man. A man who carefully explained the concepts of algebra to his son, never losing his patience when Austin had difficulty grasping the theory. The man who held her tenderly in his arms while she cried, the man who gently wiped her tears. The man who set her soul on fire.

With Jed, passion didn't begin to express their coming together. Wild would be a more appropriate term. He was a demanding lover, giving pleasure as well as taking in return. Her body heated just thinking about it.

The only doubts she harbored belonged to uncertainty and her own insecurities. She had no idea where their relationship was headed. But was she willing to take the risk to discover if they could have something more than just an affair. She didn't know what his feelings were, but one thing she was certain of—she'd fallen hard for Jed Maitland.

Hours later, Griffen still hadn't told Jed what was in her heart, despite spending the day alone with him. In and out of bed. She still hadn't worked up enough courage, and by the time they'd driven to her dad's for Sunday supper and to pick up Austin, she figured she'd just wait until they were alone again.

At home in her own dining room, she pulled items from the china cabinet and wrapped them in newspaper for the move. She still couldn't decide whether keeping her feelings to herself was selfless or selfish. Jed had some tough career decisions ahead of him, and the demons he wrestled were old and powerful. If she told him she'd fallen in love with him, she worried she might cloud the issues for him, more than he'd already done himself. But self perseverance was also at work. If she didn't tell him, he couldn't hurt her.

"Mom?" Austin called to her from the family room. "Mom, you better come here."

The anxious note in Austin's voice had her climbing down the ladder. She rounded the doorway into the great room just in time to hear Jed's ripe swear.

Dread tightened her chest. "What's going on?"

Austin pointed toward the television. "You're not going to believe this. We're gonna be on the news."

Jed swore again and stood. Griffen moved to his side and looked up at him. Anger, clear and vivid, glittered in his dark eyes. Alarm coursed through her. Since Dani's journal had been delivered to her, her life had turned into a roller coaster. She'd be the first to admit she wasn't cut out for the slow climbs, swift drops and last minute turns.

Austin's face lit with excitement. Jed stood with his hands braced on his hips, his body tense when the familiar face of the newscaster returned.

"West Texas Nightly News has this late breaking story," Vince Rawlins said. A publicity photo of Jed highlighted the upper corner of the screen and Griffen's heart sank.

"Dallas's favorite bad boy, Texas Wrangler quarterback, Jed Maitland, has been nursing more than injuries in the off-season," Rawlins continued. "Sources tell us Maitland the Maniac ordered his attorney last week to set up a trust fund in an undisclosed amount for an illegitimate son; thirteen-year-old, Austin Hart Somerfield of Hart, Texas. Lindsey Jackson has more on this story."

"So cool." Austin scooted closer to the set. "They said my name on T.V."

Griffen stared in shock as the camera zoomed to a large Spanish style home surrounded by greenery while the sultry voice of the field reporter named a few of Rafferty's more high profile clientele, Jed included. "Mr. Rafferty failed to comment on the situation, however this reporter has learned that Maitland is now residing in Hart near his son."

"How can they get away with this?" Griffen asked. He wasn't residing in Hart, he was staying at the Lakeside Motel. She looked up at him, but he kept his attention locked on the television screen. The muscles in his jaw clenched and the look in his eyes was pure murder.

Vince Rawlins came back on screen, the local sportscaster

seated beside him at the news desk. "Glen, you spoke to Maitland's agent this afternoon, right?"

"Yes, Vince." Glen Behrmann faced the camera, his perfectly coiffed hair gleaming under the studio lights. "Head Coach Deacon Rizzo confirmed his office hasn't heard from Maitland for the past two weeks. I'm sure everyone will recall the event that experts say ended Maitland's career."

A film rolled of Jed inside the pocket, arm poised to send the ball deep when a player from the opposing team broke away from the guard and slammed into Jed, knocking him to the ground. The last clip showed Jed being carted off the field on a stretcher.

Griffen slowly sat on the edge of the sofa, her heart in her throat. She felt far away, as if this were all happening to someone else. This wasn't something she'd seen coming, and she'd been a fool to not have even considered the possibility. Jed wasn't anonymous. He was a world class athlete, one of the greatest quarterbacks to ever grace the game.

The next clip rolled. A bevy of reporters waited outside of a Dallas high rise as Deacon Rizzo exited the building.

Glen Behrmann thrust a microphone at Rizzo, trotting to keep up with the coach's long strides. "Is it true that Maitland is refusing to show up at training camp? What about the medical appointments he's missed? Will that keep him off the roster next season?"

Rizzo stopped and looked directly into the camera. "That's up to Maitland."

"You bastard," Jed said, his tone vehement.

"What about this kid he's claiming?" another reporter asked. "Rumor says he had an affair that ended when he turned pro."

Griffen looked over at Jed. "How do they know this stuff?"

He gave her his attention, the fury in his eyes unmistakable. "What they don't know, they're going to make up."

The cordless phone resting on the desk rang and she stood.

"Don't answer it," he said.

She ignored him and answered it anyway. "Hello?"

"Mrs. Somerfield?"

"Yes."

"This is Wayne Woodley from the Dallas Tribune. Would you care to make a statement?"

"A statement?" How had they found them so quickly?

Jed took the phone from her and brought it to his ear. Now that word had spread about Austin, he knew it wouldn't take the bastards long to find him. He just didn't expect it to happen so soon. "No comment," he said, then punched the button to disconnect the call.

The phone jangled again. He gave her a look filled with frustration and anger. He punched the button and waited.

"Is Austin there?"

"Who is this?" he demanded.

"Jimmy Packard."

He let out a breath filled with frustration. The old anger had come back, that deep ugly rage he'd kept just below the surface since he'd left the hospital. He wanted a drink, but was afraid if he started, he wouldn't stop. Instead, he tried to focus on Austin and Griffen. They needed him right now, sober, not swimming in the bottom of a bottle of Jack Daniels. "He'll call you back," he said and disconnected the call.

"What happened?" Griffen asked him.

"I don't know yet," he said. "But we're going to lay low until I find out. I'm sorry about all this."

"This is Texas. Football is always a hot topic, but not like this. This is unbelievable," she said once the newscaster moved onto another topic.

Too bad the rage brewing just below the surface hadn't moved on as easily. He turned to her, fighting to keep his temper under control. "Get your stuff. We're leaving."

"Leaving?" she asked.

"We're getting out of town for a few days. We'll go to my place in Possum Kingdom. It'll be harder for them to get to us."

Her eyes widened. "We can't leave. Austin has school tomorrow, and I have a meeting with the principal. I only have two weeks to get moved..."

He counted to ten. He would *not* explode. Not at her and not in front of his son. This wasn't their fault. "Austin will have to take a few more days off." He kept his voice low, his words clipped. "I'll hire a tutor. I'll hire someone to move you. When things cool down, you can come back."

The phone rang again and Jed punched the button. "No comment," he said without giving the caller a chance to identify himself. He set the phone back on the desk and ignored it when it started ringing again. "The press is going to be swarming all over Hart by morning. They'll be camped out on your front lawn. Do you want that?"

The call rolled into voice mail. Seconds later, Austin's cell phone started ringing. "It's Jimmy," he said, then answered. As he walked out of the room and headed toward the stairs, Jed heard him say, "That was so epic. Did you hear them? They said my name on television. Twice."

"He won't think this was so cool in a day or two when the press won't leave him alone," Jed said. "They didn't say anything this time, but how is he going to feel when they start asking him what he thinks about his 'little sister?'"

Because of him, now his son was exposed to the bloodsuckers, and the thought enraged him. He could handle the media, he'd been doing it since he'd been nominated for the Heisman Trophy in college, but Austin was a kid. And in his experience, the press was anything but kind. No doubt they'd be dredging up the past, every rumor, every untruth, and every skeleton in all of their closets.

Griffen crossed her arms and gave him a look filled with determination. "Austin and I are not leaving. If we run away, they'll just find us."

"Dammit, Griffen." The tenuous grip on his temper slipped. "They'll eat you alive. Let me handle this."

She didn't back down. In fact, she lifted her chin and gave him a level stare. "I will not run away. If you want to leave, fine, but Austin and I are staying right here."

He pulled in a deep breath. God, he wanted a drink. "At

least let me take Austin back to your dad's. Just for a day or two until I can deal with this. I don't want those bloodhounds near my son."

She nodded in agreement, then went upstairs to tell Austin to pack an overnight bag. He watched her walk away, her back straight, her head held proud, and couldn't help but admire her. She had more strength than any woman he knew. In the face of adversity caused by the media circus, she was ready to stand and fight.

And they'd do it together.

SIXTEEN

GRIFFEN HEARD THE garage door closing, signaling Jed's return. He'd insisted on staying with her, so after taking Austin to her father's, he'd gone to his motel room for his things. He didn't bother checking out, reminding her that everything they did now would be under public scrutiny. He'd tried to make her promise to unplug the phone, but she'd refused to hide.

She set a filter in the basket and counted the scoops for coffee just as Jed walked into the kitchen from the garage. One look told her his earlier temper had cooled, but he was still upset. She could see it in the tensing of his jaw and the set of his shoulders. "We'll get through this," she said as she flipped the switch for the coffee maker.

The grin he gave her didn't soften the weariness in his eyes. He pulled her into his arms, holding her as if his life depended on it. "I'm sorry this happened," he said.

She wrapped her arms around him and rested her head against his chest. She loved being held by him, loved feeling the power and strength of his arms around her. Regardless of the threat to her sanity and her heart, she hung on tight. "It's not your fault. How could you know this would happen?"

"I should have known better. I *am* sorry, Griffen." Regret filled his voice. "I never meant to hurt you and Austin."

She leaned back and looked up at him. "None of us expected this," she said and meant it. They'd been so caught up in their own personal drama, they hadn't given a thought as to what could happen once the media got wind of their situation. She should have known better, but how could she?

She'd never been exposed to press releases and media reports. Hart just wasn't the type of town to garner much attention. Until now.

The phone rang again and Jed sighed. "Has that been going on since I left?"

She nodded. "Mattie called, but I let everything else roll into voice mail."

"I need to get a hold of Steve and find out what went wrong. Then we're going to have to unplug that phone."

The coffee maker finished, and she reluctantly stepped out of his embrace. After pouring them both a cup, she added a splash of creamer to hers, then followed him into the family room. She sat on the end of the sofa and curled her feet beneath her. She hadn't gotten much sleep the night before, and although the day had been a long one, sleep was the last thing on her mind.

Jed pulled his cell phone out of his pocket, then dropped into the chair behind Griffen's desk and called Steve. "What the hell happened?" he asked when his lawyer answered.

"I don't know what to say," Steve said. "Someone leaked the story. I've ruined my associates' weekend and have had them scrambling all night trying to find out how it happened. We do know a file clerk in the investment firm sold the story to TMZ. I've been on the phone with Yorke and your publicist. We're working damage control."

"You'd better do something," Jed snapped angrily. "I'm not going to have my son's picture plastered on every national news show."

"Calm down, Jed," Steve said in a placating tone. "They can't do anything like that without Mrs. Somerfield's permission."

"They sure as hell didn't have a problem releasing his name." The temper he'd thought cooled shot back up to the boiling point. "Sue the firm. That trust account was confidential. Isn't there some law about protecting the identity of minors?"

Steve muttered something he couldn't quite make out, but

sounded a lot like not being fresh out of law school. "I'm a step ahead of you. Half my team is in the office working on it already. We'll have court papers filed first thing in the morning."

Not exactly satisfied, Jed told Steve to get back to him later when he had more details. As he placed a call to his agent, Griffen went into the kitchen.

"Where the fuck are you?" Bob Yorke demanded the minute he answered.

"In hell," he fired back. For all his running, where had it gotten him? Nowhere, other than into the arms of a woman he knew he should've stayed away from, only he couldn't. For the life of him, he simply could not walk away—yet. They had a connection that extended beyond the past, and something he couldn't, or wouldn't, put a label on, kept him by her side. It wasn't as if she'd done what no other woman since Dani had managed to do to him. No way had he let her into his hardened heart.

Liar.

"Why didn't you tell me about this kid of yours?" Yorke asked.

As soon as this latest mess was cleaned up, he was firing Yorke. The man was supposed to be his agent, supposed to have his best interests at heart. Lately, the only interests Yorke seemed to have was in saving his own ass. "Because it's none of your damned business," Jed said. "Your business is my career, not my private life."

"Your private life keeps interfering with your career. What you have left of it," Yorke countered. "You've let this go too far. The owners are ready to pull out and your endorsements are drying up. It's time, Jed. It's over."

"It'll be over when I say it's over." Dammit, he didn't need Yorke blowing him shit, too. He had enough to handle, and he a son to protect. Only then he could think about his own future.

"Not any longer," Yorke said. "According to the doctors, you don't have a choice. Look, the owners put a generous offer on the table. Take it and make everybody happy, Jed."

Jed said nothing. He couldn't because the more he thought about it, the more retirement sounded like the option he'd end up taking. The game had been his life for so long, the thought of leaving it behind was tough to face.

"Wouldn't you rather retire with dignity?" Yorke asked, his tone snide and condescending.

Jed's temper immediately shot through the roof. *If* and *when* he retired, it would be his decision and no one else's. "Go to hell." He disconnected the call. The bastards. The dirty—

"Jed? Is everything all right?"

Her soft, husky voice drifted through the red haze of his anger. She held a plate filled with pastries, like she was Betty fucking Crocker.

"*No*," he said. "Nothing is right."

Concern etched her pretty face, and he felt like a jerk. She set the plate on the table in front of the sofa. "How can I help?"

"Get the hell away from me," he muttered, wanting to kick himself the moment the words left his mouth. God, she didn't deserve to be treated that way.

She straightened and planted her hands on her hips. "What is your problem?"

"Not a goddamn thing, all right?" he snarled, more out of his own frustration at allowing the entire situation to spin out of control. But that didn't excuse his first class prick routine, and he knew it.

Fire lined her gaze as she advanced on him. He scowled at her, but she didn't back down. Anyone else would have run for the hills when he was in a mood like this. But not her. Oh, no, she faced him, letting him see what she thought of his attitude. Which wasn't much, obviously.

"I'm not happy about any of this, either." Griffen knew she was making matters worse by snapping back at him, but dammit, this affected both of them. Jed wasn't the only one involved here. "Don't expect me to put up with your crap, Maitland. It isn't going to happen. So you can stop taking it out on me."

He gave her a hard look, then crossed the room to stand in front of the fireplace. Resting his arm on the mantle, he propped his boot on the stone hearth and stared at the logs stacked there. "You don't know what they're like, Griffen. Your life won't belong to you any longer. I don't want that for you or Austin."

Her heart snagged at the torment in his voice. True, she didn't have a clue what all the attention would be like, but she must have known somewhere in the back of her mind that it would happen sooner or later. Maitland the Maniac drew attention, whether on the football field or leading his nefarious, and often falsely reported, lifestyle.

"There will be questions," he said. "Questions you aren't prepared to answer. What you don't give them, they'll find on their own and they aren't real particular about accuracy, only their damned ratings."

"What are you so afraid of?" she asked. "Is there something else about you they can drag through the dirt to make you look bad?"

He turned on her, the hard lines of his face prominent, anger blazing in his eyes. "Not me. *You*. How does that feel, Griffen? How will it feel when they start speculating and second guessing, implying I was the cause of your marriage ending, or maybe that your ex found us in bed together. They're going to camp out on your doorstep, talk to your neighbors, wonder why you went out of business, why your house is for sale. They'll imply that you came to me for money."

"But that isn't the truth."

"They won't care."

"But I didn't even know you when I was married to Ross. Besides, what he did to me has nothing to do with you. Or us."

He crossed his arms over his chest and braced his feet apart, his stance arrogant, his voice damning. "Don't be so sure. They found out about Austin because I set up a trust fund for him. Some low level employee decided to make a few bucks by selling the story. It won't be a stretch for them to think you came to me for money."

"That's nonsense. And I've told you before, I don't want, or need, your money."

"It's done. He's my son, and it's done. End of discussion."

She didn't care for his high handedness or his going behind her back. But she understood. He was only looking out for his son. That didn't mean she had to like it, though.

"It doesn't matter," he said. "If there's a hint of sleaze, the bottom feeders will find it and exploit it to the *nth* degree."

"That's not fair."

He shrugged. "It's all about ratings. The bigger the scandal, the higher the returns."

She dropped onto the sofa. "This can't be happening."

"Well, it is. So you'd better tell me everything or I won't be able to answer their questions. And believe me, if it looks like we're hiding anything, it'll only get worse."

She looked away. Telling Jed the truth, the humiliation of her stupidity wasn't something she relished, but he was right. Unless he knew the truth, how could he defend her to the press? She looked back at him. He hadn't moved, his stance still as arrogant as ever.

She pulled in a deep breath and let it out slowly. "There was nothing sleazy about Ross's affair, unless you call running off to Jamaica with his twenty-something secretary sleazy. When he left, he wiped out everything. Our savings, CDs, our investments, even the business accounts for Antiquities. He only left me enough money to cover the mortgages on the house for a couple of months, but that was it. Thank God he left Austin's college fund alone, but I think the only reason he didn't touch it was because it wasn't in his name."

"That son of a bitch."

"I thought so, too, for a while," she said. "I was making enough money to keep the store running on its own, but not enough to manage both the business and the house, the car payments, the bills."

His eyebrows drew together. "How bad is it?"

"I was up to my ears in debt, but I trusted Ross. I let him handle everything and was foolish enough not to question him." She shook her head at her own stupidity. "I was living in a house of cards and never knew. When he left, I found out the hard way that he hadn't paid the bills in months. Nearly every credit card was maxed, and the balances were astronomical. The only thing that was current was the mortgage. Pretty sad for a professional financial planner."

"Why didn't you say something?" His demanding tone revealed the sharp edge still clinging to his anger. "You know I could have helped. I offered to help."

"And I appreciated the offer, but I had to do this on my own. You have to understand, once I got over the shock of having to dig myself out of the financial mess Ross left me in, I was angry. Not so much at him, but at myself. I couldn't believe I was so blind that I didn't see what was going on. When I quit beating myself up, I came up with a plan and went to work."

"Yeah, about that." He pulled in a deep breath "There's something you need to know."

He sat next to her on the sofa and explained how he'd not only bought her house, but every item from the auction, as well. "I bought the house through a dummy corporation, hoping to shield you and Austin from my reputation." The expression in his eyes pleaded for understanding. "I apologize, Griffen. For all of this."

She wanted to be furious with him, berate him for not believing in her, but that was her pride talking. Her heart, on the other hand, was much more understanding. The man she'd fallen for was nothing like the public persona. Beneath the barriers, beneath all those rough edges and the rotten attitude, lurked the heart of a man who felt deeply about those he cared for. Dani had seen that side of him, and now Griffen knew the truth for herself, as well.

She'd gotten to know the real Jed, and right or wrong, sane or crazy, she'd fallen in love with him. The truth was in Jed's eyes and not in his angry words, and definitely not in the bad press that followed him. He wasn't the narcissistic prick she'd once believed, either. Instead, he was a man who cared about her and his son. His concern over how his life would affect them, how his past would bleed into their lives, touched her deeply.

She scooted closer. "We will get through this. They'll find another story that's more sensational or scandalous. In a day or two, we'll be old news."

"I know you're right, but in the meantime, this isn't going to be easy."

"We'll get through it," she said again, then wrapped her arms around his waist.

He held her close. She pressed against him, finding comfort in the steady rhythm of his heart. Together. She managed a small smile. Together they would somehow weather the media storm.

He leaned back and brought his hand under her chin until she was looking at him. "I'm sorry," he said, then brushed his lips gently over hers. "I've got a lousy temper."

"Yeah, we need to work on that," she said, before he dipped his head to nuzzle her neck.

Jed marveled at the woman pressed against him. Was she afraid of nothing? His rotten temper included? He nipped his way from her neck to her ear, then teased the spot with his tongue. She moaned, a sexy little sound that hardened him in a flash.

Their lives were in a state of chaos, but the only thing he wanted to do right now was lose himself inside her and forget about the vultures swarming overhead. Which would only create more problems, he thought as he nibbled on her earlobe and unbuttoned her blouse anyway.

She trembled beneath his gentle touch. "I won't put up with your crap. You can't bully me, Maitland." There was heat in her voice, but not the kind initiated by anger.

He pushed aside her blouse and unhooked the front clasp of her lacy bra to palm her breasts. "I know," he said. "I'm sorry." He pulled off her blouse and tossed it on the floor before taking her nipple in his mouth.

Her head fell back when his tongue caressed her sensitive flesh. "Hmmm, you're forgiven," she pushed away from him. "Let's go upstairs."

He didn't need convincing. The desire darkening her eyes was enough to make him explode.

When they reached the bedroom, Griffen peeled off her jeans. He hurried out of his own clothes, and they came together in a wild explosion of heat.

She pushed him on his back and straddled him, then slid her body over his until she guided his erection between her sexy as hell thighs. He cupped one tempting breast as she tossed her head back and rode him hard. Using his fingers from his free hand, he helped bring her to completion, gritting his teeth as she shuddered through spasm after spasm, her hot, wet heat milking him with erotic contractions.

Unable to stand the sweet, sensual torture another moment, he gripped her hips and thrust upward, going deep and making her cry out as another wave of ecstasy claimed her. He rode the tide with her, finding his own release as the turbulence of their passion swirled around them, making them one.

As they came back to earth, she snuggled against him, and he wrapped his arms around her and held her close. He couldn't have let her go if he is life depended on it. Regardless of how uncertain his future might be, one thing he did know— no way in hell he was walking away from Griffen without losing his heart in the process.

Griffen slid the pancakes from the griddle and set them on the plate she had in the warming drawer. After turning the bacon one last time, she set the table, thankful to have something to keep her hands busy, even if her mind continued to wander.

Just as Jed had predicted, the news crews were out in full force. Her street looked like the scene for a story about a natural disaster rather than the hunt for the latest scandal surrounding a legendary, superstar quarterback. She'd turned on the television to watch the news while she made breakfast. Anger had burned through her when the front of her house flashed across the television screen, as well as a view of the town, including the going out of business sign hanging in the window of Antiquities. They'd even had the nerve to shoot a live segment from the Hart Cemetery where Dani and her mother rested.

Nothing was sacred.

By the time the cable news shows started airing the story, Griffen had little doubt as to the lengths the media would stoop to get what they wanted. They wanted a statement from Jed, and until he appeased them, they would continue to dredge up his past and speculate about this future.

She poured them both a glass of orange juice, then set the bacon to cool on a paper towel. Jed walked into the kitchen and she gave him a weak grin, surprised by how right her world seemed with him there, sharing breakfast, using her towels, sleeping beside her. During the night, he'd made love to her again. Slow. Tender. Making her heart ache and her body come alive under his touch. He'd held her close throughout the remainder of the night, even pulling her beneath him again before they left the warmth of the bed a little over an hour ago.

He sat at the table and waited for her to join him. "I just got off the phone with my agent. I've got a press conference this afternoon at the stadium."

She set the pancakes on the table, then turned to retrieve the bacon. "So soon?" She handed him a cup of coffee and he smiled his thanks.

"The sooner the better," he said as he scooped a short stack onto his plate.

He slathered butter and syrup on his pancakes, then helped himself to a few slices of bacon before shifting his attention to the television as a reporter from CNN told the story of an adopted boy who woke up one morning to find his biological father was the legendary Jed Maitland. He continued to eat while an interview with a child psychologist followed, dispensing with every adopted child's fantasy and advising viewers of the irreparable emotional harm such a discovery would, in his so-called expert opinion, cause Austin. Jed swore and snagged the remote off the counter behind him, flipping the station.

Griffen winced when he landed on Nancy Grace, who played hardball by bringing up the previous paternity suit. Jed's lips thinned and his jaw tightened as he stared at the screen, listening to Nancy and a trio of pundits all speculate on Jed's future relationship his son.

He turned to ESPN in time to see a panel of former and current pro football personalities dissecting his career and adding their own speculation as to his future in the sport. He rose and stalked to the coffee pot, pouring himself another cup, then leaned back against the counter and continue to listen to the less than glowing reports.

"Has it always been this bad?" She couldn't imagine having to live with this type of attention every single day of her life. She'd have cracked long before now.

"I've heard worse," he said, casting his hard flinted gaze in her direction. He listened to the panel for a few more minutes, then turned off the television.

She set her fork on the plate, her appetite ruined. How could they do this to him? The speculation about Austin was one thing, and almost understandable. Almost. To have his peers impaneled and second guessing his career and his future crossed a line, in her opinion. One had nothing to do with the other.

He kissed the top of her head and rubbed at her tense shoulders. "Sweetheart, we need to talk."

She groaned and peered up at him. "No good conversation ever started with those words," she said, her worry increasing at the concern in his eyes. "I take it this isn't pillow talk?"

"Sorry, babe." The remorse lacing his voice tore at her heart. This wasn't his fault, but considering the guilt he harbored over Linc Monroe's suicide, more than likely he was setting full blame for their current situation at his own door.

She sighed and set her plate aside. "What is it?"

"In a few hours, I'll be walking into the wolf's den."

She knew he despised the idea of her being anywhere the press, but because of who he was, she and Austin were affected, whether he liked it or not. She wanted to face them together.

She looked away, her gaze drawn to the windows. *They're outside now.* Was there some sleazy tabloid reporter lurking in her backyard hoping for a money shot to sell to the *Inquirer*? The cable networks had sent out crews in vans with satellites and remote equipment. Were the reporters speculating on what she and Jed were doing behind closed doors, making lewd comments and suggestions amongst themselves over Styrofoam coffee cups? The thought made her ill.

"I'd like to be there," she finally said, turning her attention back to him. Facing the media didn't thrill her, but she'd be damned if she'd let them crucify Jed again.

"Griffen." He kept his hands on her shoulders, his thumbs gently skimming over her neck. "I can't let you do that."

She stood and moved away, feeling Jed's eyes on her back as she cleared the table. She really wasn't ready to face anyone at this point and resented the outside world barging into their lives. But she refused to remain idle while they turned Jed's affair with Dani, and as a result, Austin, into something to be ashamed of.

She set a dish in the sink and turned to face him. "I know you want your life back, but if I'm there, it might help."

He moved in front of her and tipped her head back with his finger. "I appreciate the offer, but no. I don't want you anywhere near that circus." His voice was gentle, as gentle as the arms that had held her during the night. "Let me handle them."

Concern and something else, some other emotion she couldn't define deepened his dark brown eyes. "Why?" she asked in a strangled whisper. "Why won't you let me help? I never expected any of this, but that doesn't mean I'm willing to go into hiding and let you take the heat. Austin is here because you and my sister had loved each other. I won't let them twist that into something ugly."

He gripped her shoulders. "I won't let that happen. I promise." He laughed, a sound that held no humor. "My life has been filled with damage control for too damned long, and I'm sick to death of it."

"What if they ask about us?" She needed, yet feared his reply. She didn't doubt that Jed cared for her, but neither one of them had ever said they were playing for keeps. Was she wishing for something that was beyond them? Was she heading straight for heartbreak?

He didn't release her, just kept looking at her with a determined glint in his eyes. "I don't know," was all he said.

Neither did she, and the thought was far from comforting.

Griffen had been a wreck since Jed left around noon. He'd send a text telling her the news conference was set for five o'clock. ESPN would carry it live.

She sat on the sofa in her father's study, nervous and waiting. A reporter from ESPN recounted Jed's career, from the days when he first began to garner attention at Ole Miss, to his long association with the Wranglers. Sprinkled into the professional career was a version she knew to be mostly untruths and misconceptions, an exaggerated version of the truth, the darker, more notorious side. The basic facts were somewhat accurate, but the reporter failed to mention the real story behind the hype.

When the reporter mentioned the previous paternity suit, she stiffened. Linc Monroe's suicide was mentioned, and when the reporter added his own commentary, blaming Jed's affair with Marilee for the cause behind Linc's death, she quietly seethed. Jed had promised Linc he'd protect Marilee and her unborn child, and she knew he'd never correct the erroneous assumptions made by the press.

Her dad sat next to her on the sofa, while Austin sat cross legged on the floor, his attention divided between watching her and the television screen. His dark Maitland eyes filled with worry every time he looked at her, and it nearly broke her heart.

"We should be there," she said to her dad. "He shouldn't have to face the media alone. Provide a united front like…"

"A family?" Thomas finished for her. "Is that what you really want? For you and Jed and Austin to be a family?"

Did she? She loved Jed. There was no longer any doubt in her mind about her feelings for him. Regardless of Austin's anxiety the past couple of weeks, she knew her son adored his father. From what she'd observed, Jed's feelings for Austin were reciprocated. They deserved a chance to really get to know each other, to form that special bond between a father and his son. But where did she fit into the picture? Or rather, she and Jed?

"I don't know, Dad," she said. "Maybe."

The reporter quieted as Jed walked up to the podium amid flashing bulbs and bright lights from the cameras. He looked handsome in a suit she was fairly certain was Armani. His expression somber, he approached the podium, a sheaf of papers clutched in his hands.

"Thank you for coming," Jed said, but his tone lacked sincerity. He set the papers on the podium in front of the bank of microphones. The cameras continued to flash. "I have a prepared statement, then I'll take questions."

Griffen simply stared as Jed looked directly at the cameras and told his side of the story. He told them about the affair he'd had with her sister, and how he'd never known until a few weeks ago of his son's existence, nor had his son's adopted parents known he was the biological father. He didn't lie, but he didn't sugar coat the truth, either. He simply explained why he'd never had any contact with his son.

He finished his statement and reporters shouted questions. The demands for attention came fast and furious, and Griffen couldn't decipher all of the questions. Jed held up his hands to stop them, then called on the reporter she'd seen earlier from the sports network.

"Jed, will you be taking custody of your son?"

Griffen held her breath. Austin bit his bottom lip, his attention solely on his father. Jed had promised her that he had no intention of taking Austin away from her, but he did want to be a part of his son's life.

"No," he answered, and she breathed a sigh of relief.

"Will you share joint custody with the boy's adopted mother?"

"Mrs. Somerfield and I only have an informal arrangement at this time."

They did? If that was the case, he'd failed to let her in on the details. They shared a son. And a bed, which was pretty informal when she thought about it. Maybe that was the cause of her unsettled feelings. She and Jed had never really come to an agreement, informal or otherwise, about Austin. The only time they'd discussed their relationship was when she'd told him they didn't have one. Everything had happened so quickly, even she couldn't be certain of where they were headed. She'd worked hard to get her life back under control, and the unresolved issue with Jed only kept her feeling scattered.

"Is there any truth to the rumor that Mrs. Somerfield contacted you prior to filing a paternity action against you for thirteen years of child support?"

"No." Jed's eyebrows pulled into a deep frown. "None at all."

"Will Mrs. Somerfield and your son be relocating to Buffalo with you?" the sports network reporter asked. "Or do you plan to have a long distance relationship with your son?"

Buffalo? As in New York?

Austin looked at her and frowned. "What are they talking about, Mom? What long distance relationship?"

"I don't know, Slick."

"We haven't yet discussed the details," Jed said, then turned to answer another question.

Griffen's heart sank. Abject pain filled a place deep inside, the place Jed had touched, the place filled with her love for him. As much as he'd reiterated the uncertainty of his future, she had a sinking suspicion he'd just made a decision. If the people in Buffalo were making him an offer that would keep him actively involved with the sport he loved, he just might take it. He'd said football was all he knew. How could he not take it? He would walk out of their lives as quickly as he had walked in—leaving her and Austin behind in Texas.

"Mom? Did you know Dad was going to New York?"

Dad. She'd never heard Austin refer to Jed as dad before, only *my dad*, or *my real dad*. Dad was personal. Dad indicated a relationship.

"No, I didn't," she said around the disappointment lodged in her throat.

She had to be strong to face what she'd suspected all along...Jed simply wasn't the stick around type.

Somehow she'd have to make Austin understand that Jed's moving to New York had nothing to do with him, but everything to do with Jed's career. Fathers had careers all the time that took them away from their families for periods of time.

Only they weren't a family. They were Austin, his adopted mother, and a professional quarterback for a father.

She watched through a haze as the reporters continued to bombard him with questions about his career, his injury and his recovery. His answers were short and concise, and never once did he mention he'd entertained the idea of retirement. Football was his game, he told them. A game that was his life.

And it looked like the game could be taking Jed away.

SEVENTEEN

BY THE TIME Griffen and Austin returned home, the reporters and their news vans were thankfully gone. They had their story—for now.

Griffen had heard nothing from Jed, so she had no idea if he would come to say good-bye or catch the next flight to Buffalo. Regardless of the fantasy they'd all been living the past couple of weeks, deep down she'd known he would eventually leave. Shame on her for believing otherwise. She should have prepared Austin more than she had, too. If she'd followed her instincts and never contacted Jed to begin with, Austin wouldn't be in his room brooding over the fact that he was losing his father before he really got a chance to know him, and she wouldn't be nursing her already broken heart.

She wished he would call, send her a text. Anything. At least then she'd know what the hell he had planned. The phone had rung a few times, but since it wasn't Jed calling, she'd let them all roll into voice mail, fearing more calls from reporters wanting a statement. She ignored them, not wanting to talk to anyone.

Anyone except Jed.

The doorbell rang, and for half a second she considered ignoring it, but it could be Jed. She went to the front hall and peered out the side curtain. The sight of a sheriff's deputy standing on her doorstep had her stomach roiling. Nothing good ever came from having a cop at the door.

With trembling fingers, she flipped on the porch light and

unlocked the door. "Can I help you?" she asked, surprised her voice worked.

"Mrs. Somerfield?"

His no nonsense demeanor did nothing to dispel her fears. "Yes. I'm Griffen Somerfield."

He thrust a clipboard at her. "Sign here, please."

She scanned the form which only indicated she'd be acknowledging receipt of legal documents. "What is this for?" she asked as she signed the form, then handed the clipboard back to the deputy.

"You've been served, ma'am." He handed her a large manila envelope. "I'm really sorry."

Unable to find her voice, she nodded, then closed the door. Served? But she'd talked to Keith Shelton only hours ago. He'd been so pleased when she'd advised him she'd have all of her debts with the bank not only brought current, but paid off, just as soon as she received the check from the auctioneer. Surely she wasn't being sued at this stage.

Heart pounding, she carefully lifted the flap and withdrew a thick sheaf of papers from the envelope. She scanned the face sheet and her knees went weak.

No.

He wouldn't. He'd promised.

He lied.

She reached for the wall for support because her legs were in danger of giving out on her. A strangled sound tore from her throat as an intense pain squeezed her chest. Jed wasn't only suing her for custody of Austin, he'd filed an emergency petition, asking the court to vacate the adoption—in only four days.

In four days, Friday afternoon at two o'clock, she could lose her son.

She flipped through the documents. Just as she'd feared, he was alleging her adoption of Austin was illegal because he wasn't given proper notice that his parental rights were going to be terminated. She read the petition carefully, each line striking her heart, tearing it apart. He didn't lie. There no exaggerations of the truth. Only the cold hard facts. She had illegally adopted Austin because Dani had lied under oath at the involuntary termination hearing when she'd claimed she didn't know the identity of Austin's biological father.

The tears she had no hope of holding back blurred her vision and burned her throat. She slid down the wall to the ceramic tiled floor, clutching the court papers to her chest and sobbed.

Griffen tossed back the shot of bourbon, then poured herself another. In the two hours since she'd been served, despite her valiant attempt to numb the anguish at the expense of her liver, the pain hadn't ebbed. She had serious doubts it ever would, either.

Then there was the anger. She seethed with it, and the bourbon was more fuel to her fire than a numbing agent to her pain. After all she'd done to pull her life out of the hell Ross had left her in, she'd mistakenly believed she and Austin would have a new beginning. She'd downsized, found a nine-to-five job close to home. But after talking to her future brother-in-law, she realized she'd been wasting her time. Trenton hadn't been all that encouraging. Legally, Jed held all the cards. The bastard even had the winning hand. Because according to Trenton, no judge was going to deny restoring Jed's parental rights.

She sipped the whiskey and set the glider to rocking again. A light breeze stirred the leaves on the trees, and she heard the croaking of the frogs down by the water. While she wouldn't miss this house because of what it represented to her, she would miss the quiet nights on the back porch as the water from the lake rhythmically lapped at the shoreline. She'd miss the gentle breezes on summer evenings and the occasional wildlife that ventured across her back lawn. And the quiet. She wouldn't have that in town, but considering she could very well be completely alone, maybe being so isolated wasn't a good idea.

She didn't know what to think. Try as she might, she simply could not figure out what was going through Jed's mind. One on hand, he was generous to a fault, setting up a trust fund for Austin with more money than he'd ever need in his lifetime. She supposed since he was already paying for one child that wasn't even his, no way was he going to deny his biological progeny a secure future. Too bad the only future Austin wanted was one with his father...a father who up until she'd been served with court papers, would've only seen his son during the off season when he wasn't in Buffalo, New York.

Then there was the other hand. The one where Jed was a backstabbing, low-life cowardly bastard. Dammit, they'd discussed this. He'd promised he'd never take Austin away from her. But one fancy job offer from Buffalo and all that changed—without so much as a phone call to warn her he was going to be ripping her heart out of her chest and stomping all over it with his cleats.

The rat bastard.

The hinges on the back door squeaked and she looked up, expecting to find Austin. Instead, it was the rat bastard himself. He still wore the suit he'd worn for the press conference. His hair was mussed, as if he'd been running his hands through it all evening. He looked miserable, and she didn't care. Not any longer.

Right now, she despised him.

"Griffen—"

"I saw the press conference," she said. "There's nothing left to explain."

He crossed the porch and moved to sit beside her on the glider. "Sweetheart—"

"Don't call me that." She came off the glider as if she'd been shot from a cannon. "Don't touch me. Don't you *dare* touch me." She stood at the railing and faced the lake because she couldn't stand to look at him, couldn't bear for him to see the pain he'd caused her, how he'd broken her heart.

"It's over." The tightening of her chest squeezed and made it difficult to breathe. "I know it was just sex for you, but I can't play that game. I don't know why I thought I could."

He moved beside her and turned, propping his backside against the railing. The moonlight cast his face in haunted shadows, making the chiseled lines more prominent, more...determined. "We need to talk."

She threw him an incredulous look. "Seriously? I thought the papers I was served with tonight pretty much said it all."

"What are you talking about?"

She turned and snagged the court documents off the table next to the bottle of Kentucky bourbon. "These," she said as she planted them against his chest with a smack. He clamped his hand over hers, but she yanked it away. "Go fuck yourself, Maitland. You're not taking my son away from me."

His frown deepened as he scanned the documents. "There must be some mistake," he said. "I have no intention of taking Austin away from you."

She wanted to flip him off. She wanted to throw the half empty bottle of Jack Daniels at his head. Instead, she poured herself another shot and tossed it back. "You're goddamned right you won't."

He looked at her curiously. "Are you drunk?"

"I'm trying to be."

"And how's that working for you?"

She let out a sigh as she dropped onto the glider. "Not so good." Leaning forward, she rested her head in her hands. "How could you do this? After everything, how could you go behind my back like that and petition the court to take Austin away from me?" She looked up at him. "I told you I'd never deny you your son. Does my word mean nothing to you?"

He pushed off the railing and joined her on the glider. "I told my lawyer I wanted to make sure my parental rights were restored. I never told him to seek nullification of the adoption."

"Apparently he didn't get the memo."

"I'll take care of it."

She was afraid to believe him. "And I'm supposed to trust you?"

"Yes," he said. "I've never lied to you."

No, he hadn't. But that didn't make her feel any better, either. She'd believed her ex would never lie to her, cheat on her or rob her blind, and look how that had ended.

He smoothed his hand up her back, his fingers settling at her nape where he gently massaged the knot of tension gathered there. She trembled beneath his touch, just as she always had and probably always would. A part of her wanted to tell him to stop, the survival part of her. The weak-where-he-was-concerned part kept her mouth clamped shut and soaked in his touch.

"The court will reinstate my rights without you losing yours," he said. "Establishing shared legal custody won't change anything, other than giving me back my legal right to my son."

She straightened and shifted in her seat to look at him. "I don't know what to believe."

"Believe this," he said, then leaned in and kissed her. She should've pushed him away, but she didn't. Instead she kissed him back and allowed herself to become lost in the dizzying sensations.

He ended the kiss and looked at her. The intensity in his gaze unnerved her, but she couldn't look away if her life depended on it. She wanted to despise him. She really did. Certainly, she didn't want to trust him. Only problem was— she loved him.

"I want you and Austin to come with me," he said quietly. "To Buffalo."

She looked away again, afraid to hope. So what if she loved him? That didn't mean he loved her. Oh sure, he cared about her. That much she did know, but love? Enough to make a relationship work? They'd never last. They'd become nothing more than a temporary promise to what? Love, honor and cherish?

"I want you and Austin to live with me."

She flinched as if he'd slapped her. Her heart took a dive and landed in the pit of her booze-soaked stomach. Live with him? Did he know nothing about her?

She laughed suddenly, the sound cold and caustic and filled with bitterness. "That's convenient."

He sighed and gave her a look that said she was making this a hell of a lot harder than necessary. Too bad. He knew she was not the kind of woman to shack up with a man.

She stared at the man in question and tried to wrap her mind around what he'd just asked her. "You want us to *live* together?"

He didn't say anything, just looked at her with that hard flinted gaze. She recognized the tight clenching in his jaw as a sure sign of his frustration. Jed Maitland was not accustomed to being told no, by anyone.

No matter how much she loved him, no matter how much Austin might want otherwise, she refused to live with him without a commitment. A legal one. She swallowed the disappointment lodged in her throat. "No."

He rubbed at the back of his neck. "I thought...dammit, Griffen. What were you hoping for? A marriage proposal?"

"Quite frankly, yes." A deep ache curled inside her at his defensive tone. She'd been silly to think they could have a real, lasting relationship. They were too different. Like two roads that crossed on a journey from elsewhere. His the glitter highway and hers an old country lane filled with traditional values, like family and marriage and forever.

She turned and swiped a renegade tear from her cheek. She hurt so badly, she doubted she'd ever heal. "What did you expect me to want, Jed? After what we've shared recently..."

She looked back to the lake. She'd done things with Jed, wicked and erotic things she'd never done with another man, not even her ex-husband. She gave herself to Jed when she hadn't even realized she loved him. And that love made all the difference in the world to her. To her, it meant forever.

"It doesn't matter," she finally said. "I'm happy for you. Good luck in Buffalo."

He grabbed hold of her shoulders and turned her to face him. Anger, and something else, flashed in his eyes. Hurt? "It doesn't have to be this way."

"Yes it does," she said and shrugged out of his grasp. "I'm not like one of your gridiron groupies, Jed. I won't be packing a bag to follow you to New York. Sorry to disappoint you, *sweetheart*, but it's just not my scene."

He eased a harsh breath between clenched teeth. "I'm asking you to come with me. For you and Austin to live with me."

Her patience slipped. "That's the problem," she railed at him. "You want us to live with you. I can't do that, Jed. I have Austin to think about."

He glared down at her. "The three of us will be together. What is wrong with that?" he asked. His eyebrows pulled together in that ferocious frown that had become all too familiar to her.

Who was she kidding? Everything about the man was familiar to her. He was permanently imbedded in her mind, her heart and her soul. "What kind of message would I be sending to my son if I moved in with you? I won't do it. Austin deserves better than that, and you know what, Jed? So do I."

"I thought..." His voice rose, but then he sucked in a deep breath and let it out slowly. "I don't know what I thought," he said more calmly. "I never made you any promises."

"I never asked you to," she whispered. She looked up at him, her heart aching as she memorized every line of his face, every nuance that made him Jed, that made him the man she loved. "Good-bye, Jed."

She turned and walked toward the door. Every step of the way she fought to keep the tears blurring her vision from falling.

"Dammit, Griffen," he said, his voice filled with tension and frustration. "Don't do this."

Blindly, she reached for the door. With her hand resting on the knob, she turned back to face him. "No, Jed," she said, hating the anguish between them. But it was too late. "This is exactly what I have to do. I love you, but for me, it's all or nothing."

She pushed through the door and slipped into the kitchen, leaving the night, and Jed, outside. She leaned against the frame, waiting until she heard his Escalade roar to life before she dropped into one of the chairs at the round table. He was gone. Out of her life, and Austin's.

When Ross left, she'd resigned herself to being alone, but she'd never felt so completely isolated as she did at this very moment. Allowing the bleakness to consume her, she dropped her head in her hands and cried until there was nothing left but emptiness.

Jed was miserable as the limousine wound its way through the Wednesday afternoon traffic to Orchard Park, New York, a suburb of Buffalo. He'd known all along Griffen was the type who played for keeps, the kind of woman he should've had the good sense to avoid. Instead, he'd allowed that other, uncontrollable part of his anatomy do his thinking for him, and where had it led him? Straight to hell.

Only it wasn't her fault the path to hell was paved in her curves, in her gentle laughter, in her sweet smile. There was more to his own private purgatory than just sex. It was her, every single thing about her. Every exciting, frustrating, stubborn part of what made Griffen who she was...the woman he'd let into his heart. The hell was of his own making because he couldn't give her the promises she needed to hear.

He should be relieved. The last thing he needed was a wife and kid cluttering up his life.

He should be grateful that she hadn't taken him up on his proposition.

Instead, he was miserable.

For the past two days he'd been damned irritable, too. He'd fired his agent, his publicist and had instructed his lawyer to set up the meeting with the Buffalo people. Rambling around the empty, cavernous house in Possum Kingdom, he'd been restless, irritated, and he missed Griffen. He'd lost count of the number of times he'd reached for his cell phone to call her, but something always held him back. Something kept him from calling Griffen to tell her he'd commit to anything she wanted just so they could be together.

It's all or nothing.

He bit back a curse and shifted on the leather seat of the limo. Her words continued to haunt him. She loved him. And he'd told her what he'd wanted, and she'd still kicked him in the balls with her rejection.

He'd loved once before. He'd committed himself to one woman and he'd lost big time. He'd loved Dani and she'd left him without a word, never giving him a chance to know his son. He'd loved his parents and they'd been taken away from him. For the past thirteen years he'd committed himself strictly to his career because it'd been safe. He'd been broken and patched up far too many times, but always, his career had never failed him. He'd even been committed to Linc, and that commitment had ended when his best friend took his own life.

It wasn't your fault.

"Dammit, Griffen." His gut twisted at the image of her in the moonlight, that stupid ratty sweater she always wore pulled tight around her as she downed shot after shot of Jack Daniels in an attempt to numb the pain he'd caused her. She'd tried to hide them, but even in the moonlight he'd seen the tears glistening in her eyes.

Good-bye, Jed.

He didn't want good-bye. He wanted her.

It's all or nothing.

As the driver pulled to a stop, Jed wondered if he was making the biggest mistake of his life in letting Griffen slip through his fingers. He'd always see her whenever he spent time with Austin. Their coming into contact with each other was inevitable because of the common bond they shared with their son. And he knew it would never be enough.

He didn't want good-bye.

He didn't want strained meetings.

He didn't want polite conversation.

He wanted her, dammit.

The driver opened the door and Jed stepped out into the biting cold air, a far cry from the warmth of the Texas sun this time of year. The damp chill hanging in the air made him instantly uncomfortable and long for the warmer temperatures of home.

Home. With Griffen and their son.

He ignored the funny lurch in this chest and strode across the snow-dusted pavement to the glass door. An attractive young woman in a navy wool suit greeted him and introduced herself only as Marty Fuller's personal assistant before leading him to a conference room with dark paneling, heavy furniture and potted trees.

Marty Fuller, the assistant general manager of the team, stood and greeted him. Fuller was a small, wiry guy with a too slick grin who'd probably never gripped a football in his life. He introduced him to the team's lawyers, a pair of officious looking pricks with matching waxy complexions, followed by the publicist, Cal Palmer and two additional suits. And not a single member of the coaching staff.

"Have you had a chance to see the city, Jed?" Fuller asked, motioning for his assistant. "Drink?"

"No, thanks," Jed said, then watched as Fuller waved his assistant away. "I came straight from the airport."

He hadn't had a real drink since the first day he arrived in Hart. That didn't mean he'd lost the craving for something strong and forgetful. More than once he found himself standing in front of the wet bar at the lake house, contemplating the numbing effects of Jack, Johnny or José. Booze wouldn't ease the loneliness, at least more than temporarily. When he came out of the drunken stupor, he'd still be without Griffen and Austin, so he hadn't bothered.

"Anxious to get down to business." Fuller chuckled as he settled his scrawny frame in the chair at the end of the conference table. "I like that. Did your agent explain our offer?"

Jed leaned back in the black leather conference chair and kept his eyes on the AGM. "Actually, Bob Yorke and I parted company. Why don't you tell me about the offer?"

Fuller exchanged a look with his lackeys, then returned his attention to Jed, that slick smile on his face again. "Well, Jed," he said, leaning forward and placing his arms on the polished surface of the table. "We feel you're just the publicity shot in the arm that we could use."

"My record speaks for itself," Jed said, giving Fuller a smile of his own, one he didn't quite feel. Something wasn't right in this room, but he couldn't put his finger on exactly what was wrong. Yet.

"You do have quite a record," Cal, the publicist said, drumming his designer pen on a leather encased legal pad. "And a reputation to match."

One of the lawyers chuckled. "That he does."

"All this new publicity will bring attention to the team that we haven't had in a number of years," the publicist continued.

The hair on the back of Jed's neck rose, but he didn't so much as flinch when he leveled his stare on Fuller. "Publicity?" he asked cautiously. "How so?"

"Well, this kid of yours," Cal said. "We feel the publicity you're currently involved in is definitely to the team's advantage. My people can spin it, make you look good for a change."

Jed resisted the sudden urge to plant his fist in the middle of Cal Palmer's round face. They didn't want him or his talent, they wanted his reputation. Not the reputation of his many years as a pro, either. No, they wanted the notorious, the infamous, and the mostly untrue reputation. Bastards. "How is my son an advantage to the team?"

"Jed, let me put it to you real simple like," Fuller said, a condescending note to his voice. "You draw the press. They love you or love to hate you, I really don't care which." The guy rested his elbow on the table and pointed his finger at Jed. "Your name brings the press running. That means exposure for the team. The more attention you draw, the more air time we have and the more seats we fill. And the owners will have what they like best—more money."

"It's a win-win, Jed," Cal Palmer added. "We buy out your existing contract with the Wranglers and you get another couple years of play. In return, we garner the press coverage for just having you associated with the organization."

Jed laced his fingers together and looked around the room. It took every ounce of his self-control not to beat the crap out of Fuller, and while he was at it, he'd wipe the eager smirk off the publicist's face, too. "So you want me for my publicity, not for what I can offer the team professionally."

"The social media has exploded since the scandal broke," one of the lawyers said.

"Jed, you've got us all wrong," Cal said.

"Do I?"

"We want you," Fuller said. "The added attention is simply a perk."

"I see. You're not looking to offer me a real job, but something that will keep my name associated with your team. You want a way to catch the media's attention, fill seats and keep lining your pockets in the process."

"Oh, no, you'd definitely have a real position," Fuller explained. "Get you out in front of the crowds, pull a few publicity stunts a couple of times a year. Hell, we'll even make sure you play, you know, to keep you happy when you're working the press. With your name and reputation, well, we see it as a winning combination."

"I see it as a crock," Jed said and stood. "Thanks, but no thanks."

Marty Fuller's eyes narrowed to slits. "No? Do you know who you're talking to? We're your last chance, Maitland. Be smart for a change. Take the offer."

Jed braced his hands on the table and leaned toward Fuller. "Screw you and your offer. The answer is still no. You're not using my son to spruce up your last place image."

He pushed off the table and stalked across the room to the door. His career might be over, but he'd be damned if he'd sell out his own kid to make a few bucks he didn't even need. Or worse, become one of those glory day boys who desperately attempted to hold onto a past that was long gone.

"Jed, where are you going?" the publicist called after him. "This could be the best thing that's ever happened to you."

"I left the best thing that ever happened to me back in Texas," he said, then walked out on the bastards.

He reached the elevator and punched the button. He was going back to Texas. Back to Hart. And back to Griffen. Provided she'd have him.

The elevator arrived and the door slid open. Jed stepped into the car just as Fuller and his entourage arrived. Jed pushed the button for the first floor, but the AGM's hand snaked out and prevented the door from closing.

"The medical experts say your career is over, Jed. Think about it," Fuller said in a cajoling and highly irritating tone. "Say yes, and we'll keep you on the roster."

"You have a decent quarterback," he said. "You don't need me." Jed punched the button again. It was either the button or Fuller's face. "So you can take your offer and shove it. I just retired."

EIGHTEEN

GRIFFEN PACED THE length of the corridor of the second floor of the courthouse, her heels clicking loudly on the tiles with each nervous step she took. She hadn't heard word one from Jed all week. Not that that should bother her, but the reality was, she was close to going out of her ever-loving mind.

She tried convincing herself she should be happy about his silence. After all, wasn't she the one who'd said good-bye? She should be grateful the big jerk took the hint and stayed away from her. Only she'd never been a very good liar, and she sure as hell couldn't swallow the whopper she'd been trying to sell herself all week. Not when her heart stuttered every time her cell phone buzzed. And certainly not when disappointment tripped her up each and every time it wasn't him on the other end. The truth was, she had no one to blame but herself for her misery.

So call him. Tell him you made a mistake.

If only it were that easy.

It is. Just do it.

She'd seriously considered calling him, several times over the past four days. She had the sleepless nights and grainy eyes to prove it. But in the end, no matter how much she wanted otherwise, she simply could not sacrifice her values. If she had only herself to consider, then maybe, but she had a teenaged son to raise and shacking up with a man who wasn't her husband wasn't going to happen.

While she'd feared Austin would blame her for Jed's

departure, he hadn't. He wasn't exactly happy about it, but he hadn't asked too many questions and seemed more resigned than anything else. When she'd talked to him, she reminded him that once his dad was settled, he'd more than likely be in touch. For all she knew, he may already have and Austin wasn't talking. Which did make sense since Austin hadn't seem all that concerned about Jed's disappearing act. But she knew her son well enough to know that when he was ready to talk, he would.

She reached the end of the corridor, turned around and headed back toward Mattie. Austin had been in judge's chambers with the court appointed child advocate, Trenton, and the swarm of attorneys representing Jed's interests, for over half an hour. She could only guess at the questions they were asking Austin.

Of course, Jed was nowhere to be found. "Typical." She glanced at her watch for the fourth time in as many minutes. Her life was about to be torn apart and he couldn't even be bothered to show his face.

"Sit down, Griff," Mattie said from one of the hard wooden benches lining the corridor. "You're starting to make me nervous."

Griffen walked over to her sister and dropped onto the bench next to her. She blew out a stream of breath that did nothing to quell the quaking of her insides. "I can't believe I was stupid enough to fall for his lies."

Mattie slipped her cell phone into her purse. "What lies?"

"He said he'd drop the petition to vacate the adoption. Like a moron, I actually believed he'd do it." She looked at Mattie, but found no comfort from the concern in her sister's eyes. She looked at her watch again. "They've been in there for forty-five minutes."

"It's going to be fine, Griff."

The serenity of Mattie's tone clawed at her raw nerves. "You don't know that," Griffen said a little too sharply.

"Neither do you," Mattie said. "And don't snap at me. I'm on your side."

"I know." She let out another huff of breath. "I'm sorry.

I'm just scared."

"Chances are they're probably just doing some legal maneuvering to keep your rights intact while reinstating Jed's."

"Then why haven't they sent Austin back out here with us?"

"I don't know," Mattie said. "The judge is probably just being thorough. It'll be fine."

"You think?"

Mattie reached over and gave Griffen's hand a gentle squeeze. "Yeah, I do. I trust Trenton to handle it. He's a good lawyer, Griff. He's going to fight for you and Austin to stay together."

"I wish Dad was here."

"He will be. Soon."

She sprung up off the bench and started pacing again. A month ago, she'd have thought the worst that could have happened to her was facing financial ruin. Today, she knew that tragedy was minor in comparison to the thought of losing her son. Why did she always have to do the right thing? Why couldn't she have just thrown Dani's journal away and never said a word?

Because she couldn't have lived with herself if she had, that's why. Deception just wasn't a part of her DNA.

Given the same situation, she knew without a doubt she'd have done exactly the same thing. She didn't have it in her to deny Austin a chance to know his father. She may have had her heart broken, but that was her own stupid fault for falling in love with a man who...

"Jed."

Her heart took off at a maddening pace and her pulse skyrocketed at the sight of him walking toward her. The dark charcoal suit he wore fit his large frame to perfection. For all of two seconds, she considered launching herself into his arms and telling him she'd made a massive mistake. That she loved him and didn't care about anything except that they be together. Only she didn't. The fierce determination in his eyes, in his stride, reminded her why they were at the courthouse in the first place.

"We need to talk."

God, she was really starting to hate that phrase. "Our lawyers are doing the talking now."

He reached out and snagged her hand. "Come with me."

"Hey. What do you think you're doing?"

He pulled her along behind him, down the corridor and around the corner, into an alcove. He backed her up against the wall and her tummy flipped. God, she wanted to kiss him. She wanted to do a whole lot more, too.

Instead, she gave him what she hoped was a hard look that revealed none of what she was really feeling. "There's nothing left for us to say."

"Correction. I'm going to talk," he said, "and for once, would you please listen?"

His nearness made her common sense scatter. She balled her hands at her sides to keep from touching him, from reaching out and smoothing her fingers over the frown lines gathered between his eyes. "Fine," she said, cursing her stupidity for looking at his mouth.

"There is no Buffalo," he told her. "I turned it down."

"That doesn't change—"

"It changes everything. My life is here. With you and Austin." He leaned in, close enough so that his breath fanned her lips. Close enough that she could practically taste him.

"I love you, Griffen," he said in that familiar, low, husky rumble. "I've known for a while now, I just couldn't admit it. To myself or to you."

Stupid her, she smiled at him. He loved her. "I'm still not moving in with you." She couldn't. Not without a commitment. Love was good, but it still wasn't a commitment.

He smiled back with that killer Maitland grin, the one that had her heart melting and her girl parts paying attention. Well, that and he had told her he loved her.

"What kind of marriage is that going to be if we're not living together?"

She pulled her hand from his. "Jed…"

He took her hand back and went down on one knee, and that's when she saw them. Austin, her dad, and her sister and Trenton, all standing a few feet behind Jed. All smiling, waiting and watching them as if they knew this was coming. She looked down at Jed and her knees went weak. All the emotion rippling through her, all the love in her heart, was there, mirrored in his beautiful, dark eyes.

"I love you, Griffen," he said again. He opened a little black velvet ring box to reveal an elaborate array of diamonds in an elegant setting. "Marry me."

Only Jed could make a proposal of marriage sound like a command. She'd wanted to hear those words from him. She'd wanted that ultimate commitment from him, and there was no way she'd let him back out now that he'd put it out there.

Tears blurred her vision. "Yes, Jed," she said around the lump lodged in her throat. "I'll marry you."

With the quickness of the snap of a football, he was on his feet. She blinked and she was in his arms and he was kissing her stupid.

He ended the kiss and looked over at Trenton. "Is everything ready?"

Her future brother-in-law grinned. "Ready."

Jed planted another quick kiss on her lips. "Marry me now."

"Now?" Was he crazy? "As in right this second?"

"Why not?"

She opened her mouth to protest, but uttered no sound. For the life of her, she couldn't voice any number of reasons flitting through her mind. Apparently, she was equally certifiable.

That killer grin of his returned. "I promise I'm not going to run way with my assistant or wipe out your bank accounts or run up your credit cards."

"You don't have an assistant."

"Not yet," he said, his grin deepening. "But I will."

She hiked up an eyebrow. "Then she'd better be gray haired and over sixty with dozens of grandchildren."

The tenderness in his eyes was wearing her down. "Sweetheart, you're just going to have to trust me."

"You know that's not so easy for me, right?"

"Geeze, Mom," Austin said, "say yes already."

"Seriously, Griff," Mattie added with a laugh.

Trenton looked just as impatient. "The judge is waiting."

Her father smiled at her as he pulled a pretty bouquet of roses in varying shades of pink from a bag, holding it up for her inspection. Apparently Jed had given this whole marriage thing a lot of thought.

She looked back at the man who'd stolen her heart. A sensation between a fever and a chill eddied down her spine at the intensity, at the hope, in his gaze. "Yes. I'll marry you right now."

Moments later, gathered in the privacy of the judge's chambers with her family present, she listened as the judge first dictated an order reinstating Jed's parental rights to Austin without vacating her rights as Austin's adoptive mother. And with both her and Jed's consent, an oral petition to change their son's name to Austin Hart Maitland was also granted.

When she'd initially driven up to Possum Kingdom to tell Jed he had a son, she'd done so without any guarantees as to the outcome. But she also knew the only risks she'd ever regret in her life would be the ones she was too afraid to take. Life didn't come with guarantees. She could worry about what might or might not happen in the future. Or she could live. And love.

And in that moment, she knew. She knew without a doubt she'd much rather build a life with the man she loved with all her heart.

The judge circled her desk to stand in front of them.

Jed took her hand and she looked up at him. The tenderness in his eyes melted her heart. "I love you," he whispered to her.

She laced her fingers with his and planned to never let go again.

Judge Wentworth cleared her throat. "Dearly beloved..."

*

Three months later...

"How long did you say Mattie and Trenton were going to be in Europe?"

Griffen smiled up at her husband as he guided her in a two-step over the dance floor to a George Strait song. "Only for two weeks," she said. "It won't be that bad. I promise."

Jed chuckled. "If you say so. I was only in charge of her for twenty minutes. I can only imagine what two weeks of keeping up with that little tyrant is going to feel like."

Griffen laughed. "Stop complaining. Phoebe adores you."

"She knows an easy mark when she sees one. Now I know why Mattie calls her Phoebzilla." He frowned and looked around the perimeter of the ballroom. "Who is the little monster terrorizing now?"

"She's over there," Griffen said, indicating the long wall of windows overlooking the country club's golf course. "With Dad waiting for the fireworks to start." Phoebe, still dressed in a paler, miniature version of Griffen's dress, sat quietly on Thomas's lap, her head resting against his shoulder, looking nothing but precious and sweet cuddled up with her granddaddy.

"Don't let that angelic expression fool you," Jed warned playfully. "She's only powered down to conserve energy for her next act of terror."

Griffen laughed again at the hint of fear in Jed's voice. She'd promised Mattie they'd keep Phoebe while she and Trenton were on their honeymoon. Lord knew they had plenty of room since moving into their new home last month. Instead of keeping the house in Hart, they'd bought a house out in the country about five miles outside of town. The ranchette had plenty of trees and enough land for horses, something she'd always wanted. Plus, since they were in the country, the property offered them much more privacy. If they were in the mood for water sports, there was still Jed's monstrosity of a house out in Possum Kingdom.

She'd considered renting out the bungalow she'd purchased, but in the end, had decided to sell it instead, depositing the proceeds from the sale into a retirement account. Not that she didn't trust Jed, but she needed to maintain some degree of independence, if for no other reason than her own peace of mind. Shortly after they'd moved, the head hunting firm where she'd interviewed back in March had contacted her about a position with a financial consulting firm. She'd been offered the position during the second interview with the managing partners and had been able to turn down the job at the credit union. The money was good, four times what she would've made as a loan officer, but the hours were choice and she could telecommute much of the time. Since she essentially picked the number of assignments she wanted to take, she'd been setting her own hours. Considering the news she'd been keeping to herself the past two days, she had a feeling she'd be taking even fewer consulting jobs six months from now.

Outside the bank of windows, dusk had passed into night. The fireworks would be starting soon. "I don't know why you're complaining," she said to Jed as the music ended. "You'll be in meetings all next week in New York, anyway."

"Is that great planning or what?" he teased.

While Jed had turned down the ridiculous and insulting offer from the team reps in Buffalo, he had taken a job with one of the networks as a new co-host on one of the Sunday pre-game shows. The timing had been prime, as one of the regulars had announced his retirement. The new agent Jed had hired made the right phone calls and a series of interviews later, Jed was offered a contract with the network. He'd not only be working the pre-game show, but he'd also be co-anchoring a weekly football-based show for the network's all-sports sister station. Unfortunately, the job meant he'd be doing quite a bit of traveling, particularly from August through February, which worked out perfectly, since she wasn't due until the middle of March.

They joined her dad and Phoebe at the windows. Austin slid into a chair next to her father and handed Phoebe a plate with a piece of wedding cake. He was so good with his little cousin. Although she wasn't too worried about his reaction, she did wonder what he'd think about having a baby in the house. She wondered what Jed would have to say about a baby, too...once she told him. Which she'd planned to do later that night.

Mattie and Trenton joined them near the window, each carrying two glasses of champagne. "Here," Mattie said. "Drink." She handed a champagne flute off to Griffen, while Trenton put one in Jed's hand.

"Dad can take the kids home with him after the fireworks. We have a suite at the Anatole and a limo to take us there. Drink up, big sister," Mattie said, clinking her glass against the one in Griffen's hand. "It's party time."

"*You* have a suite. We're going home." Griffen held the glass to her lips but didn't drink. Mattie downed half the glass as if it were a Jell-O shot. "Don't you have a flight to catch first thing in the morning?" Griffen asked, handing her glass to Jed.

"Trust me," Jed said as he set both of their champagne flutes on the table. "You really don't want to fly with a hangover."

Mattie frowned at them both. "Hush. It's my wedding reception." She grinned suddenly and wagged her finger at them. "No criticizing the bride on her wedding day."

With a laugh that bordered on brittle, Mattie spun away in a flurry of champagne-colored lace and tulle. She looped her arm through Trenton's and kissed her groom soundly on the mouth. Seconds later, the first of the fireworks started, the fury of colorful sparks lighting the Texas sky.

"Look, Mommy," Phoebe said, her voice loud and excited. "They're making stars."

Someone had dimmed the already lowered lights and the crowd shifted toward the windows to watch the fireworks spectacular. Jed bent forward slightly, his warm breath fanning her neck. "Just because I'm not having anything to drink doesn't mean you shouldn't," he said, his voice low. Not that he'd stopped drinking completely, but he knew when to stop and only occasionally had a drink or two.

"I know," she said and turned to look at him.

"What are you grinning about?"

She shivered slightly as his warm breath fanned her ear. "I'll tell you later," she laced her fingers with his. Although she was anxious to tell him her news, she really wanted to wait until they were alone. This was Mattie's wedding, and it was supposed to be about the bride, not her pregnant sister.

Gently, he nipped her ear. "Tell me now."

She pressed against him, could feel the hard ridge of his erection wedged against her bottom. Her body instantly responded. Her breasts grew heavy, her nipples pilling into tight buds. "This isn't the time." Whether for revealing her news or the way their bodies were igniting with anticipation, she couldn't state with any degree of certainty.

"Is something wrong?"

She shook her head, then reached up to cup his cheek in her palm. "Everything is perfect," she said, then tipped her head back to brush her mouth against his.

"Then tell me," he said, his voice no longer an intimate whisper.

Her father turned and gave them a warning look, but she merely smiled at her dad, then waited for him to turn his attention back to the fireworks display. "Later," she said.

"Griffen." Jed's deep, velvety voice held a note of warning she couldn't ignore. "Tell me."

She sighed and turned in his arms so she could see his face clearly. So much for waiting until they were alone. "I'm pregnant."

Jed's mouth fell open, then he snapped it shut. "Are you sure?" he asked after a moment. The note of caution in his voice was unmistakable. They had discussed having more children, so it wasn't like this should've been that much of a surprise. While he hadn't been specific about the number, she really hoped they could have at least three more. Granted, she hadn't expected it to happen so soon. They really hadn't been trying, but then they hadn't done anything to prevent a pregnancy, either.

"What's all the racket about over there?" Trenton asked, moving closer and bringing Mattie with him.

"Nothing," Griffen told her new brother-in-law, but gave Jed an affirming nod. As much as she wanted to keep the news between them, she couldn't stop the smile from tugging her lips if her life depended on it. "I confirmed it two days ago."

"Confirmed what?" Mattie asked in a bad stage whisper.

"Griff's pregnant," Jed said, a wide grin on his face. He looked so proud and happy, yet completely awestruck all at the same time.

"You're pregnant?" Mattie's voice went from a loud whisper to a near shout.

Her father turned around, his smile matching the magnitude of Jed's. Austin stared at them, and she held her breath until he grinned and shrugged. "I wouldn't mind a little brother," he said.

"It could be a girl, you know," Mattie said as she reached over and ruffled his hair.

From the horrified expression on Austin's face, he looked as if his aunt had kissed him in public instead of affectionately mussing his hair. "No way," he countered, finger-combing his dark hair back in place.

"Fifty-fifty chance, Slick," Griffen said as Jed pulled her closer.

Austin looked to Jed. "Dad, you can't do that to me." A look of pure terror crossed his face. "What if she's like...you know who?"

Everyone's eyes zeroed in on Phoebe. As if realizing she was the center of attention, she scooted off her granddaddy's lap and ran to her mom. "I didn't do it, Mommy."

Mattie smiled down at her daughter. "No, Phoebe. You didn't do it—this time."

*

Hours later, after the bride and groom had disappeared for the night and the last of the guests had gone, Jed and Griffen had driven home. Both kids were sound asleep, Austin in his room and Phoebe in the guest room. The wedding gifts were all safely packed in the back of the Escalade, which they'd deliver to Mattie's place when they went to her father's for Sunday supper the next day.

She finished up in the bathroom, then walked into the bedroom where Jed sat in bed waiting for her. He had the pillows propped behind his back and wore nothing but that killer Maitland grin and a sheet slung low over his hips.

She slipped off her robe and slid under the sheet next to him. He turned off the light and pulled her against him. Moonlight streamed into the room through the sheers covering the windows, casting the room in bluish shadows. "Tired?" he asked.

"Not that tired."

He chuckled as he placed a finger beneath her chin and titled her head back for a sweet, gentle kiss that made her heart swell with tenderness. God, she loved him so much. She knew she'd taken a huge risk marrying him that day at the courthouse. They'd never once discussed the future, and they really hadn't known each other very long. What association they did have, had been somewhat contentious. But three months in, and she knew she'd made the right choice, even if they did still disagree on occasion.

"Are you happy?" she asked him when he ended the kiss.

"About the baby?" he asked, running his hands over her curves. His hand rested on her belly. "Why wouldn't I be?"

"A few months ago you were more than a little reluctant about being a father." Reluctant hardly described his initial reaction when she'd driven up to Possum Kingdom. "Plus, you weren't there when Austin was born. I just wondered..."

"If it brought up memories of Dani." He splayed his fingers over her abdomen and planted a quick, hard kiss on her lips. "I hadn't really thought about it. What matters is now. Us. The past is the past, sweetheart."

He started nibbling her neck and she nearly lost her train of thought.

"Yeah," she said. "About that." She pushed on his good shoulder until he was looking at her again. "There's something else I should probably tell you."

More than a trace of apprehension filled his gaze. "What?"

"My mom was a twin. She didn't have any multiple births," she said, "but the twin thing sometimes skips a generation."

"Which means..."

"There's a pretty good chance that I could have twins."

He smiled. "How soon will you know?"

"Around the time we hear the heartbeat." If she were carrying twins, the man's ego would know no bounds. Not that it did, anyway, but the last thing she wanted to do was create more of a monster.

"So you're saying that every time I knock you up, there's a chance you could have multiples?"

"Nice, Jed." She laughed. "Knock me up? Really?"

His smile widened into a grin. "We could end up as a reality show."

"Uh...no."

"Aw, you're no fun." He dipped his head and traced the outline of her ear with the tip of his tongue. "But, I love you, anyway."

"That's good to know." Heat pooled in her belly and she shuddered against him as he slid his hand down her body to her heated center. "Because I love you, too," she said as she widened her legs for him.

He caught her mouth in a hot, open-mouthed kiss that had her body igniting and coming vibrantly alive under his touch. As they made love into the early morning hours, Griffen knew without a doubt that loving Jed had changed her...for the better. She still wouldn't exactly call herself a risk taker, but she'd certainly stopped waiting for that other shoe to drop.

Enjoy an excerpt from

PLAYING TO WIN

A Texas Scoundrels Novel
Book #2

Coming Soon…

PROLOGUE

I know I will be called upon to perform tasks in isolation, far from familiar faces and voices . . .

The Special Forces Creed

Somewhere in Afghanistan...

FORD GRAYSON FORCED himself to concentrate on anything but the bastard methodically stripping the flesh from his back. For over five years he'd been held prisoner, believed dead by his government, and by those he loved. God help him, he would find a way to escape.

The sting of the lash seared his skin, or what was left of it. The punishment, an example to others, dealt because he'd struck a guard, violated more than the Geneva Convention, it violated the laws of man.

They could have shot him, but they enjoyed their games of torture too much to dispose of him quickly and painlessly. Regardless of his vows to gain freedom for himself and the others, he almost wished they had shot him.

The desert sun blinded him. Eyes closed, his body flinching with each stroke of the whip, he tried to numb his mind and failed. Instead, he thought of other places, other people. He

251

thought of home. Warm summer breezes coming off the lake in his hometown of Hart, Texas. The sounds of the city, of downtown Dallas. And how much he missed his wife.

Visions of Mattie filtered through his mind. Her struggle to keep the tears at bay whenever he deployed, and how she always lost it once she thought he couldn't see her. The way her cat-green eyes simmered with desire. The way she melted into him that last chilly winter morning when he'd deployed on his last mission. God, he'd give anything to hold her in his arms again.

The acrid scent of diesel fuel burned his nostrils, the exhaust fumes from the idling truck choked him, but he didn't move. He couldn't move. They'd tied his hands and feet to stakes in the dusty courtyard. Spread eagle and face down, his shirt stripped from his body, blood oozed from the open wounds. It trickled down his back and mingling with the red, talcum-like dust that had covered him since he'd first arrived in Hell.

The pounding feet and raised voices filled the courtyard. His torturer flicked the whip one last time, but Ford concentrated on the voices. From their shouts and his scant knowledge of the language, he caught enough key phrases to garner they would be moving the prisoners again. He no longer had any idea if he was still in Iraqi territory, or if they'd been moved to another region sympathetic to the Taliban. Most times they were transported in the quiet of the desert night, driven around for hours, sometimes, he thought, in circles just to confuse the prisoners. The hiding places varied, from abandoned homes and tents in the desert, to old deserted bunkers or caves in the mountains. From the urgency he detected in the voices of his captors, they feared discovery.

Someone cut his bonds, then dark skinned hands roughly dragged him to his feet. The scum who'd whipped him, the one Ford swore he'd kill with his bare hands once the opportunity presented itself, grabbed his overgrown hair and yanked up his head. Ford glared at the son-of-a-bitch.

"I should have killed you," the guard, Shalah, said in

French.

"You can try," Ford returned in the same language.

Shalah laughed, a sound just short of menacing. "You are too brave for your own good, Lieutenant. I would have enjoyed breaking you."

"I'll see you in Hell first," Ford said in English, then spat on the guard.

His reward was a rifle butt to his gut. The air whooshed out of him and he doubled over. Before he could regain his breath, the guards shoved him in the back of the covered truck and closed the flap.

"You never learn, my friend," Jacques, a fellow prisoner, said as he pulled Ford deeper into the truck. "That one enjoys tormenting you."

"He'll die." Ford winced when Jacques examined the fresh wounds. "They'll all die."

"*Oui*, but I may have a plan for our escape," Jacques whispered.

Ford ignored the burning pain and gave Jacques a level stare.

"We are the only ones being taken away," Jacques explained. "From what I overheard this morning, we are being traded for weapons."

"Traded? To who?"

Jacques shook his head. "I am not certain, *mon ami*. But it cannot be good for us, no?" The French chemist poured water from a canteen over Ford's back. "This one is too deep," he muttered in his native tongue.

Ford grit his teeth and forced the throbbing and burning pain from his mind as he digested the information. Jacques LeCuvier had value to the enemy. When they'd first brought the Frenchman to the camp, Ford hadn't expected the delicate chemist to last more than a week, but for the past two years, Jacques had continually proven him wrong.

I would have enjoyed breaking you.

"If we're the only two being traded," Ford said, "that means fewer guards, my friend."

"*Oui*, but they have guns. All we have are these," Jacque said, holding up his smallish hands.

A slow grin curved Ford's mouth. "That's all the weapon I need."

This was his chance, maybe even his last chance—and he'd be damned if he'd let the bastards live another day.

ONE

Three weeks later...

FORD PACED THE small space, anger and frustration his constant companions. He wanted to go home. He wanted to reclaim his life. Unfortunately, Colonel Benson, the base commander had kept him caged in the military installation in Brussels for the past week. He hadn't even been able to make a goddamn phone call. Criminals had more rights, and he was mad as hell.

Proving he was indeed Lieutenant Ford Grayson, U.S. Navy SEAL, to the American Ambassador to Kuwait hadn't been easy, but after two days of telephone calls, faxes and meetings, the military had finally sent Colonel Benson to confirm his identity. That process had taken another forty-eight hours of intense interrogation before Benson had been satisfied he was one of the good guys. They'd finally shipped him out to Brussels where he'd been held another week for debriefing. He'd told them everything he knew from the moment the plane carrying him and his men had been shot down over the Mediterranean Sea, to his capture behind enemy lines. He'd recounted his years in captivity, including LeCuvier's part in blowing up the chemical plant on the Pakistani border, and their subsequent escape. Ten days later, he and Jacques arrived at the Embassy in Kuwait by traveling at night, mostly on foot.

And how had his government rewarded him? By caging him like a goddamned animal.

Ford swore viciously and shoved his hands through his newly cropped hair. He continued to pace the sparsely furnished room, scowling when he passed the rack. His sea bag rested on the top, packed and ready. He'd been told he was being shipped out, but to where, he hadn't a clue. He'd been at the mercy of a band of Taliban fighters for five years. Years of hell, years of suffering the whims of cruel jailors, with barely enough food to sustain a small child let alone a man. The room they'd given him now was little better than a prison cell, but at least the living conditions during the past week had been better than that in the various camps and abandoned houses.

His head snapped around when a light rap sounded on the door. A young marine, no more than eighteen or nineteen, stepped into the room and saluted.

"At ease," Ford said.

The grunt braced his feet apart and folded his arms behind his back. "Lieutenant Grayson, Captain Ravelli has arrived and would like a word, sir."

Ford nodded, waited for the enlisted man to precede him from the room. He followed him down a long, narrow corridor, hoping maybe now he'd have some answers. Like why in the hell he couldn't go home?

The marine stopped in front of a double door, knocked twice, then stepped aside. He saluted again as Ford walked into the room, then quietly closed the door behind him.

"My God, it really is you," Paul Ravelli said, his voice gravelly. The senior officer came out from behind a standard government-issue desk to clasped Ford's hand, then pulled him into a bear hug.

Paul released him, then moved around the desk. Opening a drawer, he retrieved a bottle of Glenfiddich and poured two fingers worth into a pair of tumblers.

"Welcome home," Paul said, handing one to Ford.

"Thank you, sir," Ford said with a nod, then tossed back the Scotch. The alcohol burned his throat, settling into his stomach like a ball of fire. He hadn't had a drink in so long, he'd almost forgotten what it was like. When Ravelli lifted the bottle in silent offering, Ford declined.

Paul perched on the edge of the desk and poured himself another. "It's damned good to see you again," he said, setting the bottle aside.

"And you." Ford dropped into the chair the senior officer indicated. "Captain, huh?" When he'd first encountered Paul, he'd been a Lieutenant, like himself. "Not bad."

"Yeah, well, you know how it goes." Paul waved away the backhanded compliment. "Benson faxed me the reports of your activities. If I had my way, you'd be receiving a medal for what you've done. Unfortunately, it isn't that simple. The Pakistani Army has claimed responsibility for the lab, and the U.S. is keeping the truth quiet."

"I wasn't looking for a medal when I went in." Ford frowned. He'd been doing his job, the job his government expected of him. He'd sworn to protect his country, and that's what he'd done. Sure, he hadn't expected to be shot down or captured, but the mission had been to locate and disable enemy facilities by any means necessary. He'd done that, and thanks to Jacques LeCuvier, they'd taken it one step further and leveled the damned thing. He'd been on enough top secret missions to understand why his government wouldn't claim responsibility, but allow some other group to revel in the glory.

Business as usual.

Ford looked at Paul, still as robust as Ford remembered him. The Captain hadn't changed much in the past five years, other than his leap frogging promotions from Lieutenant all the way up to Captain.

"How are you holding up?" Paul asked before taking a sip of Scotch.

"Fine, sir," Ford replied, trying to keep a tight rein on his patience. He wanted answers.

"Cut the 'sir' crap," Paul said. "We're friends, remember? We've known each other a hell of a long time, and been in places I don't care to see again. Right now I'm your friend, not your C.O."

"Then I'd like to see home," Ford stated honestly.

"And you will. I'm personally putting you on a transport to Carswell Field." Paul stood and circled desk to drop into a squeaky leather chair. Frowning, he hesitated for a moment before opening a filed marked *Eyes Only*. "A lot has changed since you went missing." Slowly, he slid an eight-by-ten color photograph across the desk.

Mattie.

Ford's breath stilled as he stared at the photograph. God, she was just as beautiful as he remembered her. Petite and curvy, she had a bombshell body and the sweetest smile. But her eyes, she could make him hard with one look.

His wife.

At first glance, she hadn't changed, but upon closer inspection, he noted her hair wasn't fashionably cut into the short style he remembered. Instead, she'd let it grow long, the thick, rich dark brown strands straight and teasing the middle of her back. She stood in the center of what looked like a playground, supervising a group of kids he guessed to be no more than four or five years of age.

He looked closer, examining the faces of each child, hoping to spot one who could be his son or daughter. Mattie had been eight months pregnant when he'd shipped out on his last assignment. Neither one of them had been happy about it, but as Matt had reassured him, she wasn't the first military wife to give birth without her husband by her side, and she wouldn't be the last. He was a Navy SEAL. They'd always lived with the uncertainly of when he'd be shipped halfway across the world, often with little notice of him being sent to some hot spot on a mission he could never talk about. Unfortunately, neither of them could have predicted it'd take him five years to come home again.

Guilt twisted his gut. He should have been there. They'd lost five years, five years of their lives they could never have back. Not for the first time, he briefly wondered if he'd made the right choice. His mission may have been quietly labeled a success, but at what cost? Granted, he'd done his job, but was it worth the expense of five years of their lives?

The answer filled him with self-loathing.

The springs in the chair squeaked when Paul shifted in his seat. He leaned forward, bracing his arms on the desk and gave Ford a level stare. "Things are going to be different when you get home."

"Different how?" he asked cautiously. There was something Paul wasn't telling him. He could see it in the superior officer's eyes. "What do you know?"

Paul's expression remained grim. "Mattie believed you were dead, Ford. She's a young, vibrant woman. Surely you didn't expect her to mourn you forever."

Ford tensed. "What are you saying? That she moved on?" The combination of guilt and Scotch burned his gut, along with instinct that his deepest fear had been realized. During his long captivity, he'd always thought of the possibility of another man in her life. He'd prepared himself to accept it, at least he'd thought he had. Hell, he'd been "dead" for nearly five years, what did he expect?

For her to mourn you forever.

Mattie was *his* wife. She'd promised to love, honor and cherish *him*.

Until death do us *part.*

Shit.

"I'm sorry, Ford."

Paul lowered his gaze and Ford stood, dropping the photograph on the desk. He crossed the gray linoleum to the window and looked out at the cloudless Brussels sky. God, what if she'd actually married someone else? He made a sound, somewhere between a self-deprecating laugh and a grunt of pain. "Who is he?" Ice crept into his voice, seeped into his soul.

Mattie belonged to him. She'd been his since he'd first set eyes on her, shortly after he'd relocated with his mom to Hart, Texas when he was a sophomore in high school. The attraction between them had been immediate, and by the time they'd graduated, there'd never been any question they would spend the rest of their lives together. Against the advice of their families, before they'd left for college, they'd gotten married.

Those first few years of marriage had been spent working and taking classes. After the first semester, they'd decided he should take the fast track so he could graduate in three years, while Mattie worked full-time and only took classes part-time. The plan had been for him to join the Navy, attend OSC and flight school, while Mattie stayed in Texas at Baylor University to finish her degree, then she'd join him wherever he'd eventually be stationed. When he'd been invited to join the SEALs, he hadn't hesitated to enroll in the specialized training program without even discussing it with Mattie.

That had been his first of many mistakes, something he'd had five long, hellish years to realize. He'd had no right to enter into a program like the SEALs without talking to her about it first, but he'd been young and full of himself, not to mention a selfish bastard. But she'd hung in there with him, despite everything, even moving her halfway across the country to San Diego's Coronado Island, far from her family, friends and everything familiar to her.

"His name is Trenton Avery," Paul said, pulling Ford back to the present. He slipped another photograph from the file. "He's a lawyer out of Dallas. Big firm. High profile clientele."

Ford ignored the photograph. There were more pressing matters at hand. Like how in the fuck he was going to get his wife back. "How long have they been seeing each other?"

Paul leaned back in the chair. "Ford, you should sit down."

A buzzing started in his ears. He didn't want to hear this. He didn't want to hear that his wife was involved with another man. That some hot shot lawyer was putting his hands on *his* wife. Touching her, kissing her, making love to her. "How long?"

"Mattie got married two weeks ago."

Ford turned back to the window so Paul couldn't see the pain ripping through him.

"I'm sorry I had to tell you this. I think it's best if I dispatch a courier to let her know you're alive. It's going—"

"No," he said, his voice as cold as the ice settling around

his heart. "I'll be the one to tell my wife we're still legally married."

"That's not a good idea," Paul argued. "You do realize this is going to be a shock. She's going to need time to absorb the information."

"No."

"Ford, protocol demands—"

"Fuck protocol!" he roared. "She's my wife. *Mine.*"

"Was," Paul said, his gravelly voice hard. He came out of the chair, his brows pulled into a disapproving frown.

"Like hell." Ford crossed his arms over his chest and braced his feet apart. "Mattie is *my* wife."

"Think about what you're doing, Ford," Ravelli continued in a more placating tone. "I've known you for a long time, buddy. People change. After what she went through when she heard you were dead, she can't possibly be the same woman you left behind five years ago."

"She's still *my* wife. And I'll be damned if I'll let her go without a fight."

All Mattie Avery could think of as the driver of the rented town car pulled up in front of her modest ranch house, was how she'd never been so utterly exhausted in her entire life. The two week, whirlwind honeymoon trip across Europe was one she'd never forget, and had been everything her groom, Dallas attorney Trenton Avery, had promised. The crazy schedule, not to mention a serious case of jetlag after a full day of travel, had apparently caught up with her and she was beat. She didn't care that it was nearing dawn and the blistering Texas sun would be riding high in the sky shortly. All she wanted to do was crawl into bed and sleep for a week. And maybe even shake the jittery feeling that had been bothering her for the past couple of days.

"You go in," Trenton told her as the car pulled to a stop. "I'll see to the bags."

Mattie looked over at her husband and offered him a half-hearted smile. "Thank you. It's been a day," she said, then leaned toward him for a quick kiss.

He obliged, which made her smile widen. Eighteen months ago when they'd first starting dating, she quickly learned Trenton didn't go in for public displays of affection. After time, he'd loosened up, a little. While her groom wasn't exactly a stuffed shirt, appearances were important to Trenton, something she tried to keep in mind.

She pulled her keys from her purse before she left the rented town car and headed up the walk to the front door. Heavy humidity hung in the air, stifling and only adding to her exhaustion. As she slipped her key into the lock and turned the knob, she was hit by a blast of cool air and silently thanked her sister, Griffen, for taking the time to come by and fire up the air conditioning for them. Her sister and brother-in-law, Jed Maitland, the former star quarterback of the Texas Wranglers, would be over later in the afternoon, to bring her daughter, Phoebe, home. Until then, she planned to shower and sleep for the next eight hours.

She flipped the switch to light the small foyer, then headed to the kitchen for a drink. As she rounded the corner into the family room, she caught a movement in her peripheral vision and stopped cold.

Her heart pounded so hard all she could hear was the blood thrumming in her veins. She couldn't move. Couldn't scream as a tall, imposing figure slowly moved toward her.

"Hello, Mattie."

She instantly recognized the deep, smooth voice, a voice she'd heard only in her dreams for the past five years. Reaching behind her, her hand smacked against the wall as she frantically searched for the switch. Light from the kitchen flickered to life and spilled into the family room. She stared in disbelief at what could only be a figment of her imagination.

This wasn't real. She was overly tired. She'd fallen asleep on the plane and would wake up any minute now when they landed in Dallas.

She closed her eyes, then opened them again.

He was still there. Standing less than three feet away—and he was *alive.*

"Ford?" she managed to whisper, her hand reaching for the wall behind her for support. Shock, surprise and an uncontrollable sense of joy raced through her as she drank in the sight of him. "My God, is it really you?"

Somewhere in the back of her mind she was amazed that her legs held her. He was thinner than she remembered, his thick, wavy sable hair cut in the same standard military cut, but with a hint of gray starting to pepper his temples. He wore his khaki uniform, the breast pocket laden with medals and brightly colored striped bars, evidence of his valor in service to his country. The two silver bars on his collar had been replaced with a gold leaf, indicating a promotion in rank.

Her throat clogged with hundreds of emotions, making breathing difficult. Her mind swam with even more questions. Tears of joy filled her eyes. The man she'd loved heart, body and soul had been returned to her. By some strange miracle of fate, Ford was still alive.

"Oh God," she whispered. She lifted her hand toward him, tears flooding her vision, afraid he'd disappear.

"I'm home, baby," he said, his own voice a choked whisper. Closing the small space between them, he pulled her into his arms.

Mattie clung to him, finding comfort in the strong, vital rhythm of his heart. If she let go, she feared he'd disappear and she'd wake up crying from another dream. For too long she'd hoped and prayed that the news of Ford's death had been a mistake, that someone had lied to her, but after years of wishful thinking, she'd finally come to terms with the fact that he'd never come back to her. He was gone. Dead. He'd been killed when his plane had been shot down over the Mediterranean Sea and she'd been forced to deal with the reality that she'd never be held by him again, never hear his smooth, deep voice whisper hot against her skin as they made love. Never see his laughing blue eyes simmering with desire whenever he looked at her.

Somehow that had changed—Ford was alive.

He was alive, he was holding her, his scent, his hardness wrapping around her, his arms holding her as fiercely as she held him. She pulled back and looked up at him, slowly lifting her hand to cup his cheek. "How is this possible?"

He turned his face against her hand and kissed her palm. "Later," he whispered. "First, there's something I've been dreaming of doing for five long years."

He dipped his head, capturing her lips in a hot, open-mouthed kiss. Without hesitation, she opened to him and his tongue swept inside, demanding, savoring as if to steel his homecoming in reality. The sweet rush of desire instantly flooded her body. She drank, quenching a thirst that had been unfulfilled for far too long, then greedily drank some more. Time defied existence, only Ford and the feel of his rock hard body pressing against hers registered in her mind.

Until she heard the click of the front door, followed by the sound of Trenton's footsteps crossing the tiled foyer.

Trenton. Her *new* husband.

* * *

If you enjoyed PLAYING FOR KEEPS
please take a moment and share your thoughts
by going to your eRetailer to leave an honest review.
It only takes a moment and it is very helpful
in spreading the word to other readers.
Thank you.

ABOUT THE AUTHOR

Ever since she heard her first fairy tale, Jamie Denton has been a staunch supporter of happily-ever-after. For her, there's nothing quite as heart-warming as the happy ending for a hero and heroine who overcome the odds. At the age of sixteen, Jamie married her high school sweetheart. Still happily wed nearly forty years later, she still recalls the first time she saw her future husband and knew, even at *that* tender age, he was *The One*. With a history like that, what else could she write except romances?

Jamie and her hero live with two very hairy Golden Retrievers in rural Pennsylvania. When she's not writing, she's refilling the creative well with gardening plans, a needlework project or trying out a new recipe in the kitchen. Occasionally, she can even be found curled up on the sofa with a book (what else but a romance?) and her two fur babies, Dudley and Maggie.

You can write to Jamie by visiting her website www.jamiedentonbooks.com, on Twitter @JamieDenton or on Facebook www.facebook.com/jamiedentonbooks.

OTHER TITLES BY JAMIE DENTON

Bliss, an Anthology

Berkley Publishing
The Promise of Love

Kensington Brava
How to be a Wicked Woman
The Matchmaker
Remain Silent
Dead Stop
Bodyguards in Bed

Harlequin Blaze
Sleeping with the Enemy (The FBI series)
Seduced by the Enemy (The FBI Series)
Stroke of Midnight (The NYE Series)
Ready to Wear (The NYE Series)
Absolute Pleasure (The FBI Series)
Hard to Handle (Lock & Key Trilogy)
My Guilty Pleasure (Martini Dares Series)

Harlequin Temptation
Flirting with Danger
The Seduction of Sydney
Valentine Fantasy (Fantasy for Hire Series)
Rules of Engagement (The Rules Series)
Breaking the Rules (The Rules Series)
Under the Covers
Slow Burn (Some Like It Hot Series)
Heatwave (Some Like It Hot Series)
Under Fire (Some Like It Hot Series)
Light Her Fire (Some Like It Hot Series)

Harlequin American Romance
The Biological Bond

Harlequin Duets
Making Mr. Right

Harlequin Superromance
The Secret Child

23440217R10155

Made in the USA
Charleston, SC
22 October 2013